Anything But Ordinary

Anything But Ordinary

Michael DeVault

Preface to the Second Edition

This book did not turn out like I intended it.

When I sat down to the first blank pages that would become the book you are now holding, in the late summer of 2001, I intended to pen a coming-of-age tale about a young boy in a city so foreign it would shock his senses. I chose as my protagonist a young boy from a large mid-Western city, transplanted to the most foreign locale imaginable, the city of New Orleans. That it was a straight shot down the Mississippi River only added to the symmetry and symbolism. During the first months and year or so of writing, I spent a considerable number of days wandering the streets of the Big Easy, reacquainting myself with the sights, sounds and people that make New Orleans unique among American cities.

I finished the rough draft of this book in the spring of 2004 and, as I didn't know exactly what to do next, I let it languish in a drawer for a few months before dusting it off for an edit. Then, just as I was breaking ground on editing *Anything But Ordinary*, the city I had labored to capture was hit by a hurricane. I did not set out to create a portrait of New Orleans, but that is what this book has become. For contained herein are glimpses of a New Orleans that no longer exists.

This realization remained lost to me until Carolyn Meinel, whom I consider a close friend and literary confidant, suggested this potential connection in the days following the storm. As the waters of Pontchartrain receded and the world saw the devastation in the Lower Ninth Ward, I knew the city I had come to love had been forever changed.

The writer and philosopher Barbara Branden once told me a book is never "finished." Instead, writers just stop working on books and, if they're lucky, the books get published. Looking back over this story in advance of the second edition, I see myriad things that I would, today, write differently. But that's to be expected. I'm a different writer today than I was back when I first pecked out "I am a writer" all those years back. But changing these things would, I believe, make this second edition a different book. And that's not what I want. So, instead, changes have been limited mostly to minor typographical errors and the kinds of mistakes that have a tendency to creep into a book when it's in the final stages of pre-production. What you are holding is a faithful and true representation of the original novel, but with different art and better grammar. On the topic of grammar, there are people to thank.

To Carolyn, I am forever thankful for connecting the powerful images from the cable news networks to the places and people in my story. Without that tearful phone call during the Katrina aftermath, I might have left this book collecting dust in that drawer for even longer. My friend and editor Ann Bloxom Smith's eagle eye always catches the misspelled words, the missing commas, those word choice errors that plague even seasoned authors, and more than a few problems with continuity. Without Ann's work, this book's second life would seem not much different than its first. For both Carolyn and Ann, I am grateful.

Most of all, I am forever indebted to the citizens of the great city of New Orleans for living lives responsible for creating a city of such grace, power and ageless beauty.

Laissez les bon temps rouler toujours.

Michael DeVault
Monroe, Louisiana
May 18, 2014

For Kya

"Things may not be immediately discernable in what a man writes, and in this sometimes he is fortunate; but eventually, they are quite clear and by these and the degree of alchemy that he possesses, he will endure or be forgotten."

Ernest Hemingway
Address to the Nobel Committee
Stockholm, Sweden, 1954

Chapter 1

I am a writer.

Regardless of how many times I say it or in how many reviews I read "William Northrop Bradshaw, author," I never grow accustomed to seeing my name accompanied by that title. Those words are instead my link to a time and a place far removed from book tours and the minor literary celebrity that comes with publication.

I'm not sure how that gossip columnist discovered my "dark secret" of a hidden, lost summer spent in partial confinement at the Liberty Street Home for the Elderly and Infirm, but the story–or at least versions of it–have found their way into print. Now I am forced to confront not only my past, but also the myths that have evolved. Some have speculated that I was a delinquent, a miscreant in want of firm parenting. Others write that I was a sociopath barely diverted from a subversive lifestyle by the heavy hand of justice. One intrepid if somewhat creative reporter suggested that I was a murderer.

All of these things, these "facts," are false. Yet, in some subtle way, I admit that they are all true. Regardless of which version of the truth you choose to believe, the fact remains that, were it not for a fateful day almost twelve years ago, I might never have been a writer, diverted by chance or necessity to some other career, perhaps a shopkeeper or a bureaucrat or a teacher.

My story doesn't begin with a bang, a letter from a publisher or even with a brilliant idea. Instead, the march that led me here began in a city so fantastic, so foreign, that to a boy of twelve, for three short months, magic was still possible. The summer of 1990 marked the passing of the final vestiges of my innocence and childhood.

The extraordinary people I met during those brief months took the blank conscience of a young, frightened boy and molded into him the ethics and values they had spent six lifetimes perfecting. I might never have known the people of Hall B, might never have become what I am today had I not made a single mistake over thirteen years ago, a mistake that cost me a summer and gives me this story that I have, until now, refused to share. Long before I was William Northrop Bradshaw, author, I was Billy Bradshaw, convicted vandal.

This is my story.

* * *

Someone once said New Orleans is a city comfortable with her age. Modern conveniences weave themselves into the tapestry of the city, turning her trolley cars and Jazz funerals into anachronisms. ATMs and coffee shops dot the corners of the French Quarter paths through the Vieux Carre and into the Garden District where, by some miracle, my mother found the money to send me to an exclusive, private school. So, each day after class, I set forth on a crosstown trek that took me through the heart of the city to the tiny apartment Mother rented a block or so from Esplanade and the antebellum crown jewels of New Orleans.

Summers in New Orleans aren't hot. They swelter. So it was with much reticence that I stepped off the bus and started the final hike of the school year down Esplanade, bolstered only by the promise of a lazy summer under the air conditioner. About two blocks down, I came to the boarded up Georgian, her fluted columns growing darker with grime each day.

The tropical jungle back yard of this abandoned wreck backed up to the parking lot of our apartment complex and, for the last nine months, had made an easy shortcut from one world to the other. After so many treks through the overgrown boxwoods and too-tall hibiscus, I knew by heart the way to the solarium at the back edge of the property. On this particular afternoon, the sun beat down in that particularly brutal way it always does in the first heat of summer. Gold rays bounced off the glass, momentarily making it gleam before the grime showed through. I came to a stop, squinting against the reflection.

I don't know what came over me, standing there on that day, but it was a feeling that began at my feet and grew upwards. Nearby, part of a branch had fallen from a dying tree. It was heavy, the bark worn smooth, but still solid. In my hands, it was transformed into a Louisville Slugger. A couple of chunks of paving stone, pried from the walkway, became hundred-mile-an-hour fastballs. There, in that backyard, I became a New York Yankee.

"Now up to bat," I blustered in my deepest announcer voice. "Number thirty-three, Billy Bradshaw. He checks the bases, all good."

I tossed one of the stones into the air and swung. It landed at my feet with a thud. "Strike one. Bradshaw takes a minute. The runner on second has a pretty serious leadoff. Here's the pitch."

The second rock ricocheted off a cast-iron column and flew into a nearby bush.

"Foul ball. He's not doing well, here, and there's a lot on the line. Bottom of the ninth, two strikes, bases loaded. This is what it's all about. If Bradshaw can pull it off, come through, knock a homer, the Yanks take the series," I said. "Here's the pitch!"

The stone sailed through the brief space between the solarium and me, cut through one of the panes and continued traveling, taking with it glass on the other side. I throw my hands into the air, yelling in jubilation, "Home run! It's a home run! Yankees take the series!"

"Freeze, son."

I slowly turned in place to the direction of the voice. Perhaps, in the years since, he's grown in my imagination. Or perhaps I've remembered it correctly and the police officer standing behind me was nine feet tall. Either way, my feet had grown roots into the soil and simply would not follow my brain's instructions to run.

* * *

The juvenile court judge stared down from the bench across the bridge of his glasses. My mother sat beside me, impatiently tapping her foot. Since our arrival at the courthouse, she hadn't said a word. The judge glanced back at the file before him, then back at me. He heaved a sigh and tossed his glasses onto the folder.

"If I were your father, Billy, you wouldn't be able to sit down for a week. But I'm not. So listen here. Every Monday, Wednesday, Friday and

Saturday this summer you will report to Liberty Street Nursing Home. They will be expecting you at eight a.m. tomorrow. If you miss so much as one day, I'll send you to juvie for a year. Got it?"

"Yes sir, Mister Spurgeon."

"Your honor," he said sternly.

"Yes sir, your honor. I didn't mean anything," I said.

"Miss Bradshaw, I trust that you understand the seriousness of this matter?"

"Yes, your honor."

"I'll need to see you and counsel in chambers, Miss Bradshaw. Billy can wait here."

To this day, I do not know what Judge Spurgeon said to my mother, but when she returned, she took my arm and led me from the courthouse in silence. The only thing she said to me that night involved what bus I would take the next morning to get to the Liberty Street Home for the Elderly and Infirm.

Chapter 2

Her name badge told me her name was Camille Roberts and that she was the director of nurses for the Liberty Street Home. But the manner with which she greeted me told me that Liberty Street was her show. She read the letter from Judge Spurgeon again before handing it to her assistant. "Ain't this just the damnedest?"

While the assistant read, Camille studied me again. "Vandalism huh? I ain't got any room for vandals in my home. Ellie, what am I going to do with this?"

"Miss Camille, seems pretty clear to me that Judge wants him back on the Row."

"I know that, Ellie. I can read, same as you."

Ellie leaned over the stack of files on her desk and winked at me. "Don't pay her no mind. What's your name?"

"Billy. Billy Bradshaw."

"Nice to meet you, Billy."

"Don't get too attached," Camille said. "I'm sending him back. I can't put him on Hall B. They'll eat him alive."

"Miss Camille," Ellie said. She laughed, but it didn't help set me at ease. The thought of going back before Judge Spurgeon, telling him that they sent me away, and then being shipped off to juvie was enough to send me into a panic.

"I'll do anything you want me to. Just please don't send me away."

Camille read the letter again and heaved a sigh. "I swear, that man–fine. Leon!"

An orderly appeared in her door, the mop in his hand leaving a trail of suds into her office. When she growled at him, he propped the mop outside the door. "Yes, ma'am?"

"Would you mind taking Billy back to Hall B for me? I'll phone Emily and let her know you're coming."

"Yes ma'am, Miss Camille," Leon said. Camille eyed the suds on the floor and Leon nodded. "I know, I'll clean it up when I get back."

Leon started out of the office. When I didn't follow, he stopped. "You coming or not?"

The halls of the Liberty Street Home stank of mothballs, disinfectant and urine. Most of the residents were confined to their beds or reclining in chairs. Behind half-closed doors hid dressers piled with old photographs, unmade beds in need of fresh linens, televisions tuned to soap operas. One old man sat on a roll-away toilet by his bed while an orderly changed the recently-soiled sheets. The man sobbed, repeatedly apologizing for dirtying his bed again. The orderly ignored the man, his attention instead focused on the music blaring through the headphones covering his ears. A woman padded down the hallway, her left hand clutching the safety rail. Her gray house shoes slid across the floor in six-inch increments.

Leon waved. "Hello, Mrs. Toddman."

"Hello, Clifton." She motioned us over. "How are the children?"

"They're fine, Mrs. Toddman. Growing like weeds. See you later!" Leon started off, but she stopped him. "I have something for you in my room, Clifton. Come by later."

She shuffled off down the hall, chuckling.

"Your name isn't Clifton," I said. "It's Leon."

"So? Mrs. Toddman thinks I'm her yardboy from two gazillion years ago. Mrs. Toddman thinks that this is her old mansion in Pittsburgh and that Ellie is her long-lost daughter." Leon laughed and continued down the hall, but I didn't follow him.

I felt sorry for Mrs. Toddman, for her confusion about where she was. I also wondered how anyone could ever mistake the halls of the Liberty Street Home for a mansion in Pittsburgh. When he realized I wasn't behind him again, he stopped.

"Look, kid. It's because she's old. There's a man over on Hall C thinks we're in an army barracks in World War II. Don't worry, you'll get used to it."

He pointed down an empty hallway. "The Row is at the end of this hall and through the double-doors on the left. Tell the girl at the station who you are. Her name is Emily. She'll tell you what she wants you to do."

The hallway leading to Hall B was dark, and the echoes of activity from the other end of the

Liberty Street Home barely found their way to the steel doors separating Hall B from the rest of the building. Even the rancid smell of nursing home had faded, leaving the air almost breathable. As I crept toward the doors, the muted sounds of a trumpet tickled my ears. There was music playing somewhere on Hall B. I pressed my ear to the door. Someone laughed. I cracked the door just wide enough to stick my head inside.

Just as Leon had promised, a girl sat behind a small desk reading *Cosmopolitan.* Bleached blonde bangs protruded from beneath a baseball cap embroidered with Greek letters. Oblivious to the five people seated around the table only a few feet away, their laughter and the jazz blaring from a stereo in the corner did not prevent her from answering the ringing phone. "Hall B? Hey baby. Take me to the movies tonight. I want to see that new Julia Roberts movie. Okay? See you then."

Before she could return to her magazine, she saw me in the doorway. "Can I help you?"

I eased through the door. The hydraulic closure yanked the handle from my hand and slammed the door behind me. I froze under the sudden scrutiny of six pairs of eyes. "I…Miss Camille said I should come back here?"

"Billy, right? Come on in, and I'll introduce you to everybody. I'm Emily, by the way."

The people at the table watched with hawkish curiosity as I approached. Emily's voice strained under the burden of condescension. "Everybody, this is Billy. He'll be spending some time on the Row with us. Billy, these are the residents of Hall B. This is Miss…" The phone interrupted Emily's introductions. She sighed.

"I'll be right back."

"Don't rush yourself, dear," said the woman Emily had been about to introduce. With Emily's back turned, she grabbed the pink scarf around her neck and mimed hanging herself.

The man to her right snickered. "Be nice, Anne." He stood, offered to shake my hand. "You'll have to excuse our Emily there. She's not the brightest bulb in the chandelier, but we manage to keep her in line."

I shook his hand, then turned to the woman in the scarf. She smiled. "Anne Moore, sweetie. Call me Anne. That's Louise Kearney. The Louise

Kearney," she said, indicating the woman across the table from her as if the name warranted recognition.

As it quickly became obvious I had no clue who her friend was, she shook her head.

"You've never heard of her?" Anne turned to her companions. "That, my friends, is what is wrong with education in this state." She eyed me again. "Former poet for the Library of Congress? 'Ah but youth has passed away, for naught to come another day. In times of trouble may we find, that beardless peace of youthful mind.'" She stopped, allowing several seconds for the poem to settle in. " 'Ode to the Idylls of Spring.' Amazing isn't it? I cannot believe they don't teach her in your school."

Before I could respond to Anne's indignation, the poet herself sprang to my aid, slapping Anne playfully on the shoulder. "Don't you mind anything that old bat says, Billy. It's okay that you don't know me. I'm ancient. Your grandpa would remember me, though. How old are you?"

"Twelve."

"My, you're a strapping lad for twelve." A new voice. The man at the head of the table waved me

14

over. He pulled me closer and studied me over the rim of his glasses. "Only twelve? Are you sure?"

"Well, I turn thirteen on August sixteenth."

Yet another voice, this time from the other side of the table: "August sixteenth is the day Elvis died. August 16, 1977."

"No way! That's the year I was born." I frowned, sad that I shared a birthday with such an occasion.

"Well here's to Elvis and to Billy." The man at the head of the table raised his glass of orange juice. The others followed and raised theirs.

"What are we toasting?" said a voice from the hall behind me. When I turned to see who it was, a sight I will never forget awaited.

Though he stood about five foot nine, the lilac high-heels added another three inches. The hem of a matching linen skirt swayed back and forth, in tempo with his shoulder-length brunette hair curled into ringlets. He wore no makeup, but did not need it. His cheeks were full and pink, and his lips were the color of blood. The man's almost-purple eyes were his most striking feature. I did not notice them, though, until he was seated at the table and the distraction of the lilac dress and high heels were hidden beneath the white tablecloth and he was staring at me, his eyes aglow with ferocious intensity.

"Sorry I'm late, everyone," he said.

"No you're not," a couple of the others said in unison.

"You're right, I'm not. I'm just late." His eyes fixed on me again, and he smiled. "Who is our new friend?"

"Billy. Billy Bradshaw," I said. I knew I should not stare, that it was impolite. But I could not force my eyes away from what to a twelve-year-old Minneapolis boy was such a strange sight.

"Well Billy, I'm Donald Lilly and I'm damned proud to meet you." He looked around the table at the other residents, smiling in greeting. When he finally settled into his chair, he lifted a fork, but returned it neatly beside his plate. Turning back to me, he said, "You'll have to forgive the manners of these cretins. They've spent the last ten years down here and, well, proper manners have gone the way of the dodo I'm afraid. Have a seat and join us for breakfast?"

He patted the empty chair next to him. I looked nervously at the others. Having never encountered a man in a dress, I did not know what to say or how to react to the invitation. Looking back, I do not know what was more shocking, that he was dressed as a woman, or that he was at least seventy-five years old and dressed like a woman. The combination of Donald Lilly's age and abnormality was overwhelming.

"I...I already had breakfast."

"Well, would you like some orange juice?" the man at the head of the table said. Detecting my discomfort he motioned me over. "Donald is harmless. Strange as all hell, but just as harmless." Laughter erupted from the table, easing both the tension in the room and the tension in my stomach. I smiled.

"My name is Alistair Lees," he said. "Where you from?" I slid into the empty chair next to Donald Lilly, accidentally sitting on the folds of lilac chiffon spilling from beneath him. Apologizing, I shoved the fabric out of my chair to avoid sitting on it.

"I'm from Minneapolis. We just moved here," I said.

"That's nice," said the woman who had identified my birthday as the day Elvis had died. She closed the oversized leather journal she had been writing in and slipped it beneath her chair. "Minneapolis used to be a riot of a town. Back before the skyscrapers took over. I remember taking the train through there during the election of twenty-eight. Hoover was running for president, and I was traveling for the *Hartford Courant.* Filed wire reports from each stop. There was this man…" Her voice trailed off, and a smile crept across her face. "I wonder whatever happened to him? Oh well, ages ago."

"What's the Harvard Core–Cour?"

"*Courant.* It's a newspaper. Was one of the best papers in the country at the time," she replied. "I was a journalist before women were journalists."

"What's your name?"

"I'm so sorry. Zelda Groves." I looked at each of their faces, trying to recall their names.

"You're Mr. McLean, right?" He nodded. "And you're Miss Moore. Mr. Lees. Miss Groves." I stopped at the poet. "Miss Kerns?"

"Kearney but close enough. Call me Louise," she said.

"Okay, Louise."

She smiled. I looked at Donald Lilly, unsure how to address him.

"Donald Lilly," he said.

"I...well."

"Well what?" he said.

I blushed. "Do I call you Mr. Lilly or Miss Lilly?" Another round of laughter overtook the residents. Alistair Lees leaned across the table and shook my shoulder.

"You fit on the Row just fine, Billy," Donald Lilly said. Zelda piled the plate in front of me with scrambled eggs and a stack of pancakes. Though I had already eaten breakfast, the aromas whet my appetite. I shoveled as much food as I could into my mouth. They were the best eggs I had ever eaten, different from the eggs my mother cooked in the mornings. They were fluffy and smooth, spicy but not hot.

I chewed quickly and force-swallowed. "Why does everyone call it the Row?"

"I guess it was about ten years ago?" Alistair said. "We wanted a place of our own, so we commandeered Hall B. One of the nurses, this dreadful crone of a woman, did not like us very much and thought she would insult us by nicknaming it Bohemian Hall. It didn't insult us at all. Somehow, it got changed to Bohemian Row, then to just the Row."

"But what are Bohemians?" I said.

Anne stared at me as if I were an out-of-town guest who had just committed some foible of manners born of ignorance. "Why, my dear. We are!"

Chapter 3

Breakfast that first morning on Bohemian Row continued for the better part of an hour, until we had exhausted all avenues of small talk and the last of the orange juice. I learned more about Zelda Groves and her writing, about Alistair Lees and his career as a portrait painter in New Orleans, and about Donald Lilly and his family's petroleum fortune. Perhaps Judge Spurgeon never considered the effects a twelve-year-old interloper would have on the staff and the residents of the Liberty Street Home, that my presence might create problems for the staff or discomfort for the residents. The moment the last piece of toast disappeared from the table, that dreadful silence that asks "What's next?" descended.

"So," Anne Moore said, a final punctuation to the breakfast conversation. "Louise, would you give me a hand with the dishes?" The two women began clearing the dishes away from the table.

"Don, help us out," Louise said. He paused long enough to take my plate before following the two women into the kitchen. Silence returned, broken only by the occasional rustle of paper from Alistair's newspaper. Emily had disappeared sometime during breakfast, but no one could remember where or if she said she was going.

"Well that's just no good, no good at all." Alistair leaned toward the *Times-Picayune* spread on the table before him. His reading glasses slid down his nose, teetering just above his nostrils.

"What?" Zelda said without looking up from her journal.

"Another mugging in the Quarter last night. Same story, different day, I guess." He shook his head.

"What do you expect with the city the way it is today?" Thaddeus McLean said. He had migrated to the couch in front of the television and was flipping through morning soaps on a fuzzy black-and-white TV. "Crime's through the roof. Can't even walk at night."

Alistair looked up from his paper and smiled at the ceiling. "Night walks. A beautiful woman on your arm, stars filling the sky, and maybe, just maybe, if you were lucky you'd get to—"

"Stop right there." Zelda finished his sentence.

"Why?" When she bobbed her head in my direction, he cleared his throat. "Oh yes. Well. If you were lucky you got to kiss her at the door, Billy."

"Those were the days of courting lamps and porch swings, and if your parents liked the boy, you could go to the picture show," Zelda said. "And that was only if they liked him. None of this sneaking around and the like."

Thaddeus snorted sarcastically. "Don't you pay her any attention, Billy. The damned hypocrite won't tell you what her teenage years really were like. Jazz music, petting parties, all the gin she could drink—and then some."

"Those were the days," Alistair said. He again forgot I was in the room. "I remember this one place up in Chicago. Dime a dance. A buck would get you–well, you can figure it out."

Zelda slammed her journal and tossed it on the table. "Alistair Lees, you stop that! I can't believe you two." She steered me away from the table. "Billy, don't pay any attention to them. My mother was a saint. Church every Sunday morning. And she would not let me stay out past ten. Every boy I brought home had to get Mother's stamp of approval before I was even allowed to leave the parlor and sit on the porch. She was very strict."

"Which is why you rebelled the way you did," Thaddeus said.

"Rebelled?" Zelda was almost screaming.

Thaddeus jumped out of his seat and headed for the table. "Yes, rebelled. Drank like a fish, wore men's clothes, traveled the world and never kept a fella for more than a few months."

"You're one to talk, you horny old bastard," Zelda said. Her face grew red and flushed. "I may have been a little wild back in the day, but you never did settle down. Let's see if I can remember. There was Rita, Sarah, and Charlotte in Tallahassee. Then Carol, Barbara and Helen in

Frisco. And who was it in New York? The three J's, right? Judy, Joan, and who was the third J? Oh yes. James!"

After several seconds of stunned silence he said, "You're a mean old snake when you get mad."

Anne stepped into the kitchen door and whistled. "Hey! I'm not in the mood for your morning spat. Thaddeus, leave her alone. Zel, leave him alone." She dried her hands with a blue dishrag before flopping into Alistair's seat at the head of the table. An unlit cigarette dangled from her lips, the filter coated in red lipstick. She produced a match from her pocket and ripped her thumbnail across the tip. Puffs of smoke filled the air.

"Is that an order, madam?" Thaddeus said.

Anne rolled her eyes. "Who's up for a game of gin?"

Thaddeus was the first to reply. "Count me in," he said as he slid into the chair next to Anne. Donald Lilly returned to his seat next to me, mindful to tuck his skirt beneath him. Alistair turned off the television and sat at the opposite end of the table from where he had previously been sitting. Louise Kearney, who had retreated to her room during the argument, returned at the mention of gin.

Anne cleared her throat. "You coming, Zel?"

"I'm not in the mood for cards, so I think I'll take Billy to my room for a while," Zelda said. "Billy, I have something I'd like to show you." Once sequestered in her room, she tapped the foot of her neatly made bed. "Have a seat."

Zelda's room was small and confining. Sunlight fought to break through the barrier of a floor-to-ceiling bookcase shoved in front of the window, but only succeeded in casting a sickly, yellow pallor on the wall around the shelves, a halo for her collection of withering, dusty books. Straining to maintain their form, the shelves themselves had begun to sag and tilt precipitously out from the wall. Framed photos of Faulkner and Welty mixed with the snapshots of a little girl and her mother and a publicity portrait of a much younger Zelda Groves. She shoved a couple of frames aside and used the corner of the nightstand to ease herself into the chair in the corner.

"Don't mind Thad and me, Billy. We argue every morning after breakfast. And we'll get into it again before we turn in tonight. That's what happens when two people have known one another as long as Thad and I."

"How long?" I said.

"Since the war." She pulled an old-fashioned scrapbook from one of the book-lined shelves and began turning the pages. "I met him while I was a correspondent on the Italian front. See?"

She placed the open scrapbook in my lap and tapped on a faded photograph of a man in uniform surrounded by three dark-haired Italian girls.

"He fought in Vietnam?" I said. She laughed.

"Oh heavens no, Billy. The big one. World War II," she said. I looked at the picture again.

"Weren't you jealous?" I indicated the three women.

"Jealous? No, Thad and I are just friends. I guess in a way I was happy for him?" she said, more asking then stating. As she talked, I leafed through the scrapbook filled with headlines about bombs and soldiers and USO shows, pictures of men and women in uniforms, bombed-out buildings, and personal letters. "He was handsome, but not someone I could take home to Mother."

"Were you ever married?"

"Once upon a time. To a Bible salesman. Me married to a Bible salesman, can you imagine that?" She chuckled, shaking her head in disbelief.

"So what happened to him?"

"He was on his way back home from a convention in Canada when a logging truck overturned onto his car." She took the scrapbook from my lap and flipped to another page before handing it back to me. "This is my Edward."

Edward Groves was tall and lanky and had a broad smile full of teeth. His hair was dark, but since the picture was not in color, I could not tell if it was actually black. His eyes, too, were dark and alive and filled with joy. With one arm he leaned on a sleek, shining sedan, and with the other, he cradled Zelda against him.

"This was taken two weeks before he died. I didn't even know I was pregnant yet." She smiled. "I found out while he was away and told him over the phone. I was going to surprise him, but I just couldn't bring myself to keep the secret from him."

"So you have kids?"

She shook her head. "I miscarried before the funeral," she replied.

"Miscarried?"

"I lost the baby."

Though I didn't understand, I nodded anyway. As if she knew that there were only so many things I could learn in a day and we were quickly approaching that limit, Zelda slid the scrapbook back onto the shelf and ceremoniously dusted her hands.

"But life moves on. So, tell me all about yourself, Billy."

Uncomfortable with the sudden shift of the spotlight, I stared down at my shoes. Though teachers were always interested in my background, their interest never strayed beyond those factors that directly affected my schoolwork. Other kids, for the most part, had always steered clear of Billy-with-the-weird-middle-name Bradshaw. For the better part of my young life, I had never faced the reality of getting to know someone, nor had I faced the discomfort of someone getting to know me.

"So?" Zelda said, applying even more pressure for me to begin my autobiography.

"I…well what do you want to know?"

"Just tell me about yourself. I'm a writer and that means I ask a lot of questions and try to get to know people. For example, what does your mother do for a living?"

"She works for a finance company," I said.

"And your father?" she said.

"I don't know. I never met him," I said.

Zelda frowned. "I'm sorry. Is he dead?"

"Don't know. Mom doesn't talk about him much."

"Any brothers or sisters?" I shook my head.

"Grandparents?"

"Yeah. They live in Minneapolis."

"That's right," she said. "You told us you were from Minneapolis earlier. What about school? What school? Do you like it?"

"Holy Cross. Mom sent me there. I told her we're not Catholic, but she said it didn't matter, that it's a good school," I said. "What's so funny?"

"I went to a Catholic school too. Is your school run by nuns?" she said.

"Those women are just mean."

She burst into laughter. "They have to be, Billy. Otherwise it would not be such a good school." I thought about it for a minute and decided she was right.

"What do you do for fun?"

"Homework."

Zelda laughed again. "Seriously, though. Any hobbies?"

"I used to ride my bicycle a lot back home. But there's nowhere to ride it in New Orleans. And we live in a building full of old people so there aren't any other kids. So I mostly just watch TV."

"That's too bad." She frowned and shook her head.

"Not really. I do really well in school because I have a lot of time to do my homework."

"That's the spirit. Make the most of it while you can. Maybe one day, who knows?" she said. "Do you have any friends?" I ignored her question, instead looking past her, out the window. "Gets kind of lonely, doesn't it? Moving all over and never settling long enough to get to know anyone."

"I guess."

Zelda must have detected my discomfort because she stood up and patted my knee. "Billy, do you know how to play gin?" When I shook my head, she clasped her hands together. "Then it's high time you learned. I'll teach you the basics here, and then you can go out there and beat their socks off."

She produced a deck of cards from the nightstand and began shuffling. "It's really a simple game. Have you ever played Hearts?"

I shook my head.

"Poker?"

"Yeah. My grandpa taught me one time, but my mom got mad at him."

"That's as good a starting point as any," she said, dealing the cards. Thirty minutes later, Zelda Groves returned the deck of cards to the nightstand drawer, having taught me all the secrets of the universe, or at least all I needed to know to beat Anne Moore at gin.

Chapter 4

The humid air outside of Liberty hung heavy with morning haze. I lingered on the steps for a couple of minutes, still groggy from the extra hour of sleep. I half-expected to find Camille Roberts waiting with her arms folded across her chest. Stepping through the door, I breathed a sigh of relief. Camille was on the phone.

I slunk past her desk, hoping she wouldn't see me.

"Excuse me, Mr. Downing," she said. She cupped her hand over the receiver. "Park your ass in that chair until I get off this phone."

I flopped into the chair to await my fate, angry that my fate was so uniquely tied to the actions of my mother. She was the one who had overslept, taken her time getting ready, and complained of a hangover, all without regard for how her irresponsibility might draw down Miss Camille's wrath. And from what I was hearing of her phone call, she was in a rare mood.

"Yes, Mr. Downing. I know what you're saying. But you don't know what's what here at Liberty. I've been keeping the wheels on this wagon with duct tape and bubble gum–No sir, I'm not suggesting you don't know–That's not what I said. You don't listen much, do you?...I apologize for the disrespect...No sir, but you're not my boss yet...Fine, I'll send them to you in tomorrow's mail. Good bye."

As Miss Camille hung up, I heard Ellie's phone clatter into the cradle. Eyebrows raised, Ellie sighed. "Oh, Miss Camille. That man's trouble. I can tell."

"You think?" Camille said. "Wants an invalid ward. Now where the hell we going to put an invalid ward in this place?"

Ellie opened her mouth to speak, but stopped, instead sliding back into her chair and disappearing behind her files. Rubbing her temples, Camille turned back to her own desk and saw me.

"I almost forgot about you. Well, what do you got to say for yourself?"

"My mom forgot to wake me up this morning."

"That's the third time in a week. Next time, I call Judge Spurgeon."

"Yes, ma'am. It won't happen again." I prayed for a quick dismissal to the Row, but Camille continued. "I still don't know what that man was thinking, sending you down here. What are you supposed to do? Ain't like you're going to be making any friends." She dismissed me with a nod down the hall, and as I wandered away, I heard her mumbling under her breath, "Oh well, at least you'll be entertained."

I found the Bohemians gathered around the television, enthralled with one of Thaddeus's soaps. I tried to sneak in, but Emily tipped them off to my presence.

"Hey Billy," she said. The Bohemians all turned.

"Sorry I'm late. Mom forgot to wake me up this morning–again."

"Again, indeed," Anne said. She patted the place beside her on the sofa. "You should learn to set an alarm clock. So, tell us what did you do yesterday."

One of the more annoying qualities of childhood is a kid's ability to prattle on and on, without saying much. Thankfully, most children are spared embarrassment by an ignorance of the telltale slouch of feigned interest and constantly nodding heads of active listening. Such was the state in which my tale of cartoon-watching was languishing when I realized that there were only six of us. Someone was missing.

"Where's Zel?" I said.

Alistair and Louise exchanged glances. Thaddeus pretended not to hear me, instead focused on fine-tuning the television antenna. Donald just sipped his coffee.

Anne Moore finally answered. "She's in her room." When I attempted to stand, I felt Anne's hand on my knee. "I'd give her a few minutes, Billy. She has company."

Other than Zelda's husband, we had never discussed friends or family. I assumed that the Bohemians never received visitors, that their lives as I had seen them were a comprehensive whole.

Zel's door slammed and we all jumped. A dark-haired streak charged across the lobby and through the Hall B door. Through the several seconds of stunned silence that followed, I found myself unable to bear not knowing and finally cracked. "Okay. Who was that?"

Before anyone could answer, Zelda emerged from her room, blotting her eyes. "Sorry for the outburst everyone, I'm not sure why she even bothers any–well hello, Billy!" She squeezed in next to me, nudging Anne aside.

"Who was that?"

She frowned and turned away. "No one. Just…" Her voice trailed off. I considered asking again, but the faint residue of tears on her cheeks told me everything I needed to know. Whoever burst out of Zelda's room evoked great distress in my friend. And for that, I did not like that woman, whoever she was.

With the excitement of the morning past, Alistair rummaged around Emily's desk for something to read. He found a dog-eared copy of *Redbook* and retired to his room. Louise and Ann disappeared into the kitchen to cook lunch. Thaddeus alternated between talk shows and his soaps. Donald, as always, returned to his room for a nap before lunch. Zelda was the only one who deviated from her routine. Rather than scribbling in any of a dozen journals and notebooks, she sat by the window staring into the slate-gray sky. I discovered a half-completed jigsaw puzzle on a card table in the corner. Four straight edges framed parts of a ship in various stages of completion. A section of deck ended with ragged edges where a smooth line should have been. Meandering columns of sky a single-tile's width flowed down and pooled into blue seas. Huge sails billowed, full and straining against the wind even though gaping holes dotted their surface. Several gray-and-black tiles caught my eye. I struggled for a moment, frustrated that I did not know what part of the ship I was attempting to assemble. After trying several combinations, two pieces locked, then a third, a fourth. With the fifth piece, I recognized coils of ropes stacked neatly in the corner.

"Don't bother. There's a piece missing," someone said. I turned. Thaddeus stood there, watching me.

"How do you know?" I said.

He tapped the picture of a hatch cover. "All of the pieces are sorted and there aren't any that fit the door. So there's a piece missing. We just haven't bothered to throw it out yet. There're some more puzzles over in the closet. Why don't we start one of those?"

The smell of old coats threatened to derail my efforts. "Where are they?" I said, choking back a cough. Before Thaddeus could answer, I saw the ginger-bread trim of a Victorian cottage hidden in the corner. "Never mind. I found one."

We spread the pieces out on the table. At his instruction, I searched out pieces with a straight edge. "Billy, about earlier," he said.

"When?"

"Zel and that little scene." He glanced at Zelda by the window before lowering his voice. "Well, it's like this, Billy. Zelda's niece wants her to move to Chicago. But Zelda doesn't want to go. And…"

"Chicago? Why?"

"Because her niece is her only family and I guess she feels sort of protective."

"Why doesn't she want to go?"

"Because Alistair, Louise–all of us. We're her family. When her Edward died, she started drifting from town to town. Up until a few years ago when she settled here. This is home to all of us." Even though he did not seem to be paying attention to the puzzle, three sides of the border were complete. I found two orange pieces, their sides similarly shaped, but the two refused to snap together. I tried banging them into place with my fist. Thaddeus grabbed my hands before I could hit them again. "Don't force them, son. They don't go together."

"But they look like they do," I said.

He snatched them from me. "Then put them over here and just leave them be until we find the rest of them. Otherwise you'll just mess the whole thing up."

"It's just a puzzle." I could tell by the look on his face that he was about to speak, but Anne reappeared, her shirt covered in flour. "No one told me we was putting together a new puzzle."

She scooted my chair aside and wedged herself between Thaddeus and me. Donald announced he could not sleep because of all the noise and took the seat between Thaddeus and

Anne. The unsorted pile in the middle dwindled into stacks of windows, the porch, the sky. Bit by bit, the house took shape. First the porch, then the walls, the sky. We exchanged seats, took breaks, and even allowed Emily her turn at the puzzle. Shortly before lunch, Alistair cleared his throat.

"Here you go, Billy." Alistair offered me the final piece of the house. "You do the honors."

Carefully, I fitted the last pane of glass into its spot in the door. The house was finished.

Louise stretched. "Anyone hungry? The soup should be just about finished."

A rumble in my stomach reminded me that I had missed breakfast. "What kind of soup?"

"Black bean. Figured we'd go light for lunch today and have a big dinner tonight," Anne said. She and Louise returned to the kitchen. While the others set about arranging a table for seven, I could not take my eyes away from the puzzle.

Chapter 5

The apartment door slammed behind my mother. She collapsed on the sofa next to me. Her navy suit was wrinkled, and there was a patch of dust on the hem. "What a day I've had." I didn't look up from the television. After several seconds of silence, she tugged my knee. "So talk to me."

"I'm sorry, Mom. Just tired I guess. How was your day?"

"Long and unproductive. I was in a meeting all morning with Mr. Thompson. Then I had lunch with one of the girls from accounting. After lunch was even worse. I had two major accounts to reconcile and the phone never stopped ringing." She stood and started for her room.

"Where you going?" I said.

"Have a date." She shot me a wide grin. "Big date." As she disappeared into her bedroom, I turned the television back on. Her head popped out of her bedroom. "So come talk to me, silly."

"But, Mom, I'm watching TV."

"I want to hear what happened today, but I'm running late already. So you have to come in here to tell me. Otherwise I'll be late for my date," she said, giggling back into her room. By the time I wandered through the door, her navy-blue business suit was crumpled on her bed, and she was bouncing around the room in a red miniskirt and a matching red bra. "So, tell me about today. What do you do?"

I shrugged, unprepared for her question. In the weeks I had been at Liberty Street, Mom had scarcely mentioned it, much less asked questions. It had not been a fun time, but when she finally thought to ask about it, I realized just how little the Bohemians seemed to think of me.

"I don't think they want me to get in the way, so I just sort of sit there."

"Have you met anyone?"

"Yeah. A guy who was an actor and a woman who was a reporter in World War II," I said.

"Really? Sounds neat."

"Yeah. And a poet."

"A poet? Wow."

"Yeah. Her name is Louise and she has this friend named Anne Moore and they cook their own food and they don't like Emily."

She tried to watch me through the mirror as I paced around her room. "Who's Emily?" She almost jabbed herself in the eye with her mascara and tossed the tube into the sink.

"The girl at the desk on the Row," I said.

"The Row?"

"Yeah. Hall B. They call it Bohemian Row. And there is a girl that sits there and just reads Cosmo all day." Mother gestured for the blouse hanging on the door. I turned and grabbed it, but when I moved to hand it to her, Mother's attention had strayed to her fading lipstick. The more I talked, the more excited I became until, at last, I had exhausted the story and decided to do whatever it took to become part of their family.

"Bohemian Row, huh? Sounds interesting," she said.

"This one lady–her name is Zelda–she's the reporter. And she has this scrapbook and she has been to Minneapolis."

"That's nice."

"And she married a Bible salesman named Edward, but he died in a wreck in Nebraska," I said.

"That's too bad." Sometime during her mad rush to get ready for her date, Mom lost interest in my day. But my own excitement about the Bohemians shielded me from realizing that she had stopped listening. I continued chirping away details of my day.

"Yeah. A car wreck. But that's okay because she's known Thaddeus McLean since before the War and they're really good friends even if they fight all the time. So who's your date with?" She didn't answer. "Mom?"

"Huh?" She tossed a compact onto the counter and turned.

"Who's your date with?"

"Oh. This guy who came into the office last week." She snatched the blouse from the hanger and smiled. "Really good looking too. I think he'll be a keeper."

She winked, disappeared into her closet. Mother thought every man was a keeper until on the third date she discovered that he was an alcoholic or a drug addict or married. When she emerged from behind her closet door, she was wearing her blouse and a different jacket.

"Where's he taking you?"

"To some new restaurant down in the Quarter," she said. Though she had been in New Orleans less than a year, my mother insisted on referring to the French Quarter as "the Quarter," having adopted a vernacular best described as Yankee Cajun in a futile attempt to blend with foreign surroundings. What to her sounded like a fair approximation of "Nwalins" sounded, to the rest of the world, like New Awnings. But no matter how many people she insulted, my mother was convinced that she sounded like a native.

Thirty minutes after she first turned the key in the door, my mother emerged from her bedroom wearing the red miniskirt and her best heels. She grabbed her purse and emptied the contents onto the coffee table. A cigarette pack and her wallet disappeared into a smaller handbag the same shade of red as her shoes and her lipstick. I flopped back onto the sofa and returned to channel surfing.

She spun twice. "How do I look?"

"You look fine," I said.

"I look fine? Just fine?" She grew louder and more boisterous. "I spend all that time getting ready and I look just fine. Well I'll show you." She jumped onto the sofa. Pinned under her weight, I could not fight off her or laughter as she tickled my sides.

"Mom! No, Mom." I gasped for air.

"I just look fine, huh?" She tickled me harder.

"You'll mess up your hair," I said.

"Who cares? I just look fine." She unleashed another barrage of tickling.

"Okay, okay. You look great. Fantastic, beautiful, like a supermodel. Just don't tickle me anymore."

"Like a supermodel? That's what I thought you said." She stood, straightened her skirt, and retrieved her purse from the floor. "There's a sandwich for you in the fridge. And go to bed early. We have church in the morning."

"Okay, Mom. Go now or you'll miss dinner," I said.

Leaning over the couch, she kissed the back of my head before leaving. "And by bed, I mean in your room, with the lights out. Early. Got it?"

I pushed her away. "Yes, Mom. Go. Now."

"Good night, kiddo."

I listened as her footsteps faded down the stairs. Several hours later, I awoke to the sound of muffled voices outside the door and Mother's key turning in the lock.

"Shh. My son is asleep in his room," she said.

"Well I'll be quiet. I promise," a strange voice replied. When they stepped through the door, Mother was the first to see her son awake, alert, and awaiting an introduction.

"I thought I told you to go to bed early. We have church in the morning. Why are you still up?" she said.

The man grabbed her around the waist and pulled her closer. "Go easy on him, Bev. He just wants to check me out, I'm sure. Hi, Billy. Your mother has told me all about you." He shook my hand and flopped onto the sofa. "So what are you watching?"

Something about his overt chumminess bothered my mother. She slammed her purse on the kitchen counter and her date jumped. "Can I get you something to drink? Beer? Glass of wine?"

"Sure, Bev. A beer sounds nice," he said.

"I'm just flipping channels," I said.

"Do you like sports?"

I turned the television off. "Yeah, baseball."

"That's what I hear." He laughed a couple of times. He leaned close and whispered in my ear. I could smell beer on his breath as he spoke. "Don't tell your mom, but I broke a few windows in my day."

Mother returned from the kitchen with two bottles of beer. "Here you go."

"When did you start drinking beer?" I said.

"Silly. I've always drunk beer." She forced a laugh and patted Steve on the knee.

"No, you haven't," I said.

She raised her eyebrow. "Bedtime, Billy."

When Mom's words carried the weight of an order, I knew it was best not to whine. Rather than arguing, I started for my room.

"It was nice to meet you, Billy," he called down the hall. "Maybe we can watch a baseball game some day?"

"That would be cool," I said. He smiled and waved to me before I disappeared around the corner. It was the last time I ever saw him. The next morning, Mother and I ate breakfast alone before attending Sunday services at Trinity Lutheran Church. Such was the pattern with most of the men who dated my mother. The ones that stuck around were of the typically worthless, unemployed variety and did not attend Sunday morning services. Anyone worth a damn either chose not to stick around or was never invited back. Mother never said anything about them, and I never bothered to ask.

Chapter 6

The idyll of the morning's puzzle had been a deceptive overture for that afternoon. Over a lunch of black bean soup and ham sandwiches, moods began to shift. They ate quickly and talked in frantic bursts, as if the Bohemians secretly anticipated some terrific penalty should their lunch extend beyond the prescribed time. Though I had yet to grasp fully the haphazard regiment of their daily lives, I could sense that this afternoon was somehow different.

I cannot recall what day of the week it was or if these lunches fell at regular intervals or were random happenings. This was but the first of many such days I would live through on Hall B. Moods would not exactly sour, but there would be a shift, as if no one could wait to get to their own rooms and away from one another.

As the lunch dishes disappeared, so did the Bohemians. I was abandoned on the sofa, left with Thaddeus to watch his soap opera and lament the presence of his self-described archrival.

"Son of a bitch," Thaddeus said as a graying man entered through a heavy oak door and kissed his onscreen wife. I had come to expect his reactions. Entire conversations would now begin, born of an innate hatred, the origins of which were a mystery to everyone. That Thaddeus hated someone was no surprise. That none of his closest friends had bothered to ask why surprised me.

"Why don't you like him?" I asked.

He mumbled something unintelligible beneath his breath and growled. "I was supposed to be him. That was my part and he took it."

"Why?"

"Probably because I took his girlfriend." Though I sensed there was more to the tale of the soap opera, I didn't get a chance to ask. Donald stuck his head out of his bedroom. "Billy, could you lend an old man a hand?"

Donald's bedroom was the picture of orderly. Along one wall, his bed was neatly made, the blue and white stripes on the pillowcases aligned with careful precision. At the foot of the bed, a small desk and chair sat, the papers on the desk arranged with the same careful hand as his bed. Even the shoes in Donald's closet sat as if someone had laid a ruler on the ground while setting them into their places.

"So what did you need?" I said.

"These have to go up front to Camille to go out for dry cleaning. Could you take them, please?" He handed me a plastic bag full of laundry. "They can't be washed with the other laundry."

He handed me the bag, but hesitated to turn it loose. "Dry clean."

"I get it," I said and pulled the bag from his hand. Outside, in the hallway, the first chords of a piano concerto exploded from Alistair's bedroom. His door had swung open and revealed his bedroom, though I wasn't sure where he slept. Stacks of canvasses littered his bed, rested against the walls, atop a table. At the center of the room, an easel held a canvas, faced away from the door. The tile floor was a work worthy of Jackson Pollack, so speckled with paint the original substrate had long been forgotten.

I thumbed through a stack of canvasses beside the door, confused and unable to decipher the images I saw. Half-formed faces transmutated into horrid animals. A chair had sprouted horns and teeth, ready to devour anyone who sat down. Sunlight streaming through the bedroom window illuminated the painting on the easel, but I couldn't make out any discernable images.

The bathroom door opened and Alistair stepped into the room. His hands and shirt were covered in paints and he was swirling a brush around in a jar of fluid. When he saw me at the door, he froze. "What the hell are you doing in here?"

"I–"

"Get out! I don't come into your home and barge into your room unannounced! Out!" He chased me from the room and into the hall. I ran as quickly as I could through the double doors. As I turned and sprinted towards Camille's desk, the sounds of his bellows faded into the walls. When I mustered the courage to return to Hall B a half hour later, Thaddeus and Donald were on the sofa, waiting for me. The door slammed, announcing my return. Thaddeus was the first to say anything. "Billy, exactly what happened?"

I told him about finding Alistair's door open and the canvasses against the wall, how he had exploded when he saw me in his room. Both Donald and Thaddeus waited patiently for me to finish. When at last I did, they both sighed.

"I wouldn't worry about it," Donald said. "He'll be fine tomorrow. He just gets like that sometimes."

Thaddeus scooted to one side of the sofa. "Why don't you watch some TV with us?"

I shook my head. "No, I think I'll go outside." I stopped at the patio door. "Why does he paint those pictures? I thought he painted portraits."

"He did. But he always wanted to paint for museums instead," Thaddeus said. "It didn't work out."

"Why?"

Thaddeus tapped his chest with a sigh. "Heart problems. He had to have surgery and never quite got back to painting. But he kept trying until his second heart attack."

Donald continued the story. "That one wasn't his fault. He did everything he was supposed to. Ate right, took his medications, even exercised. But things got really bad for him."

Until that morning, I looked at painting as something my grandmother did to relax. That it might be stressful for someone had never occurred to me until Alistair exploded in his bedroom. Yet, even given his outburst at my intrusion, I couldn't understand why he would give up on his dream to paint for museums. I decided to ask.

"If he wanted to paint for museums, he should have. What happened?"

Donald lit a cigarette and took a long drag. "Critics happened."

Chapter 7

New Orleans has only two seasons. Summer lasts for nine months of the year and is followed by three months of what amounts to little more than a warm fall. Spring and winter have not existed since the last ice age, casualties of the city's unfortunate proximity to the Tropic of Cancer, the Mississippi River, and the Gulf of Mexico. Year-round heat and humidity combine under a sweltering sun that beats down on the Louisiana Delta to sap energy out of its unwitting victims. On the occasional days when the temperature cools, it rains. Thus the cycle of humid mornings and balmy nights perpetuate themselves. During the hottest months of the summer, the most unbearable time of day falls somewhere between late afternoon and early evening, before winds from the Gulf of Mexico replenish the suffocating moisture and after the sun has peaked in its arc across the sky. For two or three hours near the end of afternoon, in spite of the swelter, the draw of the sun proves too strong, and the citizens of the venerable old city venture out into their yards and onto their patios to plant flowers in a bed or to while away an hour or two in a hammock or a deckchair. Alistair called the time their siesta.

The Liberty Street Home had once been the residence of a prominent physician who, upon his death, bequeathed the house to the city as a convalescent home. Heavily renovated, only the art deco façade of the two-story structure had remained unchanged in the sixty years since the doctor's passing. On the ground floor, a hundred or so patients occupied tiny bedrooms, a dining room, and the living-room-cum-activity-center. The second floor was divided between storage areas, unused administrative offices, and an apartment for the administrator and his family. During the 1970's, a socialist's spending spree funded the construction of a new wing, a single-story rectangle of glass and concrete jutting into the lawn. By any measure, Hall B lacked the character and dignity of the main house.

Perhaps it was the cold, institutional lines of windows lining Hall B or the fact that builders and architects had made no attempt at blending the two structures. But for whatever reason, Hall B had languished, unoccupied and unloved, until a few years before my arrival, when the Bohemians had commandeered the wing as their home.

I always felt that the Bohemians were Hall B, both separated from the main building in the same unintegrated and unfinished manner. The Bohemians hadn't been accepted in the general population and had been discouraged from dining with the other residents. Whenever Liberty Street received new furniture, Hall B was discretely overlooked. Likewise, other than jagged wounds cut into the masonry, the only connection between the addition and the rest of the building was a brick patio, shared between the living room of the Row and the main dining room of the home. Though the patio spanned the area between the two wings, the staff and residents knew that the patio was an extension of Hall B, the place where the Bohemians spent afternoons basking in the sun and absorbing the aromas of the roses, azaleas, and the herbs that Louise grew to dry on the recycled window screens she kept stacked by the back door.

"Billy, could you pass me that spade?" Louise pointed to a green handle protruding from beneath my chair. I sent it rattling across the bricks with the toe of my sneaker.

"Anything else I can do?" I said. The constant string of tasks and errands was starting to wear thin. Washing windows, toting dry cleaning, endless stacks of dishes in the kitchen, all of it was starting to take its toll.

Louise opened her mouth to ask for something else, but as if she had read my dissatisfaction, she shook her head no, dug out a spade full of rosemary, and dropped it on the patio. She repeated this several times, and then stopped. "Actually, Billy, around the corner behind the building, there's a wheelbarrow full of topsoil and a five-gallon bucket. Fill up the bucket and drag it around here, if you would. I need to fill in these holes."

I pulled myself off the lounger and lumbered around the corner, mumbling. For the last week

I had dreaded every day. Puzzles or card games in the morning were not enough fun to make up for the four hours of yard work or ten trips to the Home's walk-in freezers for hamburger meat. As I approached the storage shed, I cursed Judge Spurgeon and the Bohemians.

The wheelbarrow was exactly where Louise had said it would be. But the bucket was nowhere to be found. "Louise, there's no bucket back here," I called.

"Check under the shed," she said. "Sometimes it rolls under there."

I knelt down and peered under the shed, but there was no bucket. A bee buzzed past my ear. I swatted him away so I could hear the Bohemians around the corner, talking in hushed tones.

"Maybe we could say something to Camille? Find him something else to do?" Thaddeus said.

Louise's spade clattered across the bricks and she heaved a loud sigh. "He is a handful, and we're old."

"And just what do you think he'd do somewhere else?" Zel said.

"Right," Anne said. "It's not like there's a playground in the Rec Room."

"I think you're right, Anne," Donald said. "We'll just have to continue to adjust."

"But Alistair," Thaddeus said.

Donald interrupted him. "This isn't open for discussion. I'm sorry, Thad, but Billy stays."

The tension hung in the air for a moment following his pronouncement, and I thought that, had I peered around the corner, I would have seen it, winding like a tightrope between them.

Finally, Alistair spoke. "You heard Donald. We adjust, Thad."

The bee returned, flying mad circles around my head. I swatted him again. This time, it landed at my feet, dazed and stumbling.

I peeked around the corner. "There's still no bucket."

Louise wiped her hands on her gardening apron and sighed. "I'm sure I put it back there the last time I used it." She shook her head. "No wait. I remember. It's on the shelves behind the shed. Sorry, Billy."

A set of rickety wooden shelves clung precariously to the rear wall. The bucket gleamed in the sun on the top-most shelf, well beyond the reach of Louise or anyone else I'd met at Liberty

Street. Climbing onto the first shelf, I wondered just how long it had been since Louise had used that bucket. At the second shelf, the bucket remained out of reach.

I pulled myself to the third shelf and froze.

The shed popped and groaned with the sickening sound of wood beginning to give way. The plywood wall to which the shelves were attached tore away from the studs, nails squeaking as they ripped from the aging timber. For the brief moment that the shelves teetered two legs, I considered screaming or jumping. But the shed made that decision for me. The entire rear wall of the shed came loose, throwing me clear off the shelves amid a shower of debris.

"Billy, are you all right?" Thaddeus called out. "What's going on?"

Part of the wall had collapsed between the shed and the rear wall of Hall B and was pinned tightly to the bricks. I rolled onto my side, surveying the damage. Louise's bucket lay dashed beneath the wreckage. A gaping hole in the shed revealed an old lawn mower, several garden tools, and various coffee cans filled with screwdrivers, pencils and nails. I lay on the ground, tried to catch my breath. My left temple throbbed, and I could taste blood in my mouth.

"Billy," Thaddeus called again. I could see him trying to pull the section of wall out of the way. "What happened?"

"The shelves fell. And I hit my head." Choking back tears, I grabbed one of the exposed wall studs to pull myself up. A pain shot through the palm of my hand and past my elbow. I screamed. Looking back to the board, I saw a bee fluttering crushed wings in its last moments of life.

"What's going on, Billy?" Alistair said.

"A bee just stung me."

I struggled to my knees, pulled myself up to my feet. A black cloud enveloped my head. Another bee stung me. And then another on my shoulder. I had risen directly into an angry swarm. I covered my face with my hands, tried to fight off the bees. The more bees I swatted, the more they stung me. My ears were about to explode, and it took me a moment to realize the shrieks I heard were my own screams, reverberating in my ears.

"Get down on the ground and hang on, Billy. We're coming," Alistair shouted. I dropped to the ground. Something banged against the plywood wall. It shook violently with the second bang. With the third, the wall disintegrated into a pile of splinters. Thaddeus tossed aside the misshapen remains of the wrought-iron chair he had used as a battering ram, reached through the hole, and grabbed my ankles. Alistair's arms, arms that at first glance seemed thin and frail, looped under my shoulders. Together, the two carried me inside and laid me on the couch. Anne pressed a washcloth full of ice to the swelling wound. I felt cold water trickle down my temple.

Zelda lightly touched each of the welts rising on my legs and arms. "Are you allergic to bees? How many got you?"

"I don't know. Seven or eight maybe." I tried to sit up, but Anne pinned my shoulders.

"Stay. Just for a couple of minutes," she said.

Emily appeared with a first aid kit and a bottle of rubbing alcohol. Zelda yanked them away. "This is going to hurt." She dabbed alcohol onto a cotton pad, she sniffed and crinkled her nose. "And smell."

I almost grinned, but the sudden, ferocious burning on my forehead killed that impulse.

Zelda swabbed the blood and dirt from around the wound. With a fresh pad, she swabbed the wound itself. "It burns," I said through clenched teeth.

Anne patted my shoulders, tried to calm me. "It's almost over."

Zelda placed a bandage on my temple and smoothed the edges. "All done. Now, where did the bees get you?"

I pointed to several spots on my arms and legs. Digging through the first aid kit, Anne produced a vial of green fluid the color of antifreeze. "This won't hurt as bad as the alcohol. And it will keep it from getting infected."

Alistair wandered to the window, absently scratching at two welts on his own hand. "I wonder where the bees came from? They weren't there last year." Thaddeus shrugged.

"Must be a new hive," Thaddeus said.

"Oh no!" Emily said. "We're supposed to call Camille. That's the rule anytime there's an injury." She bounded for her desk; my misfortune had somehow empowered her with a new sense of authority. Maybe she did serve a purpose in their lives. She dialed a number and tapped her foot impatiently. "Camille? This is Emily. Billy hit his head and got stung…Bees…No, he's all right. I can handle it… No, really. He's– okay. Yes'am." She returned the phone to the receiver, tucked her hands into the pockets of her jeans. Emily rocked back and forth for a moment. "Camille's on her way back."

Zelda and Anne exchanged glances. "It's okay, dear. One day, I'm sure there will be a crisis that will be all yours," Anne said. Emily smiled thoughtfully before disappearing into the kitchen.

"God help us when that happens," Zel said.

Camille burst through the door and was to the sofa before anyone could respond. She stooped, her hands on her knees, panting. "You okay, Billy?" I nodded, but she did not notice. Instead, she had become transfixed with the swarm on the patio. "I'll call an exterminator."

"No!" Zelda and Alistair exclaimed together.

"We'll call a beekeeper, Nurse Roberts," Alistair said.

"And they will come and capture the bees to add them to their hives," Zelda added. Camille cocked her eyebrow and leaned away. She was not buying it.

Alistair steered her away from the windows. "You're too busy as it is, Ms. Roberts. We'll take care of it," Alistair said.

Camille shrugged. "Whatever you say." She noticed me lying on the couch and remembered the reason for Emily's summons. "Do we need to take him to the doctor or call his Mother?"

Anne shook her head. "No. Just a flesh wound. He'll be fine."

"Billy, if you feel faint, tell Emily and she'll call me. No arguments." She turned to leave, pausing in the door. "Get those bees out of here today, or I'm calling the exterminator in the morning."

With Camille gone, our attention returned to the bee-infested patio. I heard Alistair on the phone. He had to dial several people before he finally found the right person. "Good afternoon. This is Alistair Lees and I'm a—yes, the one that paints portraits or at least used to… You don't say! Small world. And how is your Mother?… Oh I'm sorry to hear that. Was she a petite woman, chestnut hair, angular chin? Had a Pomeranian? I thought so. Yes. Very adamant about making sure the dog was just so. I thought we'd never get that dog to sit still. Your number was listed in the book as a beekeeper. Do you still keep bees?" A few minutes later, he returned to the sofa. "He'll be here around dusk. Says we have to give them time to settle down before he can capture the hive."

* * *

The beekeeper studied the lethargic bee crawling across the back of his hand. "Mellifera ligustica."

"Excuse me?" Anne said. "In English?"

He smiled. "Italian Honey bee. Very desirable, very desirable." He extended his hand toward her, offering a better view of the creature. "See the bands here?" He pointed toward the bee's tail.

Anne squinted through her bifocals and shook her head. "Looks like a bee to me."

"They brought these little fellers over to work from Europe in 1879. Spread all over the country," he said. "Ligusticas are calm, easier to work."

He stepped back onto the patio and released the bee. "It shouldn't take long to capture the hive. You'll need to watch out for a few days, though. There may be a few stragglers that miss the ride."

He looked out the window past the patio, where several bees still lingered, contemplating one last harvest on their flight home. He donned a hat that reminded me of the hats worn by hazardous materials teams on television, except this one was tan, not yellow. Eyeing the welts on my arms and legs, the beekeeper said, "Billy, would you give me a hand? I have an extra veil and pair of gloves in the car."

"You mean out there?"

The beekeeper grinned. "I'm sure one of these guys would loan you a long-sleeved shirt."

I shook my head. "Uh-uh. No way I'm going out there."

Zelda pushed me towards the door. "Billy, think of how good your What-I-Did-This-Summer essay will be when you get back to Holy Cross." I thought I saw Zelda wink at the beekeeper, but before I could say anything, he was out the door.

Ten minutes later and despite ardent protests, there I was, surveying the patio from beneath a mosquito-net veil, tugging at the sleeves of Alistair's too-large shirt. The cuffs tucked neatly under the elastic gloves, but the excess fabric bunched up in my armpits. I noticed the welts on my bare shins and shuddered. "Are you sure I don't need anything on my legs?" I said.

He shook his head. "No. By the time I call you back, I'll have smoked the hive and the bees will be calm."

"Why do you smoke the hive?"

"The smoke makes them think there's a fire, so they eat as much honey as they can in preparation for a move."

I was confused. "Wouldn't a fire scare them? Make them angry again?"

"They are scared, I guess, but they eat a lot of honey. And that makes them sleepy."

"Kinda like Thanksgiving," I said. His laugh sounded hollow and eerie from my protected place beneath the hood.

"Yes, just like Thanksgiving." He squeezed the handle of the canister and a puff of smoke tickled my nose. Though I'm sure that my questions were tedious, he didn't grow impatient, never criticized and responded with the thoughtful respect of a Zen master.

"Wait here until I call you." He disappeared around the corner with a stack of what looked like oversized picture frames clasped firmly in one hand and a column of smoke jetting ahead of him from a canister in the other.

Chapter 8

I sat on the edge of a deck lounger, my legs folded beneath me. I tugged the hem of Alistair's shirt down over my knees in an unsuccessful attempt to cover my bare thighs. The heavy veil draping down past my shoulders pulled at one side of my headdress, constantly forcing me to straighten it atop my head. Occasionally, I caught whiffs of smoke drifting around the corner.

I lost track of how many minutes I had been waiting while I watched the dwindling number of bees roaming the patio, my own private countdown to when the beekeeper would call for me to come help capture the hive. I figured the fewer bees on the patio, the closer I was to being finished. I did not like bees.

Finally, he poked his head around the corner. "Come on back, but be careful not to trip." He disappeared back around the corner and I trudged behind, a light breeze dragging the protective netting and almost removing my hat. I found him sprawled on his side in the dirt. He had removed his hood and was spraying smoke in between a pair of two-by-twelve floor joists. "They built in here," he said.

I knelt down beside him and peered in between the joists. A bee landed on my veil, only an inch from my nose. I moved to swat him, but the beekeeper stopped me.

"Don't swat him. You'll upset the hive." The bee lingered for a moment and then flew back into the hive to join the other buzzing bees. "See, they won't hurt you."

"Why are they so noisy?" I said.

"They're flapping their wings like that to cool the hive. We can start moving them now." John Sanders placed one of the frames flat on the ground in front of the hole. He reached into the hive with a long saw, but stopped long enough to pass me the silver canister. "When I say now, spray smoke into the hive." He began cutting along the top of the first layer of combs. Their buzzing grew louder. Several of the bees nearest the exit of the hive flew toward him. "Now."

I filled the hole with smoke. The bees immediately calmed again. He inserted a hooked strip of metal into the hive and loosened the first comb. It fell toward him, and he caught it. He secured the section of comb into the first frame then dropped the frame into a large box and fastened it into place with elastic bands. "With any luck, we'll find the queen," he said. "Smoke."

I filled the hive with smoke again. "Why do we need the queen?"

"The bees will follow her into the box. Makes things easier." He placed another frame into the box. "I may have a problem getting the entire hive. It goes way back there. We'll just grab as much of it as we can."

With a long-handled spoon, he ladled bees from the hole and deposited them into the box. I alternated a steady stream of smoke onto the box and into the hive.

"Why does that one look funny?" I pointed to a bee on the ground.

"Damn, that's a good eye, kid." He scooped the bee into his hand, carefully placing it into the box on one of the framed combs. "Watch."

The bees still in the hive suddenly flocked to the box in a mad rush of activity. "See why we should find the queen?" he said.

I watched the bees fly almost single-file to the box. "How do they know?"

"They follow her smell." A few minutes later, he secured the last of the combs into a frame. "That should do it. We'll load the hive in the back of the truck. I have a couple of jars of fresh honey for you guys."

"I've never had fresh honey, I don't think." I lifted one of the handles of the white plywood box that now contained the beehive. It was heavier than I expected, and I almost dropped it.

"Careful. It's heavy." The beekeeper gripped the handle of his end with both hands. I did the same. "Fresh honey's good. The stuff in stores has sat there for a while so isn't as sweet."

I struggled to lift my end into the back of the truck. The corner of the box hung on the hem of my veil and almost tore. He took both handles and slid the hive into the back of his truck.

"All done," he said. "Let's get you out of that gear, and I'll get out of y'all's hair."

With the hive and gear safely stowed away, John Sanders passed two quart-sized jars of thick, molasses-colored honey through the truck window. He ruffled my hair. "Thanks for your help. See you around, Billy." As the battered truck pulled away from the Liberty Street Home, I was certain that I saw several bees chasing it down the street.

Once back on the Row, I plopped the two jars onto the table. The clock above Emily's desk caught my eye. "It's five-thirty?"

Louise glanced down at her watch. "Yes. Why?"

I looked around frantically for my backpack. "Mom's going to be mad. I have to go home."

"Why don't you stay for dinner?" Anne said. Everyone agreed. "We're having Italian." The smell of roasted garlic and tomato sauce filled the air. My stomach growled.

"I don't know. I need to call her and ask if I can stay." Louise slid Emily's phone across the desk. I dialed my number. It rang several times, but she did not answer. I tried calling her office. After several rings, she answered.

"Mom, it's me."

"Hey, sweetie. I'm running a little late. And, I have plans tonight. There are some frozen dinners in the fridge. Just do one in the microwave. I'll be in later. Got to go." She hung up before I could respond. I handed the phone back to Louise.

"So?" Zelda said.

I nodded.

She clapped once. "Wunderbar. I'll set an extra place at the table."

Alistair ushered me toward the sofa. "So tell us all about it."

"Yeah. None of us has ever captured a beehive before," Thaddeus said. Alistair sat to my left and Thaddeus to my right. Donald Lilly scooted his chair in close and leaned attentively forward.

In that moment, with the three men gathered around me and the women in the kitchen cooking, something changed. During the brief time I had spent with the Bohemians, I had been the observer, hearing their stories and learning about their experiences. But suddenly, I knew about something none of them had ever experienced, and they wanted to know about it. More than anything, I wanted to recall every detail.

I told them about the combs, about the flashlight, about the hive tool he used to remove the sections of the hive. I told them how I smoked the hive and found the queen, about almost dropping the hive at the truck. They especially liked the bees following the truck down the road.

When I finished, Alistair squinted and nodded. "He should be a writer. And write stories like that. What an eye for detail."

Donald Lilly reared back in his chair, cupping his head in his hands. "Very good. Very good indeed. Why don't you write that down?"

I shrugged. "I've never written anything before. I mean, I've written stuff for school. But, well. I don't know how."

"It's not hard," Thaddeus said. He too stood and started for the table. "Zelda would help you, wouldn't you Zel?"

"Help who what?" She set a cast-iron pot on the table.

"Billy's got a story to write. You'd help him, wouldn't you?"

She shrugged. "I don't know. I've never been much of a teacher."

"Who's writing what?" Anne said. She set a bottle of wine at each end of the table. Louise appeared carrying a basket of bread under each arm.

"Where does all of this come from?" I said. They exchanged glances.

"We sneak most of it from the kitchen. What we can't get, the wine and such, Emily brings. Don't tell Camille. I mean she knows and all," Alistair said. "She just doesn't like to hear about it."

Anne poured a glass of wine. "And don't say a word about the wine. She doesn't know about that. It's our little secret."

"Cross my heart and hope to die."

Donald shuddered. "I always hated that saying. No one hopes to die."

"Sure they do," Anne said. Louise nodded her agreement.

"Like who?" he said.

Anne downed an entire glass of wine in one swallow and slammed the glass down on the table. "People not us. Really unhappy people."

Everyone settled into their customary chairs. Alistair said a brief grace. We passed our plates around the table. Spaghetti and meat balls, garlic bread, salad, a larger bounty than any of them would ever be able to consume overflowed from the bowls and baskets and pots spread before us.

Donald nudged my elbow. "I don't think I've known any really unhappy people. Have you?"

"My mom's aunt was very unhappy. Or at least that's why Mom said she was always butting into our business." They laughed. I blushed at first, thinking they didn't believe me. "No really. She was always there. Always trying to tell my mom how to fold towels or to cook macaroni. Making sure I did my homework and was a good little boy."

Louise refilled her glass. "Sounds like she was just concerned."

"So what happened to her?" Donald said.

"She died before we left Minneapolis."

Zelda's fork clattered onto her plate. "Really?"

"Yup. Fell over dead baking a cake. For my grandfather's birthday. Heart attack." I stuffed an entire meatball into my mouth.

Anne didn't bother to swallow her food before continuing to quiz me about my aunt. "So what was this aunt's name?"

"Rose."

She washed down a mouthful of lettuce with the remainder of a glass of wine. "How terribly–" Anne started. But she couldn't find the right word.

"–ordinary," Alistair said.

She nodded. "That's it! Ordinary."

"Billy, here's a bit of advice." Donald drew a long drink of wine. "If there is anything you don't want your life to be, it's ordinary."

Thaddeus raised his glass. "Hear, hear." He returned the glass to the table, empty. Anne refilled it.

"Wonderful advice from the least ordinary among us," Anne said.

Donald shot her a look. "What's that supposed to mean."

She sighed. "I was paying you a compliment."

"I may be wearing a dress, but…"

She interrupted him. "Simmer down, Don. I didn't mean anything by it." Her words were starting to slur. It took me a minute to realize they were all halfway to drunk.

"I've spent my entire life–"

Thaddeus interrupted him this time. "Donald, calm down."

"–trying to finish a goddamned sentence," Donald said. He stared into his glass of wine. "But in this group, that ain't gonna happen."

Zelda reached for another slice of bread but missed. She laughed. "I used to good drink anyone under the table."

"Could, dear," Anne said.

"What?" she said.

"You said I used to good drink. I think you meant could."

"I most certainly did not say good did when I meant to say could did." Zelda poured another glass of wine, finished off the bottle with a shake.

Anne snickered. "Could did is even worse, I think."

"You did say good instead of could," Thaddeus said.

Zelda sneered at him. "Great. I'm being tag teamed by the hack has-been actor and the madam."

"Guys, guys, guys," Alistair said, trying to restore peace.

"What's a madam?" I said, but they did not hear me.

Thaddeus was standing. Somewhere in the dinner, things had gotten out of hand. Thaddeus's indignation wasn't helping. "Hack has-been? I won awards, thank you."

"What awards?" Zelda said.

"Yeah, what awards?" Anne said.

Louise scoffed. "Surely he doesn't mean that thing they gave him in Frisco."

"What's a madam?" I said again. Still no response.

"Well, he did get that thing from the Mayor of Dubuque," Alistair said.

Zelda laughed. "And that acceptance speech." She mimicked Thaddeus. "Thank you, dearly, Mr. Mayor and City of Dubuque, for this most stupendous and unexpected of honors."

Thaddeus tossed his napkin onto his plate. "I don't have to put up with this. I'm going to watch TV."

"Oh sit down, you old fart. We're just poking at you," Alistair said.

"What's a madam?" I said again. This time, I raised my voice a bit, but it was lost somewhere in the roar.

"I rather like standing, Alistair," Thaddeus said defiantly.

Zelda peered at Thaddeus over the rim of her glasses. "Thaddeus, put your scrawny ass back in that chair. Now."

Thaddeus mumbled under his breath as he settled back into his chair. "Hack has-been. I don't remember you winning a Pulitzer or anything."

"Guys," I shouted.

Six heads snapped to attention. Louise spilled a fork full of spaghetti into her lap. "Yes, Billy?"

"What's a madam?"

Anne and Thaddeus grimaced. Zelda giggled under her breath. Louise started to answer. "Well, Billy. A madam is–Thad?"

Thaddeus shook his head. "I'm not touching this one."

The Bohemians turned to the head of the table. If I were to get an answer, it would come from Alistair. He stared at the ceiling in search of an answer and then cleared his throat. "Well, Billy, it's like this."

Chapter 9

I sat there with my mouth hanging open for what felt like hours. I turned from Alistair to Anne and back to Alistair several times as my brain processed what I had just been told.

Donald snorted into a half-emptied glass. "I think he's in shock."

"Well, wouldn't you be?" Louise said. "I mean, to find something like that out at dinner?"

I looked at Louise. A singular thought was forming, but the words would not come out. I saw the smile on Zelda's face, half mocking, half sympathetic. The words finally fought their way to my mouth. "I didn't know you could do that for a living."

Everyone laughed. I picked up my plate and started toward the kitchen, but stopped at the end of the table nearest Anne. "Did you make a lot of money doing that?"

She grinned. "Quite a bit. Too bad I didn't save any of it." Still not sure what to think, I continued toward the kitchen again, but stopped when Zelda called after me.

"Billy. Think of it like this. Anne's job was to set up meetings between people. She was the middle-man, or in this case, middle-woman. Nothing more." When I looked at her with the same confused, stunned look, she shrugged apologetically and returned to nibbling on a piece of bread.

I stopped just shy of the kitchen door. "So she didn't actually...?" I paused, embarrassed.

Zelda considered my question for a moment before realizing what I was trying to ask. She gasped. "Heavens no. Not at all."

I shrugged again. "Okay."

I left the room in silence. Somehow, in the mind of a twelve-year-old boy, it did not matter that Anne Moore had facilitated such a shocking and possibly immoral act. So long as she herself did not participate, then I could go on treating her with the same deference as before. I rinsed my plate in the sink and dried my hands on a dishtowel. I could hear hushed voices from the dining room and peeked around the door.

"Anne, you didn't, did you?" Zelda said.

"What kind of a girl do you take me for?" Anne snorted indignantly. "Did I ever? No, Zel. For the record, hell no."

"I was only asking. I mean, I never thought to ask," Zelda said.

"Just for the record," Thaddeus said, "maybe we should tell him that it was the best whore house in the Quarter?"

Louise smacked him on the shoulder. Donald blew wine onto his blouse. She handed him her napkin and turned to Alistair. "I think poor Billy has had enough shocks for one day."

Alistair studied the bottom of his glass, as if to ponder its emptiness. "Perhaps enough shocks for a lifetime."

"It's not that bad, really, if you think about it," Zelda said. She poured Alistair another glass of wine. "He is, after all, twelve years old. I think he can handle a lesson in the birds and the bees." Louise giggled. Zelda sighed and turned to her. "What are you laughing at?"

She cupped her hand over her mouth. "Sorry. But don't you think he learned enough about bees behind the shed?"

Everyone laughed, save Alistair.

"But is it our place?" he said.

Zelda poured herself more wine. "Our place to what?"

"To tell him? I mean isn't that what parents are for?" he said.

Donald poured himself another glass of wine. "I'm not sure we get to make that decision. I don't know about you, but I'm not someone else when he's around. I'm still me."

"That's just it, though," Zelda said. "We're not just us. I don't swear as much and I don't drink."

Alistair sat forward, his elbows propped on the table. "Exactly. And I don't think we need to go out of our way to–"

Zelda interrupted him. "Look. I was seventeen years old when I learned where babies came from–the stork. And my mother never saw fit to tell me what happens on a wedding night until my Edward was about to haul me off in the car after the wedding. Can you imagine how terrified I was?"

"You have got to be kidding me. You were how old?" Anne said. She turned the last of the wine bottles upside down and shook it. Her glass remained empty.

"I was twenty-five."

"You are a goddamned liar," Thaddeus said. "Didn't know until your wedding night my ass." He passed his wine glass across the table to Anne.

"Well, liar or not, he's going to hear about it from someone. Might as well be someone he trusts," Zelda said.

"I can't believe this," Thaddeus said. "Alistair? I can't believe I'm hearing this. I would think the men would be the ones all for telling the boy about, well, everything."

Louise shook her head at him. "Thaddeus, no one is advocating that we tie the boy down and tell him what's what. But I don't think we should hide anything from him either. Hell, I've felt like I was living in a monastery the last few days. Not sure what to say. Afraid to crack a dirty joke. Maybe it's time we started being ourselves again. I mean, he's learned the worst there is."

"Well, I'm not sure that that is the worst there is," Louise said. She was looking at Anne, who blushed.

"Ahem." Donald nodded in my direction as I approached the table. The same, uncomfortable hush as at my first appearance again descended over the table. I pushed part of Donald's skirt out of my chair.

Alistair fiddled with his fork. "Billy, I don't know that you should, well…"

"Tell my mom what Anne did for a living?" I said. "Don't worry. I don't really talk to my mom about what goes on up here."

"I just don't think she would understand," Zel said.

Before giving me a chance to respond, Thaddeus changed the subject. "So, Billy, tell the girls about the hive."

I told them, repeating the story exactly as I had told the three men. They nodded and gasped at the right times. When I finished, Zelda stood. "Billy, I think you deserve ice cream for dessert." She turned to leave the table.

"I can't." I pointed to the clock above Emily's desk. "I have to go home."

After we said our goodbyes, I made my way down the darkening street to the bus stop a block away from the Liberty Street Home. Twenty minutes later, the bus deposited me on the corner of Esplanade and Marais. Night had enveloped the trees, and the silvery glow of street lamps cast pools of light along my path. I walked from one pool to the next, until at last I reached our dark, empty apartment. Mother had yet to return from her date. A note on the counter, scrawled on the back of a grocery receipt confirmed what I had expected: she would not be home until after midnight. The wadded note tumbled from the overflowing garbage can beside the refrigerator. I watched it roll across the floor as I heard my mother's voice reminding me to take out the garbage. I opened the refrigerator and grabbed a soda.

Settled on the couch under a layer of blankets and pillows, I found a station that played late-night cartoons. I set the unopened soda can on the coffee table and quickly fell asleep to the sounds of the coyote's rockets and the road runner's meep-meeps.

Sometime after midnight, the loud thud of a body against our apartment door awoke me. I jumped, at first startled, until the hushed sounds of my mother's laughter crept into the apartment.

"We have to be quiet," she said. "We'll wake up Billy." Whoever was with her replied with an inebriated grunt. "Billy. My son." She laughed again. Several seconds of silence and heavy breathing followed another thud.

"Thought for a minute you had an old man in there or something," the drunk said. She giggled and slid her key into the lock. I burrowed under the blankets.

"Nope. I'm divorced. Or dee-vorsed as you rednecks say." She tossed her keys onto the table by the door. From beneath the mountain of blankets, I could hear them stumbling toward the bedroom. They stopped halfway down the hall for several more seconds of kissing. "You have to be gone before Billy wakes up in the morning," my mother said. "I don't want to have to explain to my twelve year old what you're doing here."

"Yes ma'am," the drunk said. As the door closed behind him, heavy fingers fiddled with the lock. I tiptoed into my bedroom. The last thing that I wanted to happen was a forced meeting between the inebriate and the inconvenience.

Safe behind the relative security of my door, I pulled on my pajamas and climbed into bed. Even the thick warmth of my pillow couldn't muffle the sounds of Mother's company echoing through the apartment, and I fell asleep dreading the kinds of dreams that I knew those sounds would trigger.

Chapter 10

I have been sitting at the table with the Bohemians, dipping bread into a saucer of honey for what feels like than an hour when the Bohemians vanish into thin air. I look down at my plate. It transforms into a speckled composition book. My fork disappears, replaced by the red fountain pen I have seen Zelda using on so many occasions. I thumb through the notebook. All the pages are blank. I close the notebook, but it opens again by itself. The blank pages dissolve into a mound of angry, crawling bees. I slam the notebook shut, holding it closed with my fists. The bees climb out through the speckles of the notebook and attack my hands and my face. I feel them sting my eyes, my ears. My screams are drowned out only by the roar of the thousand bees, angry that I have upset their home…

I sat up. My comforter and sheets lay crumpled on the floor at the foot of the bed. I must have kicked them off during the nightmare. The window of my bedroom was black. Even the mercury-vapor light over the neighbor's swimming pool was dark. I looked at my alarm clock.

Three a.m.

I tugged the blankets back onto the bed and rolled away from the clock. I could not sleep, my mind still consumed with notebooks and Bohemians and bees. Each time I closed my eyes, I saw bees swarming around behind my eyelids. With a sigh, I sat up and fumbled for the lamp. The sudden brightness stung my eyes. I squinted for a moment until I had adjusted.

No bees. The room was empty. Secure in the knowledge that the bees were confined to my dream, I switched the lamp off. Four hours later, the sun burst through my window and woke me, an unsubtle reminder that, despite the circadian interruptions that were my days on Bohemian Row, even on Tuesdays I had things to do. I ate a bowl of corn flakes in front of the television. Flipping through several channels, none of the shows caught my attention. Something from the dream was bothering me still. I knew what I had to do.

The drawers of my desk were empty, save for half a box of crayons and a coloring book. I opened my backpack and swore under my breath. Mother had already emptied it for the summer, just one more annoying intrusion. I tossed it back into the closet, still swearing. In the kitchen drawer where she kept pens and scissors and memo pads, I found nothing. A cardboard box marked "office" held the most promise. It was hidden in the hall closet behind a pile of winter coats we had not worn since Minneapolis. When I opened it, I was excited to find a clipboard with the cardboard backing of a legal pad still clipped in place. Maybe this was the one. But under the clipboard there were only stacks of old baby photos, a few old letters, and a newspaper. I unfolded the paper.

It was from the day I was born. A banner headline proclaimed, "The King is dead," above a full-page photograph of Elvis Presley. Not the young Elvis from the movies, but rather the old Elvis of "Aloha, Hawaii." I folded the paper into thirds, stacked the photographs and news clippings on top of it, and slid the box back into the corner. The clipboard I tucked away in the desk in my room, thinking that it might come in handy later. My sneakers were under the coffee table where I had left them the night before. I grabbed my apartment key from the table by the door, snatched five dollars from the grocery envelope in the kitchen, and started for the convenience store on the corner.

I asked the clerk where I could find school supplies. The old man behind the counter scratched his head. "Sorry, son. We don't carry anything like that."

I sighed. The air brakes on a bus sighed with me. I thanked the man and rushed for the bus stop. The driver saw my fare-card and waved me through. At the next stop, a woman carrying several heavy bags took the seat opposite mine. She dropped the bags onto the grimy floor. Her shoulders sagged, and she settled back, fanning herself with a supermarket sale paper. "What's with this heat?"

The man in the seat beside me coughed. "Tell me 'bout it. Supposed to get over a hundred tomorrow."

She fanned herself even faster, as if the temperature had risen with the man's words. "A hundred you say? Wish they'd put air on these things."

"Someone should tell them that opening the windows only lets in more hot air," the man said.

"Well, maybe I'll just stay home." She flipped her chin defiantly.

The man laughed. "Weatherman says that it's supposed to rain this weekend, though, and cool things off." He glanced out the window. "This my stop coming up. Nice talking to you." He used one of the straps suspended from the ceiling to steady himself as the bus jerked to a stop. I watched him get off the bus and then realized that I did not know where I was going.

"Excuse me," I said to the woman with the bags. "Can you tell me where I could find a store that sells school supplies?"

"School supplies?" She thought for a moment. "There's a big shopping center at the next stop. Try the dollar store. They have everything."

"Thanks." I started watching for the next stop.

"This is your stop," she said. "The seven takes you back. But you'd better hurry or you'll miss

it, and it don't come round again for an hour."
I rushed for the nearest door. As the bus pulled
away, I noticed the woman pointing at one of
the stores. I waved and mouthed "Thanks." Inside, large mobiles hung from the ceiling above
the various departments. I looked for one labeled
school supplies, but could not find it. A clerk in
a blue smock whipped past me.

"Sir, could you tell me…?"

He did not stop.

I looked again. There were mobiles for
kitchen, furniture, accessories, ladies apparel.
Maybe the store did not carry school supplies.
Near the center of the store, a mobile labeled
"Home and Office" caught my eye. I found un-
derneath it an aisle lined with folders, staplers,
and packages of paper. The notebooks were at
the very end of the aisle along both sides. A
stack of black speckled books sat perched on the
top shelf, just out of reach. Remembering that it
was my recent adventure in shelf climbing that
brought me there in the first place, I decided
against mounting an ascent. The same blue-
smocked clerk zipped past me again.

"Excuse me," I said, this time more forceful than the first.

He stopped. "Yeah?"

"I need two of those." I pointed to the top shelf.

"You want the blue ones or the black ones?"

"One of each."

He handed them to me. "Thanks," I said.

"Anything else?"

I shook my head, but he was already gone. On my way to the register I passed a rack full of pencils. I grabbed a package of them, paid a cashier by the door, and returned to the bus stop across the street to wait for my ride home. Half an hour later, I sat down at our dining room table with the notebooks, the package of pencils, and the pencil sharpener I got from my mother's makeup bag. I sharpened one of the pencils, careful not to spill shavings on the carpet.

I opened the notebook to the first page. Just like in my dream, the page was blank. I shuddered at the thought of more bees.

A knock on the door startled me. I closed the notebook with the pencil in it.

"Coming," I shouted. They knocked again. Through the peephole, I saw two of the neighborhood children. The boy's tee shirt was white with red stripes, and his jeans, fashionably faded, gaped at the knees. The other boy's shirt, emblazoned with the detached head of a rock singer screaming into a microphone, was too big and kept falling off his left shoulder the way that tee shirts seem to do in hot weather.

I opened the door.

"Hey," the boy said. He tugged the shirt back onto his shoulder. "We were wondering if you want to go with us down to the zoo." He jerked his head toward the stairs. "My mom's waiting to take us and said we should invite you, since you're new to the neighborhood and all."

"New?"

"Yeah, didn't you just move in?" the second said.

"I've lived here almost a year."

The boy in torn jeans slapped him on his bare shoulder. "See, I told you so."

The boy on the left shrugged. "Who cares when he got here?" He turned back to me. "So do you want to come or not?"

I looked at the notebook on the table. A trip to the zoo would mean that I would not finish writing the story about the bees in time to take it to Liberty the next day. I shook my head. "No. You guys go ahead. Maybe some other time."

"I told you he wouldn't want to go," the first boy said. "Come on. Mom's waiting. See you around, Billy." I closed and locked the door as they walked away. How did he know my name? I shrugged.

Returning to the table, I wondered how he knew my name. My mother had probably talked to his mother in the laundry room or at the mailbox. I picked up the pencil again. On a single line across the top of the first page, I wrote:

THE BEE STORY BY BILLY BRADSHAW

I started the story on the next line, without skipping a space.

```
It was a hot summer day. We
were sitting outside, on the
patio, and Louise asked for a
shovel.
```

The words seemed to flow from my pencil, filling the lines on the page. I tried to remember every detail exactly as it happened.

Why am I behind the shed? I am looking for Louise's bucket. She needs it for gardening. I describe the color of the shelves and how the bucket at the top reflects the sunlight. Each step up the side is its own paragraph. Then I stop, suddenly unable to describe the sound the collapsing shelves make.

```
The shelves moaned like the
wind.
```

I scribble it out.

```
The shelves groaned like a
sick dog.
```

I scratch that out as well. Perhaps such a sound is beyond description? How else can I say that the shelves fall?

```
I could feel the shelves
moving.
```

I pause for a moment; that will do. The words start flowing again. The shelves are falling. They crumble into pieces. Then the bees come. And then Alistair and Thaddeus are banging against the wall with the chair. Then it is over, and I am on the couch in the Row with a wet rag on my forehead.

`A little drop of water ran down into my eye and I was safe.`

In all capital letters beneath the last sentence, I wrote "The End" and closed the notebook. My stomach growled. It was after two and I had not had lunch.

I went to the refrigerator, wondering if Mom had been grocery shopping yet. During the summer, she kept enough frozen dinners in the freezer for an entire week of lunches. I found a TV dinner of fish sticks and corn hidden behind a gallon of vanilla ice cream.

The directions were easy enough to follow and I enjoyed the brief bit of independence afforded by preparing my own lunch. Setting the microwave on high for three minutes and then on half-power for two wasn't rocket science. I was capable of doing that much for myself. The microwave dinged for the second time. The first bite of fish stick was crunchy on the outside, but the inside tasted chewy and overcooked. I thought about trying again. Turkey and dressing sounded good. But I took a second bite and decided that it would do until Mom came home to cook dinner.

I slipped the notebooks under my arm, the pencils into my back pocket, and wandered to the living room with my TV dinner and a glass of water. I accidentally sat on the remote and the television flickered on.

"So, you're saying that we can plant this in the winter and it will come back each winter?" the host of a gardening show said. I changed the channel before the guest answered.

"We're standing here live at the foot of the stage where in just two days some of the biggest names in music will be appearing. More on that story tonight at five o'clock," a news reporter announced. I changed the station again. After several minutes of flipping channels, I still had not found any cartoons. I looked at the clock. It was two-thirty. I sighed and switched the TV off.

Maybe I should have gone to the zoo instead. No, I had to write that story before I went back to Liberty Street on Friday. Alistair and Thaddeus both had said I should write about the bees. What would Zel think when she read it? Would she like it? Or would she hate it? Maybe it was terrible. I should get rid of it since it probably was not any good.

I could rip it up. No one would ever have to know. I could rip it up and hide the notebooks in the bottom of the trashcan. My fingers curled tightly around the first few pages, ready to rip them from the spine and by doing so erase them from history, but something stopped me. I read the first line and immediately recognized the emotion that had stopped me. I was proud of those pages. They were something I produced, something that made me proud. I smoothed the pages back down and closed the notebook.

After breakfast on the Row the next morning, I asked Zelda if I could talk to her alone. Once sequestered away in her room, I settled into my customary seat on her bed, the notebook containing "The Bee Story by Billy Bradshaw" lying open across my lap.

Zelda took the notebook from me before I could even tell her what it was. "What's that you have there?" she asked.

"I want you to be the first one to read this."

"I don't know what to say. Billy, I'm honored."

"Um…I need to ask you something," I said, my thoughts trailing my voice. "The other day, when the bees got me, I…well I overheard the talk of sending me away."

I noticed her shoulders tense, as if I had struck a nerve. She waved off the suggestion. "So you were eavesdropping?"

I shook my head. "No. Well, yes. But I couldn't help it. I just overheard."

"No, Billy, we wouldn't do that. We're just…"

"I'm not worried about that. I mean, I don't want to leave."

"And we don't want you to."

"–But when Thaddeus and Alistair were talking, Donald got angry. And everyone got really quiet." Her shoulders relaxed, and I thought for a moment I saw her grin. Encouraged, I continued. "Well, why?"

She winked. "See what you can learn from eavesdropping?"

"Yes. I'm sorry about…"

"No! Don't apologize. I think any good writer has to be able to listen in, politely of course, to learn about people." She ceremoniously smoothed her housecoat and craned her neck towards the hall. "Several years ago, about eight I guess, we were all friends, living in the same apartment building. It was a wretched place, but we were for the most part content. Then the city decided to build an I-10 off-ramp through my living room, and that was that. Well, Donald had developed his diabetes and Thaddeus was still suffering vertigo–not helped, I might add, by all the whiskey. We all had these little infirmities, were showing our age, I guess. And Donald knew the administrator here, so he sort of bought this hall for us with the last of his inheritance."

"His inheritance?"

"Well, he came from a very prominent Houston family and, as you can imagine, they weren't happy about his choice of dress. His wife left him with their son. His father disowned him, giving him enough money to live off of for the rest of his life–so long as he promised never to return to Houston." She sat back, pondering the next steps in the story while absently twirling a strand of silver hair between her fingers. "At any rate, by the time they tore down our apartments, his money was all but gone. He had just enough to set us up here."

"That was nice of him."

"Well, that's what friends do for friends," she said. "Let's see what you brought me."

Her voice was matter of fact, with a finality that indicated the story had ended. Zelda took my notebook. She read each page, sometimes nodding or sometimes shaking her head. Several times she stopped, seemed about to say something, but continued reading instead. She completed the last page, flipped back a couple of pages, and read the ending again. Finally, she closed the notebook and removed her bifocals. "Well, Billy."

"Well what?" I scooted to the edge of her bed. "What did you think?"

"Not bad."

"Really? Or are you just saying that?"

"It's really good, for a rough draft."

I did not understand. "Rough draft?"

"Yes. A rough draft is what writers call the first time they write something down. You have to go back, read it, and make the necessary changes." She passed the notebook back to me.

"You mean check for misspelled words and things?" I opened the notebook to the first page.

She shook her head. "No. Well, that too. But it's a lot more than that. It's hard to explain, really." She thought for a moment then continued, "Have you read it? I mean since you finished it?"

I shook my head.

Zelda reached into her nightstand and took out a pen. "Why don't you sit here, read it, and tell me what you think?"

I was confused. "But I wrote it."

"Revising is part of writing. It makes us better." She offered me the pen again.

I hesitated.

"Don't be disappointed, Billy. I think it's really good. But I'll bet if you read it again, you can make it even better. Trust me. Try it once on your own. Then, if you need me to, I'll help you. Okay?"

I took the pen. "What do I look for?"

"You'll see." She left the room and closed the door.

I sat there for several seconds, staring at the first page without reading it. I did not understand what she meant, but I would try. My eyes followed the words to the end of the line. By the second sentence, I had already started over. At the third sentence, I lost it again. Each train of thought seemed to break down somewhere in the first paragraph. No matter what I tried, my mind refused to connect the second sentence to the third. But why?

Sitting there on Zelda's bed alone with the first words I had ever written, I saw it. And I understood.

Chapter 11

I closed my notebook and looked at Alistair, searching for some hint of encouragement. Reading the various edits of my story had taken the better part of their morning. I was afraid that it might have been time wasted.

Thaddeus raised an eyebrow toward Alistair. "I told you he was good."

"I never disagreed with you." Alistair stood and patted me on the shoulder. "Well done, my boy."

Louise reached for my notebook. "Billy, is it really the first time you've written anything?"

I nodded.

She leafed through several pages. "The revisions. Are they all yours?"

I nodded again.

"Well, this is one girl who is quite impressed." She settled in on the sofa with my notebook. "Mind if I look it over?"

I turned to the garden window where Zelda had been for the entire time. As I had been reading, Zelda was staring out into the garden, unmoving, as if she had become a statue in the chair by the window. Wanting more than anything to know what she thought, I tried to get her attention. "Zel? What did you think?"

She did not respond. I tried again. Nothing. I tapped her on the shoulder and she jumped.

"What? Oh," she said, fighting to catch her breath. "You startled me."

"Are you all right?" I said.

"Just kind of dazed." Zelda rolled her head from side to side, stretching her neck. "Guys, I'm tired. I think I'm going to take a nap."

Anne's brow furrowed and she crossed to Zel, concerned. "Nap, hon?"

"Yeah. I have a headache and am kind of lightheaded."

Anne pressed a hand to her forehead. "You feeling okay?"

"Yeah. I'm fine. Just, I don't know. Maybe I'm coming down with a cold. I'll sleep it off." She started down the hall but stopped short of her door. "Billy, very good. You see what I mean about rewriting?"

"Yes, ma'am." I thought I saw her lips turn up, just shy of a smile.

"Well, goodnight." The door closed behind her.

For several seconds after, Thaddeus looked on with concern. "Alistair, you think she's all right?"

"Why wouldn't she be?" Alistair unfolded the newspaper on the table.

"In all the years I've known her, Zelda's never taken a nap. And definitely never before lunch." He waited for a response, but Alistair did not look up.

"Alistair!" Anne said.

He looked at her over rims of his glasses.

"Zelda? The nap?" she said.

"Oh. Yes." He removed his glasses and scratched his head with the stem. "If she's not up by lunch, we'll let Emily call Camille or something. I'm sure it's nothing to be worried about."

Louise closed my notebook and handed it back to me. She headed for the kitchen, pausing briefly to rest a reassuring hand on Thaddeus's shoulder. "Yes, I'm sure it's nothing to be worried about. She is just tired," she said.

Thaddeus and I stood in the middle of the living room staring at Zel's closed door, neither convinced that we should not be concerned. Thaddeus patted me on the shoulder. "She'll be fine, I'm sure."

As much as I wanted to believe him, Thaddeus was unconvincing at best. But before I could press any further, Emily's phone rang. She looked at it for a minute, as if surprised that it was making noise. When it remained unanswered after a second ring, Anne sighed. "Emily, dear, if you pick it up, whoever is calling will talk to you."

"Oh, right." Emily closed her magazine and lifted the receiver. "Bohem–I mean Hall B, this is Emily–Yes ma'am, he's right here–Okay. Yes'am. I'll send him up." She hung the phone up and motioned me over to her desk. "Miss Roberts wants to see you in her office. Now."

My heart skipped a beat. "She does?"

Emily nodded towards the door. "She says she wants to see you in her office."

My mind raced through the events of the day. I had not broken anything. I did not think I was late that morning. Maybe I had insulted one of the residents and they had complained to her? Any of a thousand possible scenarios filled my head as I stepped into Camille's office. As usual, she was on the phone.

She cupped her hand over the receiver. "I'll just be a minute. Sit down." She pointed to a chair and returned to her call. "Yes. That's what they said. Someone from out west…No, I didn't get a name. But he's going to be here tomorrow…Yes. Tomorrow. As in Saturday…I don't know what kind of hospital administrator shows up to work on Saturday, but this one does… No, I don't know anything about him. I'm just glad they finally got around to sending someone. Maybe I can do my job now…So you'll be here in an hour to clean the apartment? Good. See you then." Camille hung the phone up. "So, Billy. Tell me what's been happening?"

"Emily said you wanted to see me?"

Camille took a sip of coffee from an oversized cup emblazoned with World Expo 84 in blue. "I just got a phone call from Judge Spurgeon. He wants a progress report."

"Well. I just hang out, I guess?" I shifted back and forth in my seat. The cushion was old, stiff, and smelled like my grandmother's attic.

"You just 'hang out?'" Camille sighed and rolled her eyes. "That won't go over."

"I help them sometimes," I blurted out.

A curious eyebrow shot up. "Help? Go on."

"Well, if they need help with gardening…"

She interrupted me. "Gardening. I got that much the other day. What else?" She jotted notes as I talked.

"I move things. Like chairs and stuff. And I help set the table for lunch. Dinner too sometimes." My head still not cleared of the panic, I tried to remember the other tasks that they had me do. Though I had at first been bothered, I'd come to enjoy helping them.

"Anything else?" Camille said.

"That's about it. Just little stuff like that. And we talk a lot."

Camille looked up from her notes. "Talk? About what?"

"Writing and poetry and prostit–" I stopped.

She dropped her pen, surprised. "Excuse me?"

"I had, well–" I choked, tried to think of a plausible cover story. "There was a story on the news the other day about these women on television. And I asked what they were. So Alistair told me."

Camille closed her eyes. She massaged the bridge of her nose between her thumb and index finger. I had never been good at lying. "Anything else?"

I wondered if she believed me. Or was she just moving on because my story was plausible enough to allow her to plead ignorance. Maybe Camille knew that Anne Moore had been a madam. If she did, then surely she knew that I was lying. Either way, I was not about to ask.

"No. That's all."

"Well, I'll let the Judge know how things are going. Just try and keep out of trouble. And out of everybody's way." Her phone rang before I could respond. "Camille Roberts…Yes, Lucy. We have a new administrator. He'll be here tomorrow…No, I don't know anything about him." I hurried from Camille's office, eager to tell every-one about the new administrator.

Emily smiled at me when I walked back into Hall B. "You weren't in trouble, were you?"

I shook my head. Everyone was scattered around the living room and kitchen, engaged in a variety of mid-morning tasks. I called them over.

"Um, I have news. Big news."

"You've been drafted?" Anne said.

Alistair laughed. "No. He's too young. Maybe he's a spy sent here by the nursing staff to report on what a nefarious life we lead back here."

I shook my head. "Nope. Even better than that."

"What?" Donald said. "Better than a spy?"

"There's a new administrator. He'll be here to-morrow." I folded my arms smugly across my chest, tossed my head back in pride. Instead of the surprise and shock I expected, they all looked to Alistair with concern.

Thaddeus turned off his soap opera. "Are you sure?"

I nodded.

He rose from the sofa and approached the dinner table. "Alistair?"

"Let's not get carried away. Maybe he'll just leave us be like the last one. I don't even remember his name." Alistair scratched his head, trying to remember. "I can't remember. He never came down here that I can remember."

"Once. But it might have been when you were in the hospital having your bypass," Anne said.

"Regardless, there is no need to panic, at least not until he gets here and we find out what he's about. Okay?" he said. They all agreed. Louise went back into the kitchen, mumbling something about finishing lunch.

I sat down next to Alistair at the table. "Why would he get mad at you?"

He glanced up from his newspaper. "Well, Billy, we're not exactly orthodox down here. I mean, how many residents in this place fix their own meals?"

"Or drink like fish," Thaddeus said. He removed a hip flask from his pocket and took a long swig. Louise returned from the kitchen carrying a tray of sandwiches.

Alistair folded his paper and dropped it on the floor. "The government has a lot of rules these places are supposed to follow. We don't like the rules, so we don't pay any attention to them," he said.

Anne sat a pitcher of lemonade in the center of the table and shouted, "Lunch!"

I moved to my customary chair next to Donald, and everyone else settled into their own places. Everyone except Zelda. Her bedroom door was still shut.

"Has anyone heard from Zelda?" I said.

Donald shook his head. "I tapped on her door a little while ago, but she didn't say anything if she heard me."

I grabbed a sandwich from the tray. "Maybe we should go get her?" I said, talking with my mouth full.

Alistair poured himself a glass of lemonade. "No. Let her sleep."

Throughout lunch, and into the afternoon, I could not help but watch her door, hoping she was okay. After the tray of sandwiches vanished, everyone gathered around the television to watch an old John Wayne movie.

Louise and I sat next to each other on the love seat. Apparently, neither of us cared for the movie. Louise spent her time working on a new poem, and I sat watching her. By the time the credits rolled, Louise had completed several drafts, but still was not pleased. She sent yet another crumpled piece of paper roll flying into the wastebasket in the corner, the twelfth in a long line of failed attempts.

I followed its trajectory into the wastebasket. "Why did you wad that one up? I thought it was good."

She looked at me, surprised. "I didn't realize you had been watching me all this time."

The happy sound of ice clinking into glasses echoed from the kitchen. Donald and Anne were arguing about the ingredients for tea.

"Mom just boils water and drops the bags in," I called from the living room. Donald and Anne laughed.

Louise patted my knee. "No, Billy. They're making Long Island Iced Teas. It's a mixed drink." She turned over her shoulder and said, "Anne, make me one too."

"Already done," Anne said.

I pointed at the wastebasket again. "So why did you throw away the last one?"

Louise shrugged. "Because it wasn't good enough."

"Is it ever?" a voice behind us said. We both looked up and saw Zelda standing there, her face puffed and lined with the tell-tale signs of heavy sleep.

"Are you feeling better, Zel?" Louise said.

Zelda shook her head. "I'm not sure. I'm awfully didthy." She took a step back and swooned, not quite a stumble. And she did not fall. She steadied herself on the corner of the television. "It's like I've been drinking or something. The room just won't stop spinning."

Louise helped her into a chair. "Just sit here for a minute, okay? Billy, go find Alistair and Thaddeus."

"No, I'm fine. Just need to rest a bit," Zelda said. She patted me on the shoulder. "Billy, I'm fine. Really. Don't bother them. They're probably busy."

Her hand remained on my shoulder, heavy and limp, almost lifeless. I placed it back into her lap, but she did not seem to notice. "Zelda, maybe we should call the doctor?"

"I'm fine, Billy. I'm fine. Really. See?" She tried to stand, but her legs were like butter. She collapsed back into the chair, her eyes closed tight. "I'm fine. Really."

I shook my head. "No, you're not fine. Something's wrong. Emily!"

Chapter 12

On most weekends, Liberty Street operated on a skeleton crew. The kitchen staff cooked the weekend's meals on Friday and refrigerated them for reheating on Saturday and Sunday. Nurses filled hundreds of tiny paper cups with the necessary pills for two days and stacked them on cookie sheets at their stations. The handful of orderlies unlucky enough to draw the weekend shift struggled through a stressful weekend of cleaning up after the residents. But this Saturday was different.

Nurses bustled about, filling orders, cleaning stations, helping residents in and out of their rooms. Orderlies scrubbed walls and baseboards. Several candy-striper volunteers wandered from room to room redistributing dog-eared magazines. And from her post near the entrance,

Camille Roberts commanded her army for the last time. She flagged down a passing nurse and handed her a stack of fresh linens. "Take these down to room fifty-seven, please. He's going to be here any minute."

I waited as she issued orders to another nurse. When she finally got to a stopping point, I stepped forward. "Miss Roberts?"

She did not look up. "I'm really busy right now, Billy. What do you need?"

"Well, I was wondering if you'd heard…," I said, my question unfinished.

"About Zelda? Not yet." She stared at me for a minute. I looked away.

"I'm sure she's fine. But look." She scribbled something on her pad. "This is my number at home. If you want, call me tomorrow. I'll try to find out something by then. Okay?"

I nodded and took the piece of paper.

"I go to church," she said. "So wait until after one to call."

I tucked the number in my pocket and thanked her. The main door of the Liberty Street Home slammed behind me, closing with it another week at the Home. Mom was waiting in the car, the windows rolled down. When the air conditioner had died within our first week in New Orleans, she had refused to get it repaired, insisting that a 1984 Buick LeSabre wasn't worth the money and that we would be getting a new car very soon. Stepping out from beneath the shade of the home and into the sun, I groaned at the thought of a fifteen-minute ride in "Myrtle," the name Mom had given the car the day my grandparents had given it to her.

She smiled at me through the glare in the windshield, calling out of the window, "How was your day, son?"

I shrugged.

"What's wrong, Billy?"

"Nothing. Just ready to go home." I wanted to tell her about Zelda, but she would not understand. So we rode home in silence. Back at our apartment, Mother asked if I wanted a snack. Without answering, I closed the door to my bedroom. At my desk a few minutes later, I promptly discovered how terrifying a blank page is when you do not know how to write what you feel.

I sat there at my desk, the pale blue light of early evening filtering through the window. And

I cried. I cried about leaving Minneapolis, about not seeing my friends and my grandparents. I cried about the loneliness of a school devoid of friends. I cried about breaking windows out of a greenhouse and losing an entire summer. I cried about Zelda.

And the words came.

Pages of them. First, just fragments of sentences. Each fragment growing to more closely resemble a thought. Short sentences followed, and then grew more complex with the passage of time. I wrote about my last day of the fifth grade. The teachers all told me how much they would miss me. The airplane ride from Minneapolis was bumpy and ended with lost luggage. Our first days in New Orleans blurred together into a sea of sketchy details about lots of loud trumpets and two young brothers doing gymnastic tap dances on the sidewalk.

I wrote about the musty smell of the little Catholic school my mother found. The sisters still wore traditional habits like the nuns in *The Sound of Music*. They behaved as if they did not like children, but we knew that they had our best interests in mind with each assignment.

I wrote about the last day of school and the sunlight in the trees along Esplanade and the shadows dancing in the breeze. The tinkling panes of the greenhouse reminded me of the noise ice cubes made when my grandfather tossed them into his Scotch glass.

I wrote about Zelda, who, since we had met, always treated me like an adult and never talked down to me. Zel, who first encouraged my writing, taught me to rewrite and to make it better. She had belonged to the Bohemians, but how quickly she had become mine. And now she was sick and I could not be there for her and could not help her, and that was the worst feeling in the world.

I hurled the notebook across the room. It landed open on the floor. For several seconds, I fought the urge to cry or to throw my chair through the window. My fists gripped the edges of the desk, all the rage bulling around in my head, building to an explosion. I closed my eyes tight and forced my chest to stop heaving.

When I opened my eyes, I saw the window above the desk. Night had fallen sometime while I was writing. The desk lamp cast a yellowish hue over the room, but I did not remember turning it on. Unable to recall anything about the previous two hours, I stretched, and got up to retrieve my notebook. The welcome sound of pots clattering in the kitchen meant that Mother was preparing for a late dinner. I laid the notebook on my desk, turned out my lamp, and headed toward the kitchen. Upon seeing me in the door, she smiled. "Well, stranger. Where have you been all this time?"

"In my room. Writing in my notebook."

"Writing? What about?"

I shrugged. "I don't know. Just stuff."

"Dinner's almost ready." She pointed to the sink. "Wash up. And then you can help me by setting the table."

Any other time, I would have pouted at the chore, perhaps even argued and stormed off. Instead, emotionally and mentally exhausted, I rinsed my hands, grabbed plates and forks. Mom set a covered pot in the center of the table. I peeked under the lid. "So what's for dinner tonight?"

"Beef stew," she said. She uncovered the pot and emptied a ladleful of stew into my bowl, then hers.

"No date tonight?" I said.

She shook her head. "Nope. Saturday night and I'm home with you. I guess no one's interested in your old mom."

I rolled several peas around my plate with my fork without looking up. She sounded almost disappointed that she was stuck at home with me.

"Depressing really. As pretty as your mom is and no date on Saturday night," she said. When I did not respond, she nudged my arm. "What? You don't think you have a pretty mother?"

"I didn't say that, Mom. I just. Well–why can't I be your date?"

Her fork clattered to her plate. "That's a wonderful idea. Just you and me out on the town for the night." She tossed her napkin on her plate and stood. "What do you think we should do?"

I shrugged. "I dunno. What do you want to do?"

"Well it's too late to catch a movie." She checked her watch. "But we could go to the video arcade?"

"Yeah!" I jumped up and ran toward my room.

Mom laughed. "Where are you going?"

"To get my notebook and my backpack," I said. She looked confused.

"I just want to keep it with me in case I need to write something," I said.

"Sounds serious."

"Oh, Mom! Writing is very serious."

She raised an eyebrow. I waited for several seconds, unsure of what she would say. She waved me off impatiently. "Well, get your stuff and let's go. I'll be waiting in the car."

We drove to an arcade in a nearby strip mall. Parents and children spilled onto the sidewalk in front of the arcade. Knowing she would not enjoy waiting in line only to watch her son play video games, I gave up. "There are too many people, Mom. Let's do something else."

She frowned. "Are you sure? We can fight our way in."

"No. I'm sure. Let's go get ice cream," I said.

"Okay. Ice cream it is."

There was a Baskin Robbins just around the corner from the arcade. We sat in the tile-encrusted parlor and ate double-dipped cones. I asked her about work and her friends there. She told me that she did not like her new boss, but at least he was good looking. She asked me about Liberty Street and the Bohemians. I told her about Camille and the new administrator's arrival.

"Maybe that's why everyone was there today," I said.

"Huh?"

"Well, usually no one's there on Saturday. But this afternoon, everyone was working. It must be because the new administrator came today," I said.

Mom glanced at the clock above the counter and jumped.

"Wow, it's nine thirty already? We've been gone over an hour. And tomorrow's Sunday. Time to go."

I shoved the last of the cone in my mouth and followed her to the Buick.

* * *

The choir's last notes echoed through the rafters of the arched ceiling. Reverend Mueller nodded to the choir director, a solemn thanks for yet another Sunday's work. Mother and I sat in our customary seats on the fifth pew, near the wall. Her Bible lay closed on her lap. Somewhere between the offertory and the choir's special, my leg had fallen asleep. I shifted back and forth on the pew in an effort to restore circulation.

"Turn in your Bibles to the book of Exodus," Reverend Mueller said. The congregation leafed through their bibles, searching for the text. Mother's Bible fell open only pages from the directed passage and she smiled. She prided herself on usually being the first in the congregation ready to read along.

Reverend Mueller squinted at his sermon notes through thick-rimmed reading glasses teetering on the tip of his nose. "Today, we will discuss the Israelites' journey through the desert."

I reached for my notebook and found the first page of the previous night's work. The pencil that I had tucked into its spine rolled into the space between the cushion and the pew. I fidgeted a bit, trying unsuccessfully to retrieve it.

Mother tapped me on the shoulder and wagged a finger in my face. "Billy, pay attention. And put the notebook away."

I rolled my eyes, even considered defying her. Mother's glare, though, was enough to tell me that arguing was the wrong thing to do. I slid the notebook back under my legs, folded my hands in my lap, and tried to pay attention.

Reverend Mueller's voice floated through the chapel with the consistency of flowing molasses. I could almost see the words drifting over the pews. "So, as God commands, the Israelites follow Moses. Men, women and children wander the desert for forty years. They believe in God's promise so much that they spend their entire lives searching."

I snapped to attention in my seat. His words sounded familiar, but I did not know why.

"And where was it God instructed them to go? Back to the land he had promised them. But why?" He paused to remove his glasses, the traditional signal that his sermon was almost over. "Pharaoh did not understand their world, their beliefs, their God. Egypt was not home. But the

Israelites knew that if they put their trust in Him, He would lead them home."

Reverend Mueller stepped from behind the pulpit with his arms lifted above his shoulders. The congregation rose for benediction, after which the congregation would file past the door where Reverend Mueller stood. As each person approached, he smiled, took their hand. With some, he spoke at length, continuing conversations as he shook the hands of the next few people in line. With others, he simply nodded in gracious acknowledgement of their compliments. Our turn finally came, and Reverend Mueller clasped my mother's hand. "Well, Beverly. I am so excited to see you back. We missed you last week." He held onto her hand as if he knew she would bolt for the fire exit if he turned it loose.

"We were out of town, visiting family." I looked sideways at her, wondering why she lied and how she did it so effortlessly.

Reverend Mueller smiled. He knew she was lying, too, but they both played their parts.

"We enjoyed your sermon, Reverend," Mother said.

"Then, I look forward to seeing you and Billy next week. I'll tell my wife to be expecting you in Sunday School." He smiled the same gracious smile that each of the congregants received. But I could not help thinking that this smile was different, that with this smile he basked in this minor triumph of guilt-tripping her into two consecutive Sundays.

"Looking forward to it," she said. Mother shook his hand again and we left. On the way home, I thought about the Israelites, about the forty years. Why had their search so caught my attention? Reverend Mueller's words seemed almost an echo. Of what, though, I couldn't quite decide. I had heard the story of the Israelites many times before. In the desert for forty years. Pharaoh behind them as they searched for their home.

Home.

Liberty Street.

Thaddeus.

Anne and Thaddeus's first argument that first week on the Row.

I remembered everything: how he shouted that he spent his entire life searching for–

something, but Alistair had interrupted him before he could finish. That was the thought that would have completed his sentence. Thaddeus spent his entire life in search for some place he would be understood, where he felt accepted and comfortable. Everything the Israelites spent forty years searching for, Thaddeus found at Liberty Street.

Chapter 13

The life of a single mother cannot be easy, especially for the mother of a boy. She does not get to divide the unique stress of raising a son with an "other" parent. The burdens of football practice and bruised shoulders, bicycle wrecks and scraped knees are hers alone to shoulder. Boys tend to live in a world where tree-branches are sidewalks and sofa is another name for the outer wall of an impenetrable fortress. So I cannot fault my mother for latching onto whatever semblance of a routine that she could find in the topsy-turvy world her son created.

Every Sunday, after church, she took a sleeping pill and locked herself in her room for the afternoon to catch up on the sleep she had missed in the previous week. Once her bedroom door closed, she would not emerge again until Monday morning, recharged and ready to face yet another week.

Sometime after I tried Camille Roberts' number for the third time with no answer, Mother passed my bedroom door. "I'm taking a nap now," she said. I scribbled a quick note, a just-in-case against the unlikely possibility that she might awaken while I was out. "Dear Mom, I'm outside, playing. Your son, Billy." The note ensured that she would not ask questions about where I had been or what I had done. That her son had no friends to play with and rarely went outside would never cross her mind. So long as I avoided trouble, I knew my mother preferred to remain oblivious to my activities. I descended the stairs to the street below. Only when faced with the vastness of a city still in many ways foreign to me did I realize that I had no plan to find Zelda, and no idea where to start. The paramedics had taken her to a hospital, but which one? How many hospitals operated in a city the size of New Orleans? I sat down on the bench at the bus stop and waited.

Twelve year olds tend to overlook simple solutions in favor of the more complex ones they think sound more adult. So it was no wonder I sat at the bus stop for a half hour, exploring scenarios in which I visited each of the hospitals marked on the route map I kept in my backpack. I calculated what buses would take me to which little blue H, which of the hospitals I could walk between, and roughly how long the various trips would take to complete. Just as I decided it was hopeless, that I might never find Zelda, a bus opened its doors and a familiar voice called down to me.

"Billy? I wasn't expecting to see you today," the driver said. He smiled cheerfully down from his perch behind the wheel. "You going to the home? You don't normally go down there on Sunday. What's up?"

I shrugged. "I'm not sure." Moving was better than sitting still, I figured, so I boarded the bus and sat in the seat immediately behind him.

"So what brings you my way today?" he said, slamming the bus into drive.

I pulled myself up onto my knees and leaned over the Plexi-glass divider. "Can I ask you something? If you had to find someone, but you didn't know where they were, what would you do?"

"Oh, that's a tough one. I think a good place to start would be the last place you saw them," he said.

I wondered why the thought had not struck me sooner. Start at Liberty Street. Someone there was bound to know where she was. "Yes sir, I'm going to the home today."

Ten minutes later, I discovered why Camille Roberts had not answered her telephone. She sat behind her desk, hunched over a stack of file folders. A tall man sat across from her, his face partially obscured by the glass divider separating her office from the entryway. At first, she seemed to be ignoring him, but as I slipped closer to the window, I realized they were discussing the stacks of forms spread out on her desk.

"Mr. Downing. I know how to read a spreadsheet. I went to college too," she said.

"Yes, well, I don't mean to imply that you do not know what you're doing here. But the fact is, Miss Roberts, you're a nurse, not an administrator." He settled back in his chair again and crossed his legs. "At any rate, I'd like to applaud your frankness for telling me what it is that you feel we need."

"Mr. Downing," she said, but he interrupted with a dismissive wave of his hand.

"Call me Christopher."

Camille ignored him. "Mr. Downing, everything I just told you is true. This place needs staff. It needs money. It needs time, and it needs a shot of–something–I don't know what. That's your job. But you gotta let my people do their jobs as best they can." She leaned across her desk and folded her hands together, adding almost with defiance, "Otherwise you're just spinning your wheels."

He stood abruptly. "I hope we'll be able to work together in the future. But. In order for that to be possible, you're going to have to accept changes around here." Leaving her office, he almost knocked over a cart filled with water cups. I thought for a moment that the orderly behind the cart shot him a dirty look before moving along.

Camille's pencil moved slowly down a column of numbers. It stopped long enough to correct a figure and then continued down the column of numbers while I inched closer to her door. Without looking up, she said, "I haven't found out anything yet."

I tried to mask my disappointment behind an understanding tone. "Well, you've been too busy to call, with the new administrator and all."

"No, I called. They've moved Zelda to another hospital for more tests."

There was no way of hiding my alarm. "Is something wrong?"

Camille tried to reassure me. "Hey, no news is good news. And that's all I know–that they moved her to a different hospital yesterday."

"What hospital?"

* * *

I stood there, staring at the door to room 453. Zelda's room.

It was directly across the hall from the nurses' station, just where the guard at the front desk told me I would find it. A quick check of the phone book for Ochsner Hospital's listing and a single bus ride and I was there, listening to voices on the other side of the door rise and fall with the disconcerting textures of an argument. Zelda's voice was strained, upset. A much younger woman and she were arguing. I pressed my ear against the door.

"Aunt Zelda, you have to come–" the woman said.

"No. No. Leave. Now," Zelda said.

Two male voices weighed in, but I could not make out what they were saying. Their voices blurred together into an indistinguishable baritone rumble.

The woman's voice returned, fiercer than before. "See, even the doctor agrees."

"I don't care what that quack says. Leave now. All of you!" Zelda shouted. I backed away from the door only a second before a doctor burst through. Zelda's niece followed close behind, dragging the second man by the hand.

The doctor scribbled notes in Zel's chart while he spoke. "She needs to be looked after. And I don't think she's getting the kind of care she needs at that place."

The other man shook his head. "It just seems that there ought to be some way we can–well, can't make her?"

"No, unfortunately. She's an adult. She's not incompetent. She's in charge. If she says she won't go, then she doesn't go," the doctor said.

Zelda's niece forced a smile. "Thank you again, Doctor." She turned to the man with her. "Let's go back to the hotel for dinner. I'm famished." The man nodded, and they left.

My blood boiled at the thought that she could think of food with Zel sick in the next room. If that's how concerned she was, then Zel was better off staying in New Orleans. There were, after all, hospitals in New Orleans. And if they were really that concerned, they should move to New Orleans. If only she were still standing there, I thought, I would sure tell her.

The doctor's chart clattered into its holder on the door. He smiled at the nurses as he passed. Sliding silently into the room, I found Zelda flipping through a magazine. She did not notice me at first. I inched closer to the foot of her bed. "Hey, Zel."

She looked up and smiled, just as she had each time I came into her room for writing advice. It took her a moment to realize that she should be surprised to see me standing in her hospital room. "Well, Billy!"

"How are you?" I said. My eyes would not settle, instead dancing around the room, at the picture of a gazebo above the dresser, the IV pole, out the window. Everywhere but at her. For some reason, the sight of Zelda in that hospital bed unnerved me. She seemed much smaller, frailer than she had at Liberty Street.

"Well, I've been better," she said. "But I'll be fine. Just normal getting-old stuff."

"Camille said they brought you here for tests. What kind of tests?" I finally looked at her. She was the same Zel that I remembered, her eyes still feisty and full of life. I relaxed a bit.

"The doctors say I've got an aneurysm."

"What's an aneurysm?"

She scratched her head, puzzling over how to respond. "You know how when you blow up one of those long, skinny balloons it sometimes gets bigger in one place?" She waited a moment for me to nod before continuing. "Well, there's a blood vessel in my brain that's doing the same thing. It's getting bigger where it shouldn't."

"Can't they fix it?"

She shook her head. "It's inoperable."

My heart sank. "Are you going to die?"

"Sooner than later, I'm afraid. After all, I'm almost ninety years old." She laughed. "But I don't think this is what's going to get me."

For some reason, I believed Zelda. I believed that the aneurysm would not get her. She would live forever, just like the rest of the Bohemians, just like me. She propped herself up on her elbows. "Enough about me. Have you been writing much?"

I nodded.

"What about?"

Remembering the pages of ramblings I scribbled the previous evening, I frowned. The pages were still rough, unedited emotions. I knew they would draw the ire of my friend. And she was in there, in those same pages. How would I explain that?

"Billy?"

I looked up. "Ma'am?"

"What about?"

"Just stuff," I said. "It's not very good."

"Well, we'll see about that when I get back home. How did you know where to find me?"

I told her about going to Liberty Street and talking to Camille. Ochsner had been easy enough to find, a single bus ride and I was at the hospital. My overly-dramatized description of the grumpy guard downstairs made her laugh. "And then I found your room and waited for you to finish arguing. Zel, where does she want you to go?"

She groaned. "Back north, to Chicago with her and that husband of hers."

"Why don't you want to go?"

"Because everything and everyone I love is here. Don't get me wrong. I love her. She's family. But you all are my family too, and I'm not ready to leave you guys yet." She yawned.

"Zel, you're tired. Maybe I should go home."

She sighed with both disappointment and relief. "I'm sorry, Billy. You see–well, she takes a lot out of me."

"When are you coming home?"

"Just a couple more days. 'Observation,' they call it. I think they found out I have good insurance and Medicare," she said.

"I'll tell everyone. They'll be glad to know." We said our good-byes and I left. On the bus home,

I could not erase the smile plastered across my face. Zelda's words about leaving home had etched it there when she said "you guys." "You guys" included me. I was part of the group. I belonged.

And it felt good.

Chapter 14

I burst through the Liberty Street door, propelled forward by my desire to tell my friends that I, Billy Bradshaw, had found Zel. That Camille Roberts was not at her desk to check me in escaped notice until I confronted the hallway leading to the Row. So accustomed was I to hearing jazz and laughter emanating from inside, the silence stunned. No music. No laughter. Only the rumble of a vaguely masculine voice greeted me. With each step toward the door the voice became clearer, and I recognized the voice. Christopher Downing was visiting Bohemian Row.

I opened the door and tried to sneak quietly inside. But as always, I failed to anticipate the moment the door slipped from my hand and slammed behind me. Immediately, all eyes trained on me, again the interloper at the door. Alistair was on the couch, his arm draped over the back. Thaddeus sat next to him and appeared to be reading a magazine or a book, obviously trying to ignore whatever conversation the slammed door had interrupted. Anne and Louise stood on opposite sides of the kitchen door, Anne holding a dishtowel, Louise a bowl full of something requiring constant whisking. Donald sat in his customary seat at the dinner table, silent, unmoving and trying to avoid eye contact with Camille Roberts and the new administrator standing in the middle of the room.

Christopher Downing looked me over once. "Who are you?"

I stuttered, tried to introduce myself, but the accusatory tone of his voice, either real or imagined, frightened me.

Camille answered. "This is Billy, Mr. Downing."

"Who?"

"The one His Honor sent over? I told you about him."

"Oh, right. The vandal."

Alistair cleared his throat. "That, Mr. Downing, was all a misunderstanding."

"Oh really?" Downing turned back to me. "Did you get caught breaking windows?"

I nodded, still speechless.

He turned back to Alistair, eyebrows raised. "I don't know what you've heard, Mr. Lees, but there is no misunderstanding."

Alistair attempted to stand, but Thaddeus pulled him back onto the sofa. "Just leave it alone, Alistair."

Downing flipped through several pages of handwritten notes on his clipboard. "Where was I, Miss Roberts?"

"You were saying that the rules in place here are–" she began.

"Thank you. As I was saying. The federal guidelines are in place for your own safety and well-being, as well as the safety of the staff and other residents. I understand my predecessor was lax in his enforcement of those rules. Unfortunately, this isn't a practice I am prepared to continue. You will follow the rules as outlined in the resident guide, which Emily will distribute later this afternoon."

Anne raised her hand. "Just where is Emily, Mr. Downing?"

"She's been reassigned."

Anne stood in the door, unmoving, her chin slightly cocked and unsatisfied with his answer. He sighed, as if to indicate he resented having to explain his decisions to a lowly tenant.

"We are incredibly understaffed. To have one full-time employee devoted to only six patients who are ambulatory and so obviously capable is wasteful. Emily will be available two hours of each day at her post on Hall B."

Anne tapped Louise on the shoulder. "We've got breakfast to finish."

Louise and Anne turned for the kitchen. Downing called after them. "Pardon me, Miss Kearney, Miss Moore. Residents are not allowed to prepare their own meals."

As if he had crossed the room and slapped her, Anne's face dropped and her cheeks went flushed. Her nostrils flared. "I beg your pardon, Mr. Downing."

Downing stared back, one eyebrow cocked, daring a confrontation. "You will eat with the other residents in the main dining room at your prescribed time." When Camille dropped her head and sighed, Downing tensed. "Do you have a problem with that, Miss Roberts?"

I thought for a moment I heard her growl but dismissed it as my imagination egged on by the look on her face.

"Well, Mr. Downing," Camille said. "The kitchen staff has gotten used to Hall B cooking their own meals. They don't fix enough food."

"That sounds like a problem you'll need to correct, then, doesn't it?" He turned on his heels to leave.

Alistair shifted back and forth in his seat, looked at Thaddeus. When Thaddeus made no move to restrain him, Alistair stood. "Mr. Downing?"

Christopher Downing stopped in front of Emily's desk and turned. "Yes, Mr. Lees?"

"No offense or anything, but we're kind of used to doing things our own way. We aren't hurting anyone back here, so why can't we just be?" Alistair glanced at Donald, who still hadn't moved or spoken.

Downing shook his head condescendingly. "Rules are rules, Mr. Lees. If I let you break the rules, then I have to let everyone, don't I?"

Donald was the next to come to his feet, the folds of a flowered house dress rustling as he stood. "Perhaps we might speak a little later?"

"About what, Mr. Lilly?" Downing said. He glanced at Donald's dress and matching shoes with disdain.

"Well, it is a private matter? About an arrangement with–"

Downing interrupted him. "I'm aware of the arrangement you made when you came. You paid a little $120,000, correct?"

Donald nodded.

"That money has long since been used up in the upkeep of your rooms, your groceries, and your expenses. I'll be happy to review the figures."

"Mr. Downing, that arrangement was supposed to be for the rest of our lives," Donald said. When Downing was unmoved, he continued. "It was all I had left of my inheritance."

"I'm not unsympathetic, Mr. Lilly, but surely you understand this is a business decision. The home is hemorrhaging money, and I cannot afford to support the policies of my predecessor as relates to your care. You will be well taken care of, all of you. However, you'll have to begin abiding by the rules–my rules."

I recognized the smile on Thaddeus's face as the same smile I had seen a dozen times in his fights with Zel. He calmly rested a hand on Donald's shoulder. "Mr. Downing, I don't think you understand my friend here. What he's trying to tell you is, well, how can I put this delicately? Mr. Downing, you can take your rules and go to hell."

* * *

Camille Roberts stood in the center of the room in a whirlpool of tension. Her eyes were focused on the door, which had just slammed behind a red-faced Christopher Downing. Alistair started to speak, but she held up her hand and silenced him. When the new administrator's footsteps had faded, she turned away from the door and burst into laughter.

"Lord, son, I can't believe you just did that!"

Anne and Louise reappeared in the kitchen door, dumbstruck and silent. But the mocking corners of Anne's half-grin hinted that the shock was subsiding.

"Nurse Roberts," Thaddeus said. "I apologize for swearing in front of you."

She flapped her hand in protest. "Oh, I'm a big girl, Thaddeus. You don't have to apologize. I ain't never seen anything like that. Did you see how red he turned?" She gripped her side, still unable to control the laughter.

Alistair grinned. "If that's what you call delicate, I'd hate to see straightforward."

Thaddeus winked at me. "I didn't think he understood Alistair's subtlety. Do you, Billy?"

Anne scoffed. "He outright told us to eat in the dining room or starve."

"Speaking of starving."

We all turned to the voice at the table. In all of the excitement, everyone had forgotten Donald. Louise tried to apologize. "You're right. Breakfast is already late. I'm sure everyone is hungry. Breakfast will be out in about ten minutes."

Camille stopped at the door and shook her head at Thaddeus. "Son, that was brave." The sound of her laughter echoed around the room for several seconds after the door slammed behind her.

Alistair crossed to the table, sat down, and unfolded the paper. "Now that we have that out of the way, we can get back to life as usual."

Anne made her way back into the kitchen. "Good morning, Billy," she said.

"Good morning," I replied. Within seconds, four more good mornings came at me from various corners of the room.

Alistair patted the back of Zel's empty chair. "Billy, have a seat." The sky-blue place mat was devoid of silverware and china. I sat down, rather uncomfortable to be occupying her spot, especially without having yet told him that I had seen her.

"I have news," I said. "I saw Zelda yesterday."

Thaddeus slammed his magazine onto the coffee table and rushed over, nearly tripping over his house slippers. "What?"

"She says to tell everyone she's fine, that she'll be home soon, and that she misses us."

Alistair patted me on the shoulder. "Good work, Billy. Good work. How did you find her?"

I told Thaddeus and Alistair and Donald about my Sunday trip to the home, to Ochsner and the conversation I overheard between Zel and her family. Alistair shook his head. "The niece means well, Billy, so don't be angry at her." I stopped short of telling them how she had included me in the group. Perhaps Alistair or Thaddeus or Donald might disagree. The risk of again becoming an outcast was too great and one risk I wasn't ready to face.

Anne and Louise returned from the kitchen, their arms loaded with plates. Louise passed a tray of biscuits around the table while Anne served omelets with a pair of tongs. They sat down and Alistair said a brief blessing. At "amen" everyone reached for their forks but froze momentarily as he added, "Oh yes! And thank you for allowing Billy the wisdom and safety to find our dear friend, and for ensuring her safe return. Amen."

Louise looked up, surprised. "You saw Zel?"

I nodded and told the entire story again.

Chapter 15

I lay in bed for several minutes while the war between consciousness and sleep waged within my body, my head buried in my arms in a futile attempt to muffle the noises of morning's arrival. But the steady paiter of water in Mom's bathroom resonated with the same anti-rhythm of the city around us. Six-thirty was too early for a summer morning. I sighed and rolled out of bed.

The shower stopped just as I opened the kitchen cabinet. A cartoon tiger smiling down from the side of a cereal box yielded only two tablespoons of powdered cornflake remnants. I tossed the empty box into the garbage can and opened the pantry. It was empty except for half a loaf of molded bread and a box of cornbread mix. Dismayed, I decided to watch television until my mother was ready for work.

The gardening program was on again. I fumbled with the remote for a second and was about to flip channels, but something caught my attention. The host ran her fingers across a palette of lush, red blossoms, the same flowers Louise had been planting beside the patio only a few weeks before. "Jim, what is your secret to such beautiful amaryllis?" the host said.

"When planting the bulbs, I make sure to use a good soil that has been pretreated with a nutrient pH balanced specifically for young plants." The camera panned across several boxes on the table beside the flowers. "Now all of these are good. But for flowering plants, I prefer to use this."

He held up a sea-foam colored box. "Just follow the steps on the side of the box and you won't go wrong."

The host indicated another tray full of small purple and white flowers. "These impatiens look ready to go in the ground. Want some help planting them?"

"Sure, Kathy."

The host turned to the camera. "We'll be right back."

"Would you like healthy, hearty tomatoes?" an announcer's voice said as a picture of the seafoam box faded in. "How about vibrant, strong marigolds? Three out of four gardeners agree that NutriGrow is the perfect soil additive for your garden!"

An older gentleman appeared, presenting a basket overflowing with carrots and green peppers. "I always wanted to grow fresh produce in my backyard, but the soil was rocky and didn't have the nutrients my plants needed. With the help of NutriGrow, my bell peppers won this blue ribbon!"

I heard the door of my mother's room open and footsteps in the hall. She patted the top of my head as she walked past the sofa and into the kitchen. "You're up early."

I rested my head on the back of the sofa and watched her fix a pot of coffee. When she spotted the empty bowl I had left on the counter, she looked at me apologetically. "Are we out of cereal again?"

She disappeared behind the pantry door. "Guess we need to go shopping, huh? Since you're spending so much time at the home, I've started slacking." She closed the pantry door and sighed. "Next time, tell me when we're out of cereal and bread. I'll just run something home to you at lunch."

"You don't have to do that, Mom."

"What will you do for lunch, then?"

It was a fair question and one that I might not have been prepared to answer only a couple of months before. But I had changed and I was capable of caring for myself. Mother's repeated intrusions into my newly-forming independence were starting to bother me. If I wanted to find my own lunch, she should let me. "I could get something close," I said.

"It won't be a big deal, Billy. I'll come back and bring you something for lunch."

"No. Don't. It's too far for you to come, and you don't have time."

She shook her head. "You can't just go get something. I'm not going to let you run around New Orleans on a bus."

"Why not? I take the bus all the time."

"But that's different."

"Why?"

She looked up, breathing slowly. I braced for the second she began shouting. But when she didn't, I knew I had won. "I'll go straight down to Canal and back. I'll be fine."

She opened her purse and held out a five. I reached for it and pulled, but she didn't let it go. "Straight there, straight back. And be careful."

"Okay," I said. She released the five. The coffee pot gurgled and the smell of fresh coffee made me even hungrier. My stomach growled. Mom laughed when she heard it. "Want me to fix you breakfast?"

"Sure."

She took a carton of eggs out of the refrigerator and a skillet from the cabinet next to the stove. "Come sit at the table while I'm cooking and talk to me. I have good news."

Something beneath the burner of the stove started to smolder and I wrinkled my nose. Whatever was burning didn't mix with the smell of frying eggs and fresh coffee. I opened the window as far as it would go and inhaled the explosion of fresh, warm air streaming into the kitchen.

Mother alternately stirred the skillet of eggs and sipped her cup of coffee. "I found out I'm up for a promotion at work."

"Really?"

She set a plate of scrambled eggs on the table. "Yep. One of the men thinks I'd make a good loan officer. It would be more work, but more money too."

The skillet clattered into the sink. She turned on the faucet, sending a stream of water sizzling into the hot pan. Mom wiped her forehead with a paper towel and sighed. "Well, I'm off to work. Can't be late if we want that raise." Her lips brushed my cheek and then she was gone, the change in the bottom of her purse rattling as she went.

Nothing highlights loneliness more than the subdued cacophony that is an apartment building in the morning. The tines of my fork scraped quietly against the plate with a tonal value barely distinguishable from the whir of the air conditioner. The refrigerator rumbled to life. The pipes of our sink rattled their response to the anonymous toilet flush somewhere in our building. Our upstairs neighbor thumped back and forth above my head. Somewhere down the hall, a television blared a morning traffic report. I began to wish that I had not gotten out of bed.

Then the unmistakable crack of leather against wood yanked my attention out of the kitchen and into the empty lot behind our building. At first, I thought I had imagined it, but cheering soon followed. I ran to the window and looked out across the parking lot and over the fence to where a group of children had assembled and were playing baseball. I didn't know who they were, but I didn't care. Baseball was baseball, and I could hardly wait to play. My baseball glove was still hanging on the hook above my desk. I grabbed it and flew from my bedroom without stopping to pick up the notebook I knocked to the floor.

By the time I reached the landing between floors I was bounding over two and three stairs at a time. The sunlight slammed my face and enveloped me in the warm, humid glow of that is an early summer morning. As I turned the corner and started toward the wooden fence that divided our apartment complex from the empty lot, another report of ball against bat sounded.

"Foul!" someone cried out. I quickened my pace, and broke into a run for the fence.

There was a gap only a few feet away, just big enough to allow me to squeeze through and enter the field. The ditch separating our complex from the empty lot wouldn't be much of an obstacle. Another loud crack and a round of cheers. I eased down the embankment, careful to keep my balance, but the dirt was still soggy from a morning shower. My foot sank into the muck and I grasped at the weeds in an effort to steady myself. I was completely unprepared when the entire side of the ditch collapsed and sent me hurtling towards the fence.

Despite my best efforts to brace myself for the impact, my cheek made contact with the nearest fencepost, just beneath my eye. I felt my neck twist around. The muscles in my back tensed and then it was over. I was in the bottom of the ditch, covered in mud. My eye was throbbing, and I couldn't see. Somewhere in the lot beyond the fence, I could still hear the kids cheering a runner around third base, shouting for him to take home.

Chapter 16

The receptionist had to be wrong. There was no way my mother would leave work in the middle of the morning. Having seen how she had reacted to the police department summons, I only phoned her offices as a last resort when the swelling would not go down. Listening to the hold music, I tried to imagine her reaction when she had to leave work because I was a klutz. But, instead, the receptionist returned to the line and told me my mother wasn't there. I hung the phone up and returned to the bathroom. My eye throbbed in pain, and each time I looked at the mirror, I winced. The first sight of my swollen, bruised cheek had sent me into nightmare visions of a trip to the emergency room, a place that, through an incredible run of good luck, I had avoided my entire life.

I turned on the cold faucet and, with a damp rag, tried to wash the dirt from my face without further aggravating the bulging purple sack beneath my eye. Each brush of the soft cotton cloth felt like sandpaper. I blotted my face dry and returned to the living room, just in time to hear the door open and see my mother appear.

"I'm home!" she called out before noticing me in the hall. "Oh, there you are."

Her keys rattled into the tray by the door, and her purse landed on the floor with a dull thud. When she finally noticed my eye, she covered her mouth with both hands and gasped. "Billy! What happened to your eye?"

"I fell."

She brushed it lightly with her thumb. "Does that hurt?"

I nodded.

"Well, let's get something on it." She led me into the kitchen. I watched as she filled a rag with ice. The anger and resentment of our morning argument faded into a thankful ambiguity. Though I resented that she was there, caring for me, I was thankful for her unexpected return.

The cold cloth soothed my eye, and Mom's presence slowed my racing pulse.

She sat in the chair across from mine. "So. Would you like to tell me what happened?"

I told her about the baseball game, how I had been running, was trying to cross the ditch, but slipped. She watched attentively for a few seconds before becoming absorbed in some far off place that had little to do with the baseball field or my eye. Only after losing her interest did I wonder why she was home so early. Even if she had decided to come for lunch, she wouldn't have been there until much later.

"What's wrong, Mom?"

She shuttered off whatever she was thinking about and smiled at me. "I'm sorry, honey. What?"

"You weren't listening."

She shook her head apologetically but didn't look up. "Mom!"

The back of her chair slammed into the floor as she jumped up. "Nothing, Billy. Just shit at work."

I stared at her for a minute. She had sworn in front of me many times, but rarely when she knew I was listening and never without anger. I stared blankly at her and her at me, both waiting for the other to break the tension. She rolled her head from side to side, massaging her shoulder. Stooping, she righted her chair and returned to her seat.

"I may lose my job," she said.

"What? I thought you were up for a promotion."

She dropped her head into her hands. "Remember the man I went out with from work a few weeks ago? Well, he tried to make me go out with him again," she said. I knew from the look on her face that she had not told me everything.

"And?"

"And when I said no, he threatened to fire me."

Her company had sent us to New Orleans to get her away from one boss that she had gotten involved with, and now it was all happening again. Whether the anger welling inside me was directed at my mother or her boss, I couldn't tell. All I knew was I didn't want to go through another forced relocation.

"Are we going to have to move?"

She didn't reply.

"Mom!"

"I don't know, Billy! I don't know, I don't know, I don't know!"

Cubes of ice slid across the table and the back of my chair slammed into the counter with a loud crack. I slammed the door behind me and imagined that it barely missed Mom's face.

"Billy," my mother called through the door. "Billy, I'm sorry. Billy, come talk to me, please."

"Just go away!" I shouted.

"I'm sorry," she said. I heard her hand on the knob and expected her to come in. My bedroom door didn't have a lock and in all honesty, I had never wanted one until that moment. A few moments passed before I heard the door to her bedroom. My eye started to throb again. I thought about the icepack, discarded and melting on the kitchen table. The last thing I wanted to do was ask Mom to make another. I didn't need her for anything.

Finally convinced that she had gone into her room for more than a few minutes, I slipped quietly down the hall. The rag was still lying on the kitchen table where it had landed. A thin trickle of water flowed from the corner of the rag and spilled over the edge of the table.

With a fresh rag full of ice, I returned to my room to figure out what would happen if we moved again. Thoughts of a new school and yet another strange city exhausted my last bits of energy. I plunged headlong into a fitful, restless sleep haunted by dreams of mudslides and ditches, the dissonant rhythm of baseball games ringing in the background.

* * *

It was still daylight outside when I awoke.

I looked around my room for the source of whatever sound had startled me. My door was still closed, and everything appeared as it had been before my nap. Whatever the noise was, it had come from outside of my room.

The door to my mother's room was still shut, but the television was on and a fresh pot of coffee was brewing in the kitchen. I poured a glass of orange juice and returned to the living room to watch television, but couldn't find the remote. A search of the couch cushions yielded a hairpin, a rubber band, and forty-two cents, but no remote.

I sighed and knocked on her bedroom door.

"Just a minute," she called. The door opened a few seconds later. "What do you want? I'm on the phone with Grandma."

"You have the clicker."

She handed me the remote control and disappeared behind the door again. As I settled back onto the sofa, her door opened.

"No, Mom. I don't know what I'm going to do," she said. "No, I can't afford one. Besides, what could a lawyer tell me?… Fine. I'll call. Goodbye, Mother."

She hung up the phone and sat down beside me. "Hungry?"

My stomach ached to remind me of a missed lunch. "Yeah, a little."

"I think we deserve a treat. Want to go out for supper?"

I shrugged. "I guess. Can we afford it?"

"At this point, Billy, I don't know what we can afford." She tossed the phone on the couch and stretched her arms over her head. "But I want to go out. So, I'm going to go shower and change.

If Grandma or Grandpa call back, tell them I'm not here."

When she emerged ten minutes later wearing a black skirt and lavender blouse, she made a single trip around the coffee table, as if to ask how she looked.

"You look nice, Mom."

She prodded me off the sofa with the toe of a pump. "Go dress up for Mom. I'm hungry and ready to go."

I quickly changed into the khakis and button-down I normally wore to church and returned to the living room. Mom had the phone pressed to her ear, her hand cupped over the receiver, and was quietly muttering obscenities. She playfully banged her head into the doorjamb and cupped her hand over the receiver. "Grandpa now."

I rolled my eyes and flopped on the sofa to wait.

"No, Dad. No, I didn't do anything to provoke him…Yes, I know. I'll get a reputation…I don't know. But I can't go back to the office as long as he is there…Mom said the same thing…You what? Dad, I didn't want you to do that…fine. What's his name?" She jotted a name and phone number on a piece of scrap paper before launching the pencil across the room. "Dad...Dad. Whatever, Dad. Is he any good?... Okay. Love you too. Bye."

Her shoulders sagged, and her body went limp against the counter. Her fingers, clenched tightly around the phone, turned a ghostly white, the only hint of the intensity of the anger she was straining to hide. The tension within her built into a quiet rage until, at last, she hurled the phone into the floor and screamed. The handset shattered and gouged into the linoleum. Just as quickly as it came, the outburst subsided. She tossed her head back, smoothed a wayward strand of hair back into place.

As if nothing had happened, she smiled at me. "Ready to go?"

We followed the maitre d' through an arched entryway into the restaurant. The smell of crab boil and fresh fish drifted through the air. Men in suits and women in dresses huddled around tables that seemed too small for the oversized plates of seafood piled high with crab claws and fried catfish.

A waiter lingered beside a table set for two. We settled into our seats and began reading the menu as our waiter filled our water glasses. "Would you care to see the wine list?" he said.

Mother shook her head.

"I'll give y'all a few moments to look the menu over." He disappeared as quietly as if he had faded into the wall.

I scanned the list of entrées. Each dish had a name that was almost as indecipherable to me as the descriptions. The column of numbers to the far right read more like a complex list of math problems than a list of prices. "Mom, this place is really expensive."

"Yes it is." She winked, closed her menu and laid it on the edge of the table.

"You know what you want already?" I said.

"Just a seafood platter."

I closed my menu and placed it beside hers. "I'll have the same."

The waiter reappeared, pad in hand, ready to take our orders. She smiled up at him in such a way that he blushed. "Two seafood platters. I'll also have a Bud over ice, please. And Billy would like a glass of iced tea."

"Right away, ma'am." And the waiter vanished again. We sat in silence for a few seconds. But unlike earlier, neither of us were searching for conversation to fill the void. I thought about the previous day at the home and Christopher Downing. Maybe now would be a good time to tell her about my trip to the hospital to see Zel. Still distracted by the day's crises, she probably wouldn't want to hear about Sunday morning's trek. I assumed that she was preoccupied enough with work that she might appreciate the silence.

Before either of us had completed our separate mental journeys, our waiter rematerialized and presented us with a bottle of wine. "Ma'am, an eighty-six Chateau Neuf."

She tried to protest, but he had uncorked the bottle and began pouring before she could stop him.

"But I didn't order this," she said.

"Compliments of the gentleman at that table." He pointed to the far corner of the restaurant. When she turned to see who had sent the wine, two men in dark suits raised their glasses. Mom shrank down into her chair.

"Shit."

"Pardon?" the waiter said.

"Nothing. Tell them thank you." She dismissed the waiter with a wave of her hand, propped her elbows on the table and began rubbing her temples. "That's Mr. Thompson, the head of the New Orleans office."

I didn't know what to say. But I didn't have to say anything, because one of the men had arrived at our table and was smiling down at me. "You must be Billy. I've heard a lot about you. That's one hell of a shiner, son."

He turned to my mother before I could respond. "I'm glad you're here, Beverly. I was going to call you in the morning and let you know how sorry I am about what happened."

Mother managed a half-smile that more clearly said that she knew he was lying than that she was happy to see him. "Well, Mr. Thompson, I can't really talk about it right now." She shot a sideways glance in my direction. "You understand."

He smiled at me again. "Of course, Beverly. May I call you in the morning?"

"Actually, it would probably be better if you contacted my attorney," she said.

He coughed. "Attorney?"

"Well, considering that one of your vice presidents told me if I wanted to keep my job I would–" she broke off momentarily before continuing, leaving the blank space unfilled and understood between them. "I thought it best to protect my interests."

He frowned. "I had hoped it wouldn't come to this, Beverly. But I do understand."

She cocked her head slightly and smiled again. "I'm sure you do, Mr. Thompson."

His gaze shifted around the restaurant, as if he were searching for an escape route or an ally. Perhaps an attorney of his own or his friend at the table in the corner would rush in with whatever words were an appropriate response. When no one appeared, his eyes reluctantly settled back on her. "Listen, Bev. We all really like you. Hell, you're like family. I wouldn't want you to make any hasty decisions. So, why don't you take a week off, with pay? Just to think about what needs to happen so that no one gets hurt. Okay?"

She tensed. I thought for a minute she was going to slap him, but the tension in her face eased and she managed a smile. "Thank you, Mr. Thompson. I'll do that."

With a nod, he turned to leave the table but stopped short. "By the way, order what you like. Dinner is on me."

She returned his smile dismissively and watched him walk back to his table. He stopped long enough to shake hands with two men a few tables over. When he had escaped earshot, she turned back to me. "Remember this conversation, Billy."

"Why?"

"Because you'll have to testify about it in court."

Chapter 17

With two leathery fingers, Zel turned my cheek from side to side. She shook her head. "At any rate, it makes a nice souvenir for an eventful day."

"And another thing," Alistair said, "when you get into court, remember–tell the truth."

"If I can remember it," I muttered. It was more than fair to say that I was overwhelmed by the events of the previous day. My memory might fail under the stress.

Alistair reassuringly rested his hand on my shoulder. "I know you'll do fine. But if you're really worried about it, write it all down."

"Yes!" Zelda said. She darted down the hall toward her room. "Make it a story."

With the black eye and Mom's boss so fresh in my memory, the diversion of breakfast at the

Home was more than welcome. I had been so excited to share everything with the Bohemians that I had almost forgotten to tell Camille that I had arrived. By the time I phoned the front desk to let Camille know that I had arrived, Zelda had dropped a notepad and pen on Emily's old desk.

Thaddeus reappeared from the kitchen after clearing the dishes away and flipped on the television for his morning soaps. Zelda assumed her seat on the couch beside him, her leather journal open in her lap. Louise and Anne had retreated to Anne's room to play checkers about the same time Donald had gone for his nap. I glanced at the head of the table where I expected to find Alistair reading the *Times-Picayune*. To my astonishment, the space in front of him was empty and he was staring out into the garden. The missing paper was yet another reminder of Emily's departure.

Her desk was empty. The magazines, her pictures and the potted fern she kept on the ledge behind her were all gone. Only the clipboard and telephone remained. We had not seen her in the two weeks since she had left, and I wondered what she was doing now and if she liked her new job. Emily's absence had not gone unnoticed. Without the constant ringing of the telephone, our mornings had become a long, uninterrupted span of silence. Even Anne, with whom Emily clashed most frequently, had not taken the sudden void easily. Alistair's missing *Times* was only one of many reminders of all the things she had done for the Bohemians, things that I had never considered. Fresh flowers for Zelda from the market, Anne and Louise's special coffee that she brought each week from the French Quarter. Thaddeus had become quite the grouch. It seemed that for as long as she had been there, Emily had smuggled a bottle of Irish whiskey to him every couple of weeks.

I wandered over to Emily's desk and ran my hand across the top of it. Camille's inquisition sprang back to mind. I could almost hear her voice demanding to know what I did with my time. And then it occurred to me. While I couldn't buy Thad's whiskey or Anne and Louise's coffee, I could get flowers for Zel on the way and pick up Alistair's paper. Maybe there were other things I could do for them, too, things that they hadn't thought of.

I tapped Alistair on the shoulder and he turned.

"Would you like me to go get you a paper?" I said.

His face lit up. "That would be very nice."

"I know there was a lot that Emily did for you guys, and no one has been doing it since she left. A lot of the stuff I won't be able to do, but I could do some of it. Like Zel's flowers." I studied Alistair's face for some signs of response. But it was Thaddeus that spoke first.

"That's an idea with merit, Billy," he said.

I pressed forward, my mind racing faster and faster. "After all, I was sent down here to help. So why don't I help?"

Alistair scratched his head. "I definitely miss my morning paper. Why not?"

I spun around to leave, but he stopped me. "Where are you going?"

"To get your paper!"

Standing in the open door, I beamed with the sense of accomplishment. "And if you will make me a list, I'll get what you need–or at least whatever I can." I let the door slam and started down the hall.

Making my way up to the front desk, I smiled at two orderlies who were polishing the floor. They nodded back. Within my first week at the home, I'd grown used to the smell of disinfectant and air freshener. The stale smell of age didn't hold its same disquieting effect. I had even learned the names of many of the residents and would greet them as we passed in the halls. The staff all knew me by name, and we would exchange smiles. I was just another member of a team, providing my own small contribution.

Approaching the last turn to the main hall, I saw a woman in a wheelchair making her way from the opposite direction. "Hello, Mrs. Markowitz," I called. She smiled and stopped beside me.

"How are you doing today, Billy?"

"Can't stop. On a mission!"

I turned the corner and stopped dead. Staring back at me, at eye level, was a pair of ice blue eyes, barely inches away from my own. Wisps of blonde hair fell over her eyes, partially obscuring them from view. She wore a white sundress and looked like something from an old photograph.

We looked about the same age. I stood frozen for several seconds, unable to speak.

I heard Mrs. Markowitz's wheelchair squeak up behind me. "Keep up the good work, Billy," she said.

I turned back to Mrs. Markowitz. "I will." When I turned back around, the girl was gone. I looked up and down the hall for some hint of her, any trace, but she had vanished. Rushing back to the corner, I called after Mrs. Markowitz.

"Did you see a little girl in the hall just now?"

She looked at me confused and shook her head no. "I haven't. Sorry. Were you looking for someone?"

I stared back down the empty hallway. "No, ma'am. She was just standing here." I pointed to the spot where I'd seen the girl.

She leered at me with an angry glare in her eyes. "Don't you try and play jokes on me, Billy. I know very well that there was no little girl there because I just came through there."

She wheeled away, looking as confused as I felt. I knew what I had seen, but if Mrs. Markowitz was right and there was no little girl, it had been my imagination. Or worse, a ghost.

I moved cautiously down the hall, past several open patient rooms. Approaching the third opened door, I heard something, a voice, barely a whisper. With Camille's desk in sight now, I could see Alistair's paper on the corner, waiting. But the whispers from the room beckoned me inside.

Slipping silently into the dark room, I waited for a moment while my eyes struggled to adjust to the darkness. The voice, still a whisper, seemed to be coming from somewhere near the bed. I tiptoed up to the edge of the bed, expecting to find someone awake and talking. But the green-and-white-striped wristband of an invalid patient meant that the whispers I heard were not from the man in the bed.

"Shhh. He's in the room," again came the whisper.

I turned around, thinking it had come from behind me, but there was no one there. "I don't know if we can get out or not," it said again. This time, it was coming from the other side of the bed. I dropped onto the floor and checked under the bed. No feet. No girl. Nothing.

Standing, I dusted off my knees and glanced at the closet. But the door was closed and I knew from the rooms on Hall B that, if someone were whispering behind the thick, heavy doors that hung throughout the home, it would not penetrate into the bedroom.

Something in the corner of my eye caught my attention. I thought for a moment that the dusty drape had moved. I stepped around the bed and pushed the drapes aside. A blinding shaft of light cut into the room and stung my eyes.

Through the harsh glare of the midmorning sun, a barely detectable blur shot across the room and into the hall. Creaking hinges and footsteps receding down the hall confirmed what my eyes had tried to see. Rushing from the room, I tripped over an empty wheelchair in the hall and slammed hard into the floor. Undeterred, I still made pursuit. But as the footsteps receded, I came to a dead-end at a set of heavy steel doors. I had to look twice to make sure, but I was standing in front of the entrance to the Row.

The hall was empty, and there was nowhere else for someone to have run. If the little girl I had seen was real, then she would be in Hall B. Pushing open the door, I looked around the common room, first behind Emily's desk, then beneath the table. Alistair and Thaddeus eyed me curiously.

"Lose something, Billy?" Alistair said.

I shook my head without looking up, instead peering into the kitchen. "Have you seen a little girl run through here?"

Thaddeus shook his head. "Nope. No little girl. Sorry."

"Who did you see?" Anne said.

"A girl. By Camille's desk. But she disappeared."

"Disappeared?"

"Yeah. Like she was never there."

Anne shrugged. "Maybe she was a ghost."

That was the last thing she should have said. I was already afraid that the girl was not real. After all, with as many people that died in the house over the years, it was probably haunted. I shuddered.

"I hope it wasn't."

"Wasn't what, dear?" a voice said from over my shoulder. I turned and saw Zel.

"A ghost. I saw a little girl in this white dress. Anne thinks she was a ghost."

Zelda shot Anne a sideways glance. "Don't scare the poor boy. This place is spooky enough as it is." Turning back to me, she smiled. "I'm sure there is a perfectly logical explanation. There is no such thing as ghosts."

"Bullshit," Thaddeus said. He quickly corrected himself. "Sorry, Billy. Didn't mean to swear. But there are ghosts. I've seen them."

Zelda stared at him incredulously. "And just where have you seen a ghost?"

"Not a ghost, Zel. Ghosts. An entire troupe of them. Standing on stage at the Orpheum in Chicago."

She rolled her eyes. "Let me guess. They were a Shakespearean troupe performing MacBeth?"

He shook his head. "Hamlet."

She scoffed. "Figures." Turning back to me, she put her hands on my shoulders feigning seriousness. "If I ever teach you anything, it is to not pay a damned bit of attention to that man."

I grinned. "Yes, ma'am."

Alistair cleared his throat. "Billy, did you forget something?" He looked at both of my hands, then the floor around him.

I thought for a second before sighing. His paper. "I'll go back and get it."

"I would very much appreciate it."

During the trip back to Camille's desk, the halls seemed to have grown narrower, taller, and the lights didn't light as well as they had on my first trip. Each open door that I passed was a potential cave from which any number of specters might spring at any moment.

Upon reaching the front door and Alistair's waiting newspaper, the ghost of the little blonde girl had not manifested itself, and I picked up the paper and began the journey back to Hall B. Camille appeared from a near-by office and stopped me. "Good morning, Billy."

"Good morning," I replied half-heartedly.

She eyed me over the top of her clipboard. "What's wrong? You look like you've seen a ghost."

I shrugged. "Maybe I did."

"What?"

I explained to her what I had seen only a few minutes before. Her face broke into a wide grin. "A little blonde ghost?" I nodded.

"About this high?" She held her hand up a few inches shorter than me. Camille's face turned red, she stopped breathing for a second, and then burst out laughing. She gripped her sides, gulping for air in between heaves. "Oh good heavens, boy. The things you come up with!"

She shooed me away, unable to control her laughter. As I turned the corner heading to the back of the home, Camille's cackling chased me along my journey back to Hall B.

Chapter 18

For the remainder of the day, I sat on the couch between Thaddeus and Zelda, getting up only to eat lunch and help Anne transplant two potted plants on the patio. After running into the ghost, exploring the home or venturing too far from the reclusion of Bohemian Row didn't seem like a good idea. At five thirty, the phone on Emily's desk rang and I rushed to answer it.

"Hall B."

"Billy, your mother's here," Camille informed me. I thanked Camille and returned the phone to the cradle, said my goodbyes and started for the front door. A few days before, Mother had decided that, since she wasn't working for a few weeks, she would deliver me and pick me up each day. When I was scarcely out the door, a voice called after me. I stared in disbelief at Alistair standing in the hall. With the exception of Zelda at Ochsner, I had never seen any of them anywhere other than Hall B.

"Glad I caught you, Billy." He panted for a second to catch his breath before continuing. "Thaddeus and I were just talking, and we would love to meet your mom. Ask your Mother if she would like to join us for lunch on Friday, will you?"

The prospect of my mother meeting the six people so important to me made me both elated and worried. Alistair, picking up on my concern, smiled reassuringly. "I will make sure that Donald dresses appropriately and that Anne and Louise are on their best behavior."

Their willingness to perform for my mother surprised me. I hadn't been concerned about how my mother would react to the Bohemians, but rather what the Bohemians might think of my mother. I shook my head. "No. That's not fair."

He stiffened in response. "Billy, she just might–"

"No," I insisted. "She should accept you for who you are."

Alistair grinned. "Around noon?"

"Sure."

"And Billy, I'm quite proud of you."

"What for?" I said, but he had already turned and gone.

* * *

All day Thursday, I debated whether I should have a convenient episode of amnesia and forget about Alistair's invitation for lunch. It would be simple, I convinced myself. Just tell him she didn't want to have lunch, that she had other plans. But that would require lying, and lying to Alistair wasn't something I could bring myself to do. Sitting alone in my room sometime before dinner, I decided that Alistair's respect wasn't something I was willing to lose to save my mother the shock of the Bohemians.

I found her in the living room, watching the same soap Thaddeus watched. "Hey, Mom?"

She looked up from the television in acknowledgement.

"Alistair wanted to know if you, well, maybe if you–" I began, but stopped. She raised her eyebrows expectantly.

"Spit it out already, Billy."

"Well, Alistair asked me to see if maybe you wanted to come to lunch tomorrow?"

She chewed on her bottom lip for a second. I thought she didn't want to go. "It's okay, Mom. I'll just tell them that you can't–"

"No. I want to. I'm just worried that it might make me late for an appointment with the attorney."

"Oh," I said. "So you'll come?"

"Sure."

I telephoned the home and left a message for Alistair, returned to my room, and sat down at the desk in front of my notebook.

Baseball, By Billy Bradshaw

The bat popped and called my name. I ran down the stairs and into the bright, hot sun. When I got to the baseball

```
field, I saw a girl getting
ready to swing.
```

I filled page after page with details about the fight with my mother and the ice pack. I thought about the look on Mom's face when she opened the door and saw my eye, rivulets of water mixing with tears streaming down my face, and ice, skimming across the table and shattering on the floor. The words stopped after our dinner at the seafood restaurant. I closed the notebook, placed the pencil in the jar on the desk, and climbed into bed. The next morning, I awoke from a dreamless sleep to the sounds of pots and the unmistakable slam of a cabinet door. Stretching, I yawned and crawled out of bed.

When Mm saw me standing in the kitchen door, she smiled wearily. She hadn't slept. "Good morning, honey."

"Don't fix me anything."

She stared at me for a moment, as if my request hurt her feelings. "It's not that, Mom. I just have breakfast with everyone else on Hall B."

She rolled her eyes.

"What?"

"Nothing, Billy. It's just that you spend so much time talking about everyone on Hall B or whatever it is they call it. The Row? You're my son after all. It's—well, I can't wait to meet these people." She returned two eggs to the open carton and placed it back in the refrigerator. Glancing around the kitchen before sitting down opposite me, she took a moment to rinse her hands. "Well, finish your milk and get ready. I don't want you to be late again."

Thirty minutes later, and with only seconds to spare, we pulled up in front of the Liberty Street Home and I hopped out of Myrtle. Her mood had softened considerably, and I dismissed her anger as sheer exhaustion. "I'll see you at noon, sweetie. And if I'm a little late from my meeting with the lawyer, start without me. Okay?" I slammed the door.

The cold blast of air from the lobby rushed around and greeted me. Camille smiled up from the front desk. "Good morning, Billy." She looked at her bare wrist, as if checking a watch. "Barely made it."

"Yes ma'am."

She handed me the *Times-Picayune.* "Give this to Alistair, please. See you this afternoon." As I started down the hall, she chuckled, adding, "And watch out for ghosts."

With the pending lunch at which my mother would finally meet all of my friends, writing down the story of the baseball game and the lawsuit, and worrying about what would come of her meeting with the lawyers, I had almost forgotten the ghost of only two days before. With a weary, tentative sigh, I set off for a waiting breakfast feast and an apprehension-filled morning. Everyone was just gathering around the table when the door slammed behind me.

"Morning, Billy," they said in unison without looking up. I tossed the paper on Emily's desk and found my customary seat between Donald and Thaddeus, slid up to the table and dished a spoonful of eggs onto my plate.

Thaddeus nudged a tray of sausages to my side of table. "So Billy. We finally get to meet your mother?"

"Mmhuh," I said. I swallowed and wiped my mouth apologetically. "Sorry. She'll be here around noon."

Donald shifted uncomfortably in his seat and twirled a dark ringlet of his wig between two fingers. I eyed him curiously, expecting him to say something about lunch. But he didn't speak through the entire breakfast. After the dishes were cleared away, he disappeared into his room and closed the door.

Thaddeus and Anne had decided to serve meatloaf and fresh vegetables. Alistair promised to fix his mother's cornbread and Zelda would provide raspberry iced tea and dessert. They were certainly pulling out all the stops, I thought.

At eleven-fifty, Donald emerged from his room wearing an off-white dress printed with small gardenias and green leaves. He had clipped his hair behind his ears with matching tortoise shell clips. A pair of ear bobs matched the tiny flowers on his dress. When he saw me sitting at the table, he smiled and turned in place. "Suitable?" he said.

I smiled back. "I just want everyone to be themselves today. Okay?"

* * *

"So Billy tells me that you were a painter?" Mother said.

"Yes. Portraits mostly," he said. "Some landscapes and still-lifes. But portraits, mostly."

"That's nice."

Again, silence fell over the table. Mother shifted in the folding chair that had been placed between Donald and me. Anne eyed her across the table, occasionally slipping a glance to Louise as if communicating her thoughts.

I noticed her staring at Donald's dress and kicked her under the table. She quickly shifted her gaze back to her plate, then to Zelda, who smiled at her behind the rim of her iced tea glass.

Thaddeus tapped me on the shoulder. "Would you please pass the cornbread?"

"Sure," I said.

Mom shot me a sideways look. "Yes sir, young man."

I opened my mouth to correct myself, but Thaddeus preempted it. "No, Beverly. It's quite all right. He wasn't being rude. We're all family here."

Almost imperceptibly, her shoulders tensed. Zelda, sitting across from her, apparently noticed it as well and decided to attempt defusing the situation.

"Billy is quite the little writer. You should be proud."

"Oh? I know he keeps a journal in his room," she said. Zelda raised an eyebrow. "You don't know about the stories he's been writing?"

Mom shook her head.

"Well, he's quite the writer, isn't he, Louise?"

Mom glanced at me and smiled. "Everyone needs a hobby."

"Writing can be more than a hobby," Alistair said. "Billy may have what it takes to make it a career later."

"He's only twelve. He doesn't know what a career is."

"Are you sure about that? I decided to become a painter when I was younger than him."

Mother ignored him, eying Donald curiously. "So, Donald? Where are you from?"

"Houston," he said.

"What brought you to New Orleans?"

"Family," he said.

Mom did a double take. "You have children here?"

"No. I was moving here to get away from my family," he said.

I thought for a minute that maybe Mom realized the connections she and Donald shared, but she turned away in silence and continued to pick at her meatloaf.

Donald tapped her lightly on the arm. "So how was the meeting with your attorney?"

She glared at him, stunned. "Fine," she said through pursed lips. "Just fine."

When she turned back to me, she said nothing, but her eyes warned me of the lecture that was to come. I leaned over the table, resting my elbows on either side of my plate.

"Billy, have you completely forgotten your manners?" Mom snapped. I looked up, confused.

"What did I do?"

"Keep your elbows off the table." She apologized to everyone.

Alistair placed his napkin beside his plate and leaned forward, resting his elbows on the table. "It's okay, Beverly. We don't much stand on formality around here. Your son is such a joy to have around. Indispensable, really."

Twenty minutes later, after a half-hearted attempt at salvaging their meeting over dessert, Mom stood to leave. "Well, Billy. I'll be back to get you at five."

I started to rise, but she stopped me. "Don't get up. I can find my own way out."

I sighed with relief when the door slammed. Alistair settled comfortably back into his chair and smiled. "Well that went as well as could be expected, wouldn't you say?"

* * *

After passing the rest of the afternoon helping Louise pull weeds out of the flowerbeds around the patio, I was washing dirt from my hands over the kitchen sink when the phone rang.

Zelda answered it. "Hello?...Yes, Miss Roberts, thank you. I'll send him up."

I shook the water from my hands and started for the door before Zel could tell me to go. "I'm already on my way."

Mother half-smiled at me when I slid into the vinyl seat of the Buick. "How was your afternoon?"

"Fine," I said.

As the car turned into the street, I caught a glance at the second-story windows of the new administrator's apartment. All of the windows were open, and lights blazed in several of the rooms. But the last window was dark, and the lace sheers blew lightly in a breeze. For a split second as Mother pulled into traffic, I was almost certain that I had seen the outline of a girl and the unmistakable shimmer of blonde hair lurking in the darkness just behind the lace.

Chapter 19

Mother surprised me that evening by avoiding talk of lunch and the Bohemians. By the time supper rolled around, I was convinced that she had chosen to forget about lunch. I spent most of the evening in front of the television, my attention riveted to a Twins game while she fixed dinner.

Without a word, she set my plate on the coffee table, dropped onto the sofa beside me, and flipped through the TV Guide. "There's a movie coming on tonight. You want to watch that with me?"

I shrugged, munching on macaroni and ham. When the Twins game ended, she turned to her movie, having missed the first five minutes. I went to my room and returned with my notebook. When I came back down the hall, I could hear a quiet rumbling sound. She had fallen asleep on the sofa and was snoring. I covered her up, returned to my room, and sat down at my desk, pencil in hand.

I awoke with a start.

"Billy, wake up!" Mom shouted through the door. I stumbled out of bed and squinted at the alarm clock. Seven forty, less than twenty minutes to be dressed and at the Home.

"What do you want for breakfast?" she called through the door as I fought with a pair of blue jeans.

"Nothing. I'll eat there."

"Whatever. Just hurry." I could hear her storming away from the door. Buttoning my shirt, I slipped down the hall and tried to find her. The television was off, there was no coffee in the pot, and the house was silent except for the quiet whir of the air conditioner.

The front door was open. I found her waiting in the car. We rode in silence across town. Something had obviously made her angry, and I wasn't about to try and find out what. If she wanted me to know, she would eventually tell me.

Pulling up to the Home, she finally broke.

"I shouldn't even be bringing you back here, after yesterday," she said.

I looked at her blankly.

"Lunch. Not minding. You remember."

"Yes, ma'am."

"It's just I expected more of you than that, Billy. And that man–what's his name again?"

I stared blankly out the window. "Alistair."

"Yes! Putting his damned elbows on the table to try and–I wonder what's happening here?" she interrupted herself.

An ambulance was parked at the doors, open and waiting. I got out of the car and made it to the front door just in time to see paramedics removing a stretcher covered in a white sheet. As they stepped out into the sunlight, I noticed the form of a body beneath the sheet. Camille Roberts was just behind, signing forms on a stainless steel clipboard and talking to Christopher Downing.

"Well, if you're going to go, that's the way to go. Quiet. In your sleep," she said.

Downing shrugged her off. "Just take care of the paperwork and when we receive the coroner's report, put it in my box."

He disappeared into his office before she could respond. Camille passed the clipboard back to one of the medics and spotted me. "Morning, Billy."

"Good morning," I said, pausing as the paramedics brought the body down the steps. "What happened?"

"Mrs. Toddman passed away in her sleep last night," Camille said. "Poor dear didn't have no family."

She shook her head. I noticed only the faintest hint of a tear in the corner of one of her eyes. She ushered me inside, placing her arm around my shoulder and steering me away from the back of the ambulance.

"Don't you worry yourself with that now. She was old."

The name rang familiar, but I couldn't remember from where. And without seeing her face, I might never have remembered. As the door closed, though, I saw a face that I remembered all too well, sitting in the waiting area, noticeably distraught. It all came back to me—my first trip back to Hall B with Leon and the encounter with the woman who thought that the Home was her family's estate. I sat down next to him. "Leon, what happened?"

He didn't look up from the floor. "She just died in her sleep," he said. "It normally don't get to me this way, but she and I was close. She was always making me little trinkets out of things she found."

I had been to several funerals before with my mother, but only for people whom I had never met, usually friends of my grandparents. Faced with the death of someone that I'd met, that so obviously distressed someone I knew, I was speechless and didn't know how to comfort him.

He snorted a half-hearted attempt at a laugh. "Remember that time when we saw her your first day?"

I nodded. "She had something for you."

"Well, she had made a church out of popsicle sticks in crafts a few days before. When I got to her room, she swore up and down it was a cake she baked especially for my birthday. Remembered my birthday but couldn't tell the difference between a cake and a church. So I took it home. It wasn't until three days later, when she informed a nurse that someone had stolen her diamond earring, that I thought to look close at the steeple. Sure enough, right in the cross, there was her diamond." He tried to force a laugh again, but it died in his throat.

The door opened, and Camille appeared. She saw me talking to Leon and gestured toward the *Times-Picayune* on the corner of the counter.

As I walked away from the counter, two sounds competed for my attention. While Camille tried simultaneously to comfort Leon for his loss and chide him for getting too close to the patients, a tiny whisper of a voice wafted through the air, a whisper that I recognized for its eerie, hollow ghostliness.

I stopped in the middle of an intersection of two halls and looked both ways, trying to discern from which direction the voice had come, but couldn't. Several seconds passed, filled only with the usual noises of the Liberty Street Home. I sighed and continued on to the Row.

When the door slammed behind me, Alistair's head materialized out of the kitchen. "Good morning, Billy."

Zelda and Donald echoed hellos from inside the kitchen.

I tossed the paper onto Emily's desk and flopped down onto the sofa next to Thaddeus. He glanced my way and patted my knee. "You saw her again didn't you?"

I shook my head. "Just heard her."

He turned off the television and turned to me. "Oh really? Where at?"

I told him. He stared back for a moment, pondering his response. Before he responded, though, Alistair called everyone to the table.

Over the course of breakfast, everyone tactfully avoided the subject of my mother's visit. Later, as I helped Alistair clear away the dishes, he stopped me. "I hope that I didn't offend your mother too much, yesterday."

I shrugged. "She'll get over it."

He sighed. "Now don't take an attitude, son. I probably stepped over a line I shouldn't have crossed. But that doesn't give you license to be disrespectful. Got it?"

"Yes, sir."

"Good. Now let's get the dishes done so we can go outside. I've a couple of projects on the patio I need your help with."

* * *

We had not been on the patio very much over the past couple of weeks, and after two hours spent outside pulling weeds I understood why. The heat, when combined with overexertion, would induce a raging headache.

"Here you go, Billy," Camille said. She dropped two aspirin into my palm and offered me a cup of water. "You two should really take it easy out there in that heat."

I downed both aspirin and the cup of water in one gulp. Camille passed me an envelope. I nodded, thanking her for the aspirin and taking the envelope. "Head on back and give this to Zel, would you?"

I passed Mrs. Markowitz talking to a group of people in a small sitting room and waved. Leon seemed to be back to his old, passive self again and barely acknowledged my presence. I was almost to Hall B when I noticed the sounds of someone crying coming from one of the doors directly opposite Hall B, from one of the doors that I had never seen open. I was sure that, between sobs, the woman inside was calling out for help. I looked up and down the hall, but as usual, there was no one this far back in the home.

I thought about going for Camille, but when I started to walk away, the woman apparently saw me and called out. "Help." Whatever was wrong, it was now up to me to find out. I pushed the door the rest of the way open.

"Is everything all right?"

"Andy," said the woman in the bed. She waved her hand in the air, flexing her fingers as if asking for my hand. I slipped my fingers in hers.

"Ma'am?"

"Andy!" she repeated. I looked around her bed, for the call button, but couldn't find it.

"I'm Billy. Not Andy."

"Andy!" she said again, and broke down into sobs again. I didn't know what to do or what she wanted. I had become so accustomed to the independence and utility of my friends on the Row that an encounter with someone so devastated by age frightened me.

"I'll go get help," I said. I turned to leave. Her wrist locked. Pain shot up my arm as my knuckles ground together.

"H-h-handy!"

I tried to pry my hand free, but my foot lost grip and slipped on something spongy lying on the tile floor. I looked down. Between my feet, a crude face smiled up from the floor. I reached down and picked up a white cotton gardening glove. Someone had stuffed it and stitched yellow and red yarn to each of the four fingers and the thumb. The smiling face on the palm had been stenciled on with a permanent marker and the name Andy was scrawled across the bottom.

I held the crude doll up so the woman could see. "Is this what you want?"

She released my hand and yanked Andy, clutching it to her breast. Rocking gently back and forth, she mumbled the doll's name under her breath.

I remained beside her bed for a few minutes, until her breathing had returned to normal and I was sure she had fallen asleep. I turned for the door and there she stood. Silhouetted against the flood of fluorescent light from the hall was the blonde ghost. She stepped out of my way. I closed the door behind me and turned to face her, expecting to find that she had again vanished. She was still there.

"At least you're not a ghost."

Her eyes didn't stray from the closed door. "What's your name?"

"Billy Bradshaw."

"That was a nice thing you did for her." She raised her hand to her mouth and took a bite of a red apple. She wiped the juice from her lips with the back of her hand and then extended her arm to me, the red orb balanced in her upturned palm.

"Want a bite of my apple?"

Chapter 20

I could have run, bolted past her, out of the home, never to return. In the luxury of hindsight, Judge Spurgeon's month and a half in juvenile detention would have been such a small price to pay to avoid those final weeks of summer. But I didn't flee from Liberty Street that day. I stayed and took an apple from an outstretched hand and bit into it, letting its juices run down my chin and onto my shirt.

"I told you it was good." She giggled and took the apple. "My name is Cassidy. Come on. I have something I want to show you."

I wanted to protest, but her hand closed around my wrist with the tingle of a jolt of electricity. Cassidy dragged me off down the hall, around a corner, and into a service closet. The door closed, plunging us into almost total darkness. I tried to make out the shadows of movement as my eyes adjusted to the darkness. I gasped when she released my wrist, cutting me loose in the darkness.

"Don't be such a baby. Turn on the lights." Her voice was fading into the darkness. I fumbled along the wall next to the door. Brooms rattled in their containers, and I knocked a mop bucket onto its side.

"Shhh! You'll get me in trouble," she said. I heard her flip a switch, and the room lit up. The room was smaller than I expected it, filled almost to capacity with brooms and rolling garbage cans. Her fingers closed around my wrist. Each time Cassidy touched me, my hands went numb and my stomach tingled with nervous tension. She was dragging me up a narrow set of stairs, hidden behind the mopsink.

"Where does this go?" I said.

"Upstairs."

"Where?"

She turned and faced me, halfway up the stairs. "You mean you've been here all this time and never found the stairs?"

I shook my head. "I haven't done much exploring."

"Well, this one leads to my bedroom. There is another one, the main one, behind the front desk. It goes to Daddy's upstairs office. And I found one from our kitchen to the kitchen downstairs."

"Why are we going to your room?"

"Do you always ask so many questions?"

"I guess so," I said, hearing my mother's voice chide me for being too nosy after her dates.

Cassidy continued through the darkness, mumbling under her breath about annoying habits. Just as my eyes began to adjust to the pitch black of the narrow staircase, Cassidy came to a sudden stop ahead of me, and I slammed into her, stumbling backwards.

She caught me by the wrist. "Clumsy."

I tried to apologize but was too embarrassed. When at last I was able to speak, I didn't know what to say. My hand was grasping hers, and I didn't want her to let go.

But moments aren't meant to last forever. With her other hand, Cassidy opened a door led me into a room barely larger than a closet.

Daylight streamed in through an arched window that stretched the width of one wall. I recognized it as the same window in which my ghost had appeared. On the opposite wall, a musty, moldy mattress had settled into a swaybacked frame. Directly across from that door was a much smaller, closed door.

"What's through there?" I said.

"My bedroom."

"Bedroom? Then what's this room?"

"A napping porch. Before air conditioning, ladies would take naps in the afternoon." Cassidy disappeared into her bedroom, as if no further explanation were necessary. Glancing around the room, I noticed a shelf recessed into the wall, obscured by a shabby lace curtain. Through the dingy lace, I could barely see the outline of a picture frame and what looked like a couple of books. Moving closer, I reached for the curtain. She grabbed my hand. I spun around. Cassidy had returned with a large scrapbook.

"I had to make sure my dad wasn't here right now."

"Why?"

She shrugged. "I don't think he'd approve of me hanging out with you."

I wanted to ask why, but she had opened the scrapbook on her bed and was pointing at an advertisement torn out of a newspaper. I looked over her shoulder. The contorted lines of a shrunken head glared back from the inside of a blood-colored altar. I shuddered. "What is that?"

"It's a shrunken head from the altar in Marie LaVeau's voodoo shop. We have to steal it."

"Why?"

"I can't tell you. But it's a matter of life and death," she said. She leaned closer, her lips almost brushing my ear. "If you get it, then I'll know that you're the one and I can trust you."

Her hot breath tickled my ear and sent chills down my spine. I wanted to tell her no, that I would not steal anything. Stealing was wrong. But she acted as if she already knew the answer. It was written in fate, and I, a mere boy, would not be able to change fate.

She stepped away from me, closed the scrapbook, and slid it beneath her bed. "So now, it's time for you to go home."

I looked at the clock on her bedside table. It was almost five. "The Bohemians!"

We both heard the door to their apartment open and Christopher Downing's voice announcing his return. She shoved me toward the sleeping porch and through the door to the stairs. "You remember the way, right?"

I nodded. "I think so."

"Bye, Billy Bradshaw. I'll see you tomorrow."

I started down the stairs, but stopped. "No. I don't come on Sundays."

"You'll be here tomorrow."

"Why?"

She smiled. "Because you'll want to see me. Now go!"

Cassidy eased the door shut, plunging me into darkness. I stumbled down the stairs and out of the broom closet.

Arriving back at the door to Hall B, I could hear the phone ringing over the opening bars of the Ike and Tina version of "Proud Mary."

Everyone was gathered around the dining room table, playing cards, except for Alistair, who had just lifted the phone from the cradle when I stepped into the room. "Hall B...No problem, Miss Roberts. He just walked in. I'll send him right up." He returned the phone to the corner of the desk. "Your mother's here to pick you up."

Thaddeus fixed an eye on me from his seat at the table. "More ghost stories?"

I panted, trying to let my mouth catch up with my mind. "She's not a ghost. She's real. I met her. Her name is Cassidy. She lives upstairs."

Anne grinned. "So you finally met her. What did you think?"

"You knew about her?"

She giggled. "Of course. Louise and I met her yesterday after you left. She came in asking questions."

"What kind of questions?"

"About us, about the Row," Louise said, to which Anne quickly added, "But mostly about you."

"Me!" I gulped. She opened her mouth as if about to answer my question, but Zelda stopped her.

"His mother is here. You can tease the poor boy on Monday." She shoved me to the door. "It's time for you to go. We don't want your mother any angrier at us than she already is."

My shoulders sagged. "Yes, ma'am."

When my mother saw me, she mistook my quiet mood for exhaustion. "Camille told me you were outside today and got overheated."

"I guess," I said half-heartedly.

She steered me towards Myrtle, rubbing my shoulders sympathetically. "You can take a nap when we get home. I'll fix spaghetti for dinner."

Spaghetti, my favorite, would normally excite me, but my mind was still lagging far behind, up a narrow stair hidden behind mops in a janitor's closet. My ghost wasn't a ghost at all. She was a girl, confined to a pink bedroom above the dying remnants of a generation, winnowing away the last days of summer in a listless haze.

Chapter 21

I hadn't expected to find Camille at the front desk on a Sunday morning. So when I stepped through the door and found her in her normal perch, I was more than a little surprised.

"Good morning, Billy. What brings you down here on a Sunday?" she said.

I reached into my pocket and pulled out the letter addressed to Zelda. "I forgot I had it last night when I left."

She shook her head. "I thought you said you were going to give it to her right away. What am I going to do with you?"

"I meant to. But Cassidy–" I began.

"Enough said. Get on back there."

I stopped a few feet away from her desk. "Where is Cassidy?"

Camille stepped in front of the door to Cassidy's apartment. "Nope. Letter first, then Cassidy."

"Yes ma'am." I was about to turn the corner when she called after me. "Hey, Billy."

"Yes ma'am?"

"Did you get dressed in a hurry this morning?"

"How did you know?"

She laughed and wandered back into her office. I stood there for a second, wondering how she had known. My shirt was tucked in and, as far as I knew, I looked as I did every day. I had said and done nothing that might indicate I had slept late, had to convince my mother of the dire importance of delivering the letter on a Sunday, and had wanted nothing more than to get to Liberty Street to see Cassidy. Walking back to Hall B, I didn't notice any of the normal traffic in the halls. Most of the doors I passed were closed. At the few that stood ajar, the lukewarm glow of mid-morning slumber spilled into the halls. I passed Leon at a nurses' station halfway back, his headphones securely over his ears, blaring away to drown out the silence.

Even the passageway to Bohemian Row was dark and quiet. No Jazz, no laughter. The Bohemians weren't at the breakfast table, and the television was off. The only sounds were the clatter of dishes coming from the kitchen. I found Alistair with a towel tucked into his pants, drying pots.

"Morning, Alistair," I said. He turned with a start.

"Well hello, Billy. What on earth are you doing down here on a Sunday?"

I showed him the letter. "I forgot to give this to Zel yesterday."

He eyed the postmark and growled. "Melanie." He shook his head and took the letter. "Want me to take care of getting that to her?"

I shook my head. "No sir. I'd rather do it myself."

He smiled. "Well, before you do, why don't you help me put away the dishes? It won't take long, and then you can get back to looking for Cassidy."

I froze. "What do you mean?"

He pointed to my shoes. "I can't imagine that you were in that big of a hurry to get this letter to Zelda."

Looking down, I saw what Camille had seen. On my left foot, I was wearing a white tennis shoe. On my right, plain as day, a black hiking boot. My face burned with embarrassment. "I...uh–"

"No need to be embarrassed. Happens to the best of us," he said. We dried the last few plates, and when they were safely back on the shelf, I followed Alistair back into the living area. He sat down on the sofa and opened the newspaper. "I'd imagine you'll find Cassidy in their apartment." I thanked him and started for the door but Alistair cleared his throat. "Aren't you forgetting something, Billy?"

I stopped and turned. "Sir?"

"The letter."

I pulled the letter from my pocket. He pointed down the hall. "Zelda is in her room. Everyone is taking it easy. It is Sunday after all."

I didn't quite know what he meant, but as I passed the closed doors to their bedrooms, I gathered that they were all taking naps. The only two doors that were open revealed the empty beds of Alistair and Louise. When I reached Zel's door, I knocked twice. A feeble voice called from inside. "Come in."

Her room, like the others I had passed, was dark. But her drapes were not drawn. Instead, the tree outside her window provided a thick blanket that blotted out the sun. Zelda was nestled back against two oversized pillows. She smiled. "Well good morning. What brings you down today?"

I showed her the letter. "I forgot I had this."

"Who's it from? I don't have my glasses on."

"Melanie, I think."

She shook her head. "Just leave it on the nightstand. I'll read it later."

I slipped it beneath her journal, but she took my wrist. "Better give it here. No use putting it off."

After retrieving her glasses, she opened the envelope with the letter opener from a jar of pens on her nightstand, withdrew a single page, and unfolded it. With each movement of her eyes, her face fell further until she got to the bottom of the page, closed her eyes, and let the letter slip from her hands and into the wastebasket.

She shrank back against the pillows, closed her eyes, and forgot I was there. After several seconds, I moved toward the foot of her bed. "Zel?"

Her eyes barely open, she smiled. "Sorry, Billy. Can I see you tomorrow?"

She closed her eyes again, and I left. Alistair's paper lay draped across the arm of the sofa, and the kitchen was empty. I wandered out into the empty halls of Liberty Street. By the time I made my way back to the front desk, though, I had begun to wonder if Cassidy was there. "Nurse Roberts?"

"Hmm?" she replied without looking up from the chart she was reading.

"Cassidy?"

"Upstairs. Knock before you go in."

"Yes ma'am."

But when I got to the top of the stairs, I found the door standing open. I reached up to knock, but stopped when I heard a voice inside.

I edged closer, slipped into the apartment, careful not to make a sound. Just beyond the door, there was a foyer connecting two small rooms on either side. The room on the right appeared to be a living room. The room on the left was partially hidden behind a folding screen. A man's shadow moved across the screen, and I saw him reach for the telephone.

After several seconds, he began speaking again. "John, this is Christopher Downing over at Liberty Street. Listen, I have a question. How many available beds do you have?... Well ideally I would need six. But I think I can take however many you have–Two? Okay. Hold them for me for a couple of weeks. I'll make it worth your while... No nothing special. Just got a few plans. I'm remodeling an underused area into an invalid ward... You remember Hall B?... That's the one. I'll move on it next month sometime. I'll let you know."

* * *

"Slow down, Billy," Alistair said. He was sitting on the couch with Donald and Thaddeus, trying to follow my somewhat excited story of

Downing's plans. "Now, start over. What exactly did he say?"

"That he's planning on renovating Hall B into an invalid ward. Why would he want to do that?"

Alistair shrugged. "I don't know. But if I had to guess, I would say he plans on putting more people down here."

"That certainly makes sense," Thaddeus said. "I mean, he said himself that he's losing money with us down here. Only six in this big hall."

Donald turned back to Alistair. "Right. So what do we do?"

Alistair slid back against the sofa and pursed his lips as if deep in thought. "I don't know."

Louise and Anne appeared from the hall. "What's all the ruckus about?" Anne said with a yawn. Alistair shrugged.

"Looks like Downing's planning on moving us out," he said.

Louise gasped. "Can he do that?"

Thaddeus shrugged. "It's his place. If he wants us moved, we move."

"Would that mean splitting us up?" Anne said.

"What can we do? We need a plan," Louise said.

Alistair sighed. "I don't know that there's much we can do. I mean, we could fight it, but I don't think it would get us very far. We don't know why, how, or when."

Donald heaved a sigh, dropped his head into his hands, and wept. Thaddeus moved to console him, but Louise stopped him, shaking her head. After several seconds, he blotted his eyes. "I'm sorry there isn't something I can do. I wish..." but his voice trailed off.

I stood up. "I think I can help."

They all turned and faced me. The looks on their faces were a mixture of skepticism and futility. Louise was the only one who responded. "What do you have in mind?"

"Don't you get it?" Zel said. She had emerged from her bedroom without notice and was padding her way to the sofa. She yawned, settling in beside me. "He's going to ask her."

Chapter 22

Alistair shook his head and stormed away. "No, I said. Absolutely not. We are not involving that girl in this. It isn't right to even ask her to go against her father."

"You heard Billy," Anne said. "She doesn't even like him. Why not ask?"

"It's a principle, Anne. You don't encourage rebellion against parents. Where would that get us?" he said.

She shrugged. "A hell of a lot closer than where we are now."

"Maybe she's right, Alistair," Thaddeus said. He pinched the bridge of his nose.

Donald nodded. "Yes. We can't do anything or even try to stay together unless we know why."

"Alistair, listen to them," Zelda said. Alistair's head snapped to attention, and for the first time since I had suggested Cassidy could provide us with information, he seemed shocked.

"This from you, Zel? I wouldn't have expected it."

"I just don't see what the problem is," she said. "The girl goes in, opens a drawer, and brings it here. Big deal."

Alistair made for the patio but stopped short of walking out the door and turned. "I don't like it. But it appears I'm outvoted. Billy, you may–" he said, but the phone cut him off.

Anne lifted the receiver. "Hello?... Yes, Ms. Roberts. I'll send him right up."

I sighed. "I know. My mother's here," I said before the phone was back on the cradle.

"Billy," Alistair called. "I wouldn't say anything to anyone about this. We're obviously not supposed to know. It will probably be better if we don't let on just yet."

"I understand. I'll try to find Cassidy on my way and ask her. Okay?"

Zel and Thaddeus nodded.

When the door closed behind me, I stood in the hall for a second, leaning against the door. So much had happened that I was having trouble processing everything. Instead of a plan of action, we had questions, questions that we had no way of answering without Cassidy's help. And even with it, I wondered what we could do. There didn't seem to be any way to stop him.

I turned at Camille's desk and headed up the stairs, but she stopped me. "Billy!"

"Ma'am?"

"Your mother is waiting."

I sighed. "But I need to see Cassidy."

"Nuh uh. Your mother was angry enough that she had to come in for you. But the girl ain't here anyway. She's fixing to go see her grandparents." Camille jerked her thumb over her shoulder. I could see my mother's car through the window. "You'd better get going," Camille said.

"What time will she be back?" I said, reaching for the doorknob.

"Billy, get out here, now," Mom shouted.

I stepped into the door so she could see me. "Mom, I need to find Cassidy. I have to ask her something."

My mother shook her head and took me by the arm. "I'm in a hurry, son. You can tell her tomorrow."

"She's leaving tomorrow morning for Seattle," Camille said.

"Seattle!"

"Yeah. She's going to spend the week with her grandparents."

I turned back to my mother. "Mom, please. It is very important. I just need to ask her something."

"What's so important?"

Unable to answer, I looked down at my feet. I couldn't tell her about Christopher Downing, especially not in front of Camille. And I had promised not to say anything to anyone–and that included my mother. Without a reason I could give her to stay, I skulked to the car and slammed the door.

When Mother got in, she turned to me. "So what is all of that about?"

"Nothing."

"Who's Cassidy?"

I stared out the window. "No one."

She playfully bopped my knee. "Is this a no one you have a crush on?"

"No!"

"Then what is it?"

"Nothing, Mom."

She sighed. The Buick roared to life as she threw the car into gear. "Fine. You don't want to tell me, then don't tell me."

"It's not that, Mom. It's nothing. Really."

"Nothing." She steered into traffic and pointed the car toward our apartment. We came to an abrupt stop behind a stalled bus.

"I know what you're thinking, Mom. I'm not hiding anything from you."

She fiddled with the knob on the radio, stopping on an oldies station. The sounds of an Eagles tune faded through into the opening of Fleetwood Mac's "Don't Stop." As we pulled forward again, Mom drummed quietly on the wheel, keeping tempo with the music. "Billy, I know boys have their secrets. I don't expect you to tell me every single thing. But don't lie to me."

"What do you mean?"

She swung the car into the other lane and passed the stalled bus. "I mean if you don't want to tell me something, then say 'I don't want to talk about it' or 'it's none of your business' and I'll respect that."

"Really?"

"Of course."

"It's none of your business," I said flatly. She grinned. "What, Mom?"

"I knew you were lying."

* * *

"You have one new message," the recorder said. Mother pressed play again, and a male voice thick with a drawl filled the apartment.

"Bev, this is Danny. Was gonna see if maybe you want to go out tonight. Call me and let me know." Mother jotted the man's number on the pad by the phone.

"Who was that?" I said.

"Danny," she replied. "A guy I met the other day. He asked me out, but I turned him down." She dialed the number. After several seconds, she smiled. "Hello. Danny? This is Bev…Northrop…I'm good. Listen, I can't go this evening, but what about Monday night?…Tonight only, huh? Well hold on." She cupped her hand over the phone and raised her eyebrows at me, a silent request for my blessing.

I shrugged.

"What time and where?…See you then." She hung up the phone. "I've got a date tonight."

I rolled my eyes, but she didn't see. While she was in the shower, I tried to find something on television but ended up turning it off and grabbing my notebook instead. No matter how hard I tried, the day's events stifled any attempt I made at writing a sentence. By the time Mother finished her shower and was ready for her date, I had ruined three whole pages with half-filled lines scratched through.

"What are you working on," she said.

I closed my notebook before she could look over my shoulder. "Nothing. It just isn't working today, I guess."

"Well, it'll come," she said. She kissed me on the top of the head. "I'm meeting him for dinner in about an hour. I guess I'll be back later. You'll be okay?"

"I'll be fine."

She slipped a ten-dollar bill into my shirt pocket.

"Order a pizza for dinner. Okay?"

After she left, I watched a sitcom, called and ordered pizza, and tried twice again unsuccessfully to kickstart a story. When at last the pizza arrived, I ate two slices and fell asleep on the sofa in front of the TV.

* * *

"Wake up, Billy."

I opened my eyes and found my mother awash in the glow of early morning. She smiled. "You'll be late. Go get dressed."

I stretched. "What time did you get home?"

"Late. Now go wash up."

As I closed the door to the bathroom, I could hear her in the kitchen, beginning breakfast. There wasn't enough hot water for me to take a shower, so I tried as best I could to scrub down at the sink. I ignored the pool of water forming beneath my feet. After brushing my teeth, I returned to the kitchen.

She had cooked herself eggs and toast and poured herself a glass of orange juice. Instead of sitting down at the table, I climbed onto the counter. "Hey Mom, when do you go back to work?"

She shrugged. "Not sure, really. You have to meet with the attorneys tomorrow. Is that okay?"

I thought about it for a second. "Yeah. That's fine. I wrote it all down."

The look on her face seemed more amusement than shock. She smiled. "You what?"

"I wrote it all down. In my notebook."

"Go get it."

I jumped down and rushed to the living room. My notebook was still on the table where I had left it the night before. There, on the pages after "The Bee Story," was a facsimile of the entire night. I handed it to her.

While she read the three-page story of our dinner at the restaurant, I sipped on what was left of her orange juice. She stopped every once in a while and would chew on her lip before continuing down the page. When she finished, she read it again.

"This isn't bad, Billy," she said. "Why did you write it down?"

"That's what Zel said to do."

"Who?"

"Zel. At the home."

"The home! Damn it all to hell. Get your things. You're going to be late."

There comes a time in the life of children when they are suddenly and unavoidably confronted with some great truth of the universe, a truth that comes with neither effort nor warning. The days stretching before them are filled with a finite number of new experiences. Chocolate ice cream won't always be their favorite food. School will end, and the children will wander out into the world, a reasonable facsimile of their parents. Riding across New Orleans, through the Quarter and past a cemetery, my great truth came with a thunderclap: I would never be like my mother. Whatever I had to do and wherever I had to go to get away from her lifetime spent chasing after elusive dreams that refused to materialize, I would not fall victim to a lifetime of nothingness. I knew what it was I was going to do and how I was going to do it. I would become a writer.

And Zelda Groves would show me the first steps.

"Zelda!" I shouted as I burst through the doors to Hall B. Alistair and Thaddeus were sitting at the table. There was no breakfast, no sound of pots and pans, and no music from the stereo. "What's going on?"

Alistair motioned for me to sit. "Billy, we have something we need to tell you."

While not threatening, his tone dripped of frightening urgency. The once wide expanse of the Hall suddenly seemed tight, confined, and I was having trouble breathing.

"Please sit down, Billy," Thaddeus said. As I sat, I noticed the tell-tale streaks of dried tears on his cheek.

"Billy," Alistair said. He almost began to cry again, but staved off tears long enough to catch his breath. "Zelda had a massive stroke last night."

"What does that mean?" I said.

"It means they don't know if she's going to get better."

Chapter 23

The reception area of the Law Offices of Buddy Quinn reminded me of a doctor's office. Solemn, but not depressing. Bright, but not glaring. The door was heavy, probably oak, and painted the same almost-white color of the walls. Directly through the door, a receptionist kept watch from a small window. On the wall opposite the leather sofa on which I was told to wait, there was a set of shelves filled with *Reader's Digest* condensed books, a statue or two, and potted ivy that spilled over the top of the shelves and hung almost to the floor.

On the two walls on either side of the door hung at least twenty pictures of billboards. Some were orange and yellow and red. Others gleamed with the warm colors of autumn. A few followed a patriotic scheme. The one thing each billboard had in common was Buddy Quinn. Buddy Quinn wearing a gray suit, smiling down from a red-white-and-blue billboard. Buddy Quinn, stern-faced in a black suit, on a gold-and-white billboard. Buddy Quinn in a red polo laughing amid a flurry of hundred dollar bills.

The door separating the reception area from the back office opened, and another woman, older than the receptionist, stepped in. "Billy? Mr. Quinn will see you now."

She led me to a conference room where my mother was sitting in the chair nearest the head of the table. Beside her, Buddy Quinn stood hunched over my notebook. "So you wrote all of this, kid?"

"Yes, sir."

He glanced up and shot me the same, toothy smile from the billboard. "So why did you write it down?"

"Zel told me to."

"Who?"

My mother interjected quickly. "A friend of his at the Liberty Street Home."

"Yes, the home," Buddy said. "Well, Billy. Good job."

He reached across the table and pressed a button on the phone. "Phyllis, could you step in for a moment?"

The woman who had led me to the conference room reappeared. "Sir?"

"Take this for me, please, and type up the first," he paused to count the pages, "four pages."

"Right away, sir." The woman disappeared with my notebook. Buddy Quinn leaned back and shook his head.

"I don't know what to say, Bev. You've got a home run. Right down the middle. They're toast." He smiled again, and I recognized just what that smile was made of. Money.

"Mr. Quinn, I just want my job back," Mom said.

Buddy Quinn's smile vanished. He propped one elbow on the table and leaned into my mother. "I have to be honest with you. I don't think that's going to happen. We've already discussed this."

She wiped a tear from her cheek and tried to force a smile. "So what am I supposed to do?"

Buddy Quinn smiled again. "Mount the bastards on the wall of your living room."

Lying before me on the table was a document I didn't recognize. The front page made no sense to me. I recognized only my name, typed beneath a blank for me to sign. Behind it, and bound to the cover with a blue piece of paper, was a single page that I recognized too well. It was my story. Buddy Quinn had handed it to me and asked me to read it.

When I finished, I looked up. Buddy Quinn and my mother were both watching me. He raised his eyebrows. "Is there anything you want to change in there?"

I shook my head. "No. Why?"

He slid a pen across the table, closed the document, and pointed to the blank above my name. "Sign it there."

Buddy Quinn's pen was heavy in my hand. The gold metal, cold to the touch, shimmered in the sunlight as I signed my name. Buddy took his pen, twisted it closed, and tucked it into his coat pocket.

"Good job, kid."

"How long?" Mom said.

He shrugged. "It just depends. If they think I'm out for blood—which I am—then two, maybe three weeks at the most. If not, then we go to trial."

"Try to avoid that," Mom said.

"I always do, Beverly."

Buddy Quinn extended his hand to me. It was cool, too smooth. He smiled down. "Billy, you keep taking good care of your mother, you hear?"

"Yes, sir."

Mom hugged Buddy Quinn on her way out of the office. By the time we reached the car, she had returned to her normal, quiet self. "So, Billy. What do you want to do now?"

"What do you mean?"

"Well, I think you've earned yourself a treat. Ice cream? Video games or pizza?"

I shrugged.

She backed the car into the street and put it into drive. A billboard attached to the side of a convenience store advertised Ochsner Hospital. I turned and pointed to the billboard. "Take me there."

"What on earth for?"

"That's where Zel is. I need to see Zel," I replied. I was prepared to make my case for going to the hospital. I had, after all, unwittingly done something very important and had signed the deposition for Buddy Quinn. She had given me the choice of what I wanted to do and where we were going to go. I would stand my ground and fight until she took me to see Zelda. But she didn't protest. Instead, she drove me directly to Ochsner. A candy-striper at the front desk told us that Zelda was in the intensive care unit.

"Are you family?" the girl said. "Only family is allowed to visit."

I sighed. Defeated by rules.

"She's my great aunt," I heard my mother say.

"Go on up, then," the candy-striper replied.

On the elevator, I felt my mother's hand rest on my shoulder. "It will be okay, Billy. I'm sure."

But I wasn't. The doors opened, and by the very nature of the place I knew that it wouldn't be. The ICU was unlike any other hospital I'd seen before. The elevator emptied into a small waiting-and-receiving area in front of the nurses' station. A woman was sitting on the green, institutional couch, reading a magazine.

She looked up, smiled, and then returned to her magazine. Behind the counter, the attending nurse looked up.

"May I help you?"

"Zelda Groves, please," Mom said. The nurse pointed to a sliding glass door across the room.

"Number six."

"Thank you." Mom knelt down beside me. "Do you want me to go with you or wait here?"

I looked across the floor to number six, not knowing what I would find when I stepped through that door.

"I guess just wait here." I said.

"Billy, I'm not–"

"Mom."

"Okay. I'll just read a magazine or something."

I walked away without registering what she had said. The sliding glass door to room number six was open, but the interior was separated from the hall by vertical blinds that swung gently back and forth in the gentle, air condition breeze. I pushed back the shades and stepped into the darkness.

Everything in room number six looked blue in the dull, florescent light from above the bed.

Along one wall, several machines were recording various readings onto rolls of paper. As my eyes accustomed to the dimness, I realized that the room was much smaller than the last hospital room I'd seen. Zelda's bed took up over half of the floor space. There was a single chair at the foot of the bed, and in that chair, an unopened suitcase.

"Zel?" I said.

I stepped closer to the bed, and finally was able to see her face. There was a tube sticking out of her mouth and her eyes were taped shut. Moving through the darkness of the room, my foot kicked a cable that snaked across the floor connecting two pieces of equipment.

I moved closer and called out again. The only response I got was the slow, uninterrupted rise and fall of her chest in tempo with the ventilator beside her. I reached out, took her hand. It was cool, but not the cool, alive hands of Buddy Quinn. Zelda's hands were ice.

I folded her hand back across the other on her chest, wiped the single tear from my eye, and backed out of the darkness of her room and into the bright, sterile hall.

My mother saw me, smiled. "How did it go?" she said.

I said nothing, pressed the button to call for the elevator. On the ride down, she placed her hand around my shoulder and awkwardly tried to hug me. "Everything all right?"

I shook my head. "She didn't wake up."

Mom sighed. "I'm so sorry, sweetie. Maybe she'll get better."

I couldn't force my brain to believe her. I wanted to wake up the next morning and rush into Bohemian Row, smile as I ran past the table, raced down the hall and knocked on Zelda's door only to find her with her journals. I wanted things to be like they were before. Before Christopher Downing, before Zelda's stroke.

That night, again in the safety of my bedroom, I sat down at the desk and opened my notebook. Nothing. I couldn't write the raw emotion of standing beside Zelda's bed. Every part of that room, every image was burned into my eyes. When I blinked, I saw the IV snaking from her wrist or the tube taped in her mouth. The machines were there too. The words to describe them would not come, instead locked behind an unbreakable dam somewhere between my head and the end of the pencil.

If the words for Zelda's room would not come, then, I would write about Buddy Quinn's office. I didn't understand why my story had made him so happy, but I didn't care. He had no right to read my story, much less give it to some other stranger to type.

Sitting at my desk, as the shadows grew longer on the wall and the sun descended beneath the horizon for yet another day, I was torn. While Zelda wasted away in a hospital room, all I could think of was my anger at my mother for giving Buddy Quinn my notebook.

Chapter 24

I stomped down the hall to Mom's room and glared. She was pacing back and forth on the phone. "Mom, I have to go," I said.

She shushed me with a dismissive wave and slammed her bedroom door. Her muffled voice still filled the apartment as she shouted at Buddy Quinn. "But Buddy, this was my livelihood and now they've fired me! Fired! I've got a kid, Buddy. And an apartment and credit cards. I wasn't–No, I know what you're saying…No. What's arbitration? Contract? I never signed a contract…A noncompete? I signed all kinds of papers when they transferred me. They said it was standard operate–So what does that mean?" She was silent for several seconds, occasionally sighed. Finally, she giggled. "Okay. Yes, Buddy. Fine. I'll make sure we're there."

She opened the door and smiled. "I think I'm ready."

"Finally."

Grabbing her purse, she checked her makeup in the mirror beside the door.

"Why the big hurry?"

"Because. I've been late enough," I said. She pursed her lips to make sure that her lipstick was smooth. "And it's really important that I get there today."

I was halfway down the hall by the time she locked the door. She had to jog a few steps to catch up.

"What are you doing down there, anyway?" she said.

"Um, nothing much, really," I said.

My compulsion to lie was as much to shield Cassidy from involvement as it was to prevent my mother from discovering my role in the fight to save Bohemian Row. Though my mother knew of Downing's plans, she would not have accepted my involvement, much less the complicity of Downing's own daughter. As far as she was concerned, each day was filled with phone calls and visitors, people Alistair and Anne had known over the years. The *Times-Picayune* had even agreed to write a story on Downing's plans to close Hall B and had promised that a reporter would visit in the next couple of weeks. To her, my only involvement was my presence. I still filled my hours with menial tasks like washing dishes and cleaning windows.

Driving down Marais, my mother hummed quietly. At a red light, she turned to face me. "Billy, if there's anything I could do, you'd let me know, right?"

"Of course I would."

"I mean that. They mean a lot to you. I have to appreciate that, I guess. So if you need something, you'll tell me?"

I nodded without a word. Through the exaggerated sincerity in her voice, I knew she meant it. Aside from there being very little she might be able to do, I knew my mother and her track record with men. And meeting Christopher Downing was the last thing any of us needed. So I rode on in silence, hoping that she would not notice the ten dollars missing from her wallet, ten dollars that I intended to put with the ten-dollar contribution the Bohemians had made toward renewing the bus pass that had just expired.

When we pulled up to the home, Mom had to let me out on the street. Three pickup trucks, each bearing the name of a different construction company, blocked the driveway. I found their owners just inside the door, knotted around a set of construction plans in the small parlor opposite Camille's desk. One of the men saw me and smiled. I scowled back and rushed off down the hall.

Camille wasn't at her desk, so I jotted a note to let her know I had arrived. The doors to Hall B were propped open, and I discovered Camille at the dining table with Alistair. She fell silent in the middle of a sentence when she saw me. "Well, there he is! We were just talking about you. Alistair tells me some interesting stories." She turned back to Alistair. "I think we're done, aren't we?"

She stopped at the door. "Billy, don't let them do anything stupid, like burn the place down or anything."

I smiled. "Yes, ma'am."

She leaned over, pulling me closer. "And I wouldn't go nosing around on my desk if I were you. You won't find anything there. It's all on his desk."

I paused. "I'm not sure I understand."

She smiled wryly. "And I'm sure you do."

She waved at Alistair before closing the door. Before I could speak, he held up his hand to stop me. "Shhh. Just a moment."

I stood motionless, wondering what he was listening to. After several tense seconds, he smiled. "There. Now you were going to say?"

"What was that all about?"

"I wanted to make sure she didn't overhear anything she would feel compelled to report," he replied.

"But she–"

"I know. I know. But trust isn't always mutual. While we may be able to trust Nurse Roberts, she doesn't quite trust us. So I didn't want her to hear what I'm about to tell you." He gestured to the seat beside him. "Pull up a chair."

As I settled into Louise's chair, leaned conspiratorially across the corner of the table, I felt like a gangster in a seedy bar. Alistair was the godfather and I his henchman, ready to carry out his orders.

Alistair pulled me even closer. "I've been talking to everyone and it seems that Mr. Downing is planning to move forward with the renovations much sooner than expected."

"How soon?"

"August twentieth, so I'm told."

"August! That's not even a month away. What are we going–"

"Calm down, Billy. I already told you. We have a plan."

He outlined everything. The letters, the newspaper article, the phone calls. Somewhere, there was a charter for the Liberty Street Home, dating back to the days when the old doctor left the house to the city. Maybe something in there could help, but he wasn't sure. "The one person I need to reach is a city councilwoman. I painted her entire family, three generations of it. But I cannot get through to her on the phone. She's virtually unreachable."

"Write her a letter."

"I already have. But now, I don't know that it will get there in time. I can't chance it. So I want you to take it to her, Billy."

"To who?"

"To whom, Billy," Louise corrected me. She had apparently just finished the breakfast dishes, her hands still damp.

"Never mind, Louise," Alistair said.

"Well if he's going to be talking to city councilmen, he needs to speak properly," she said.

I swallowed hard. "Okay. So how do I get there? And what am I supposed to say?"

He slid an envelope across the table. "Just give her this note, and wait for a reply."

I stared at the letter for a moment, wondering what it might say. Without protest, I slipped it into my backpack. After retrieving a notepad from Emily's desk, Alistair jotted several instructions on a sheet of paper and handed it to me. "It's not too far, only a couple of miles. Take the bus to Perdido Street, and then it's just around the corner." He handed me two dollars for bus fare. "You can't miss it."

I folded the directions and placed them in my pocket, next to the letter. Louise met me at the door and hugged me. "Take extra care crossing the street, young man. And you might want to call on a certain young lady upstairs to see if she would like to tag along."

Had it already been a week? It seemed like only a couple of days since Cassidy had gone to Seattle. Now that she was back home, she would probably help us in exchange for help securing Marie Laveau's shrunken head. I checked the hall for traffic before cutting into the broom closet for the climb up to the napping porch. Waiting in the darkness of the stairwell for her to answer the door, I resolved to ask what precisely it was she wanted with the shrunken head in the first place.

My second knock opened the door widen enough for me to peek inside. "Cassidy?" I said, my voice barely breaking a whisper. The napping porch was empty, but the door leading to her bedroom was open. I shoved past the coats and dresses, through her closet, and into her bedroom. She was kneeling on the floor in front of her shelf, hunched over an encyclopedia.

Cassidy's bedroom was the polar opposite of the napping porch. If there was a dresser in the room, its existence was pointless, as every scrap of clothing she owned was strewn about the floor. Books were tossed, haphazardly, onto the shelves in no particular order, and loose sheets of paper spilled off the desk and onto the floor. The only art on the walls was a pair unicorns posters, the corner of one ripped away and fluttering in the ceiling-fan breeze.

I tried to tiptoe across the room without stepping on her clothes, but my foot hung and I tripped. Looking down in horror, I discovered a pair of her panties wrapped around the toe of my sneaker. When I tried to kick them away, they became even more entangled, and I almost toppled over. Cassidy looked up from her book and laughed.

"It's not funny!" I said.

"Yes, it is," she replied, pulling the panties from my shoe and waving them at me. "Don't worry. They're clean."

"How can you tell?" I said, looking around the room.

"Because the dirty ones are on the bathroom floor, silly."

She shoved a pile of socks out of my way and patted the floor beside her. "Pull up some carpet. I'm reading about Druids."

"What are Druids?"

She rolled her eyes and closed the book. "Don't you know anything?" With a sigh, she crossed her legs beneath her and assumed a professorial bearing not unlike the nuns at Holy Cross. "The Druids were ancient pantheists–they believed in many gods and that gods were in everything. The rocks, the trees, anywhere there was creation, there were the gods."

"So why are you reading about them?"

"Because," she said. "My mother was an Ovate."

"An Oh-what?"

"Ovate. A seer."

"What did she see?" The more she attempted to explain, the more confused and befuddled I became. Growing equally frustrated with my ignorance, Cassidy opened the book to a marked page and pointed.

"Here. See? They see the future."

I looked down at the picture. A woman stood above an altar, holding an apple in one hand

and a sword in the other. Where in a picture of Mother Mary there might have been a halo, around the woman's head were pictures of animals. "What are those," I said.

"Those are zodiac signs. You know. Like horoscopes?"

I shook my head.

"When's your birthday?" she said, rolling her eyes.

"August sixteenth," I replied.

She pointed at a picture of a woman wrapped in a flowing gown. "See? This is you. You're a Virgo." She pointed at another picture, of a ram. "This is me. Aries. It's a shame, really."

"What is?"

"That you're a Virgo. It means we're completely incompatible."

Though I had become completely fascinated by everything she was saying, Alistair's letter crinkled in my pocket, a subtle reminder of my reason for coming to her in the first place.

"Cassidy, I have to go to City Hall on an errand and was wondering if you would come along," I said.

She shrugged, returned the book to the shelf, and dusted her knees. "I don't know. I mean, my dad doesn't really let me go into the city by myself."

"But you wouldn't be alone, would you?" I said with a smile. "Besides, I need your help."

She scoffed, stormed across the room with the book. "Why should I help you? It's not like you helped me," she said. I tried to calm her, hoping her dad hadn't heard her shouts. It was a side of Cassidy I had not seen before and was anxious to send back to wherever it came from.

"Hey! You've been in Seattle. It's not like I could have done anything while you were gone." When she didn't register a response, I conceded. "Fine. If you go, I'll help you. We'll get your head thing. Together."

She turned for the door to the apartment, rested her hand on the knob, but hesitated. "Fine. Whatever. Let me get my things. Stay here–and don't make a sound while I'm gone."

She disappeared through the closet. The curtain covering her alcove fluttered in the draft from the door barely enough to reveal Cassidy's collection of artifacts. An old hair comb still had hair in it from its last use. There was a photo-graph of a woman with the same almost-white hair as Cassidy's standing with her back to the camera. Before her spread an ocean so blue that it blended seamlessly with the sky above. Beside the photograph, a single leaf of paper, yellowed and cracking at the edges, contained a handwrit-ten poem under a title, "Ariadne Awake." In the farthest corner of the small shelf, an imprint in the dust outlined the footprint of a box or a book. I reached in, about to draw my finger through the dust, but the door slammed. I hastily dropped the curtain.

"What do you think you're doing?" Cassidy said.

I shrugged. "Nothing. Just looking."

"Well, don't." She grabbed me by the arm and dragged me down the stairs. At the front desk, Camille Roberts saw both of us and smiled.

"Where are you two off to?"

Cassidy and I glanced at one another, our si-lence providing a more-than-adequate answer to her question. Camille sighed, threw her hands up and shook her head. "I don't even want to know. Just don't leave until I ain't looking."

Cassidy cocked an eyebrow. "Why, Miss Roberts?"

"Because I want to be able to say I didn't see you two leave when all this backfires." She turned around and began shuffling through a filing cabinet. "And be careful, you two."

Chapter 25

The City Council receptionist had taken our names and told us to sit. We had been sitting for almost half an hour when Cassidy started for the receptionist's desk again.

I caught her by the wrist. "Where are you going?"

"I'm not waiting anymore. It's not like we don't have other things to do," she said. She yanked her wrist free.

Feeling somewhat helpless and abandoned on the couch, I decided to join her at the desk. The receptionist at first didn't notice we had returned. Cassidy cleared her throat and the woman looked up. "Oh, you're still here?"

"Excuse me? Yes we're still here. We've been waiting just like you said to wait. Over there?" She pointed to the waiting area.

"And who was it you were here to see?" the receptionist said.

"Catherine Marx," I said.

The receptionist shook her head. "I'm sorry. Councilwoman Marx is very busy and can't see you."

Cassidy folded her arms across her chest. "And just how do you know that? Have you asked her if she has time to see us?"

The woman sighed, shaking her head. "Look, little girl. I don't have time for this. And unless–"

"See this?" Cassidy said, ripping Alistair's note from my pocket. "This is a note from a very important person. And we're not leaving until we see Catherine Marx."

"How about I just call security, then?" the receptionist said. She lifted the phone, but a hand fell onto the receiver.

"You're here to see Councilman Marx?" a man said. The man was tall, his seersucker suit hanging from his frame by the two great circles of fabric bunched tightly around each corpulent bicep. His face was friendly and warm, deeply lined and ruddy. Though he didn't say anything else, his smile seemed to be asking our names.

"Billy Bradshaw," I said. He nodded, turning to Cassidy.

"And you are?"

"Cassidy Downing. You know Councilwoman Marx?"

"You could say that. Why?"

"We have this letter for her." She snatched Alistair's letter and showed it to him.

He took the envelope and examined the address. "Who is this from?"

"Alistair Lees," I said.

He smiled. "Ah yes. Follow me." As he led us down the hall, Cassidy could not refrain from turning back and sticking her tongue out at the rather miffed receptionist. Three doors down, he motioned us to stop. "Wait here for a moment."

He stepped inside with Alistair's letter, leaving the door halfway ajar. Inside, a woman's voice. "Well, I thought you'd left!"

"I came back," the man said. "With company."

"Oh? Well, give me just a second, will you?" the woman said. I could hear paper rustling inside and tried to picture what her office might look like. I imagined a dark wooden desk in the center of the room and a Persian rug on the floor.

The walls were paneled with walnut, and I could almost smell the faint aroma of musty old books. When Catherine Marx spoke again, my mind returned to the hall.

"So who is this company? Anyone we know?"

"I don't know," the man said. "They brought this note and said it was from Alistair Lees."

"Alistair? I've not heard from him since I was what, in college?" she said.

"I don't know. The only reason the name rang a bell was–" he said, stopping abruptly. A second later, she laughed.

"Well, by all means show our guests in, Jacques."

The man opened the door and ushered us into her office, a small, almost cramped room that glared in the late morning sun. The walls, painted a drab battleship gray, shimmered in the light reflecting through a tree outside. Sitting behind a wholly unceremonious steel desk was a gaunt, lanky woman with flowing brown hair. She smiled, leaned back in her chair and cocked her head to one side. "So this is who the great Alistair Lees sends to do his beckoning these days?"

Cassidy and I shared a sideways glance. She motioned me forward. "Ma'am? Alistair–Mr. Lees–said we should wait for an answer."

She nodded. "I know."

"How?" Cassidy said.

"It's in the note," Councilwoman Marx said. She indicated the opened envelope on her desk. "My god, I've not seen him since before college."

Her eyes went to the wall over her desk. "When he painted that."

I hadn't noticed the portrait when we came in, and by the look on her face, neither had Cassidy. Presiding over the room, a younger version of the woman at the desk stared down from the staircase of a house. Her hands rested, one folded atop the other, on a marble banister just as Councilwoman Marx's hands now rested atop her crossed knees.

"Jacques overheard you say Alistair's name and invited you in. He's probably heard me say a million times how much I always hated he retired. I wanted Alistair to paint my Taylor. He painted my mother, my grandmother, and me. Was kind of a family tradition, I guess." She sighed with a smile reminiscent of something outside the walls of her City Hall office. Jacques cleared his throat.

"As fun as all this is, Catherine, you've got a luncheon with the Mayor's auxiliary this afternoon."

She rolled her eyes. "You're no fun, Jack." Without picking it up, she read the letter again through the bottom half of her bifocals, perched perilously forward on her nose. "So what sort of trouble has our Alistair gotten himself into?"

Ten minutes and several orders to slow down later, Councilwoman Catherine Marx looked to Jacques. "So what do you think we can do?"

"I dunno, Catherine. Federal housing is sticky. Maybe, though, a little muscle would scare off this–what did you say his name was?"

"Christopher Downing," I said.

"He's my dad," Cassidy added. Both Jacques and Councilwoman Marx looked up, surprised.

"Your father, child?" she said. She leaned across her desk. "Why are you here?"

"It's not right, what he's trying to do," Cassidy said. She hesitated for a moment, and I wondered if she had contemplated telling them about our next stop. If that was what she had in mind, she decided against it. After all, the city councilwoman and her assistant weren't any more likely to approve of two children traipsing off to Marie Laveau's than either of our parents.

Catherine Marx shrugged. "I can't imagine ever challenging Big Daddy like that."

Jacques laughed. "Hell, Cat. Big Daddy would have smacked you dead."

She flopped back in her chair and propped her feet on an open desk drawer. "I'll see what I can do–but!" she said. "But, I can't make any promises. Tell Alistair I'll come see him tomorrow or Thursday, okay?"

We swaggered down the hall, smiling. I couldn't help but notice that Cassidy was as pleased as I with our accomplishment. Walking out of City Hall a few minutes later, two cold sodas in our hands, our fates were united. The Bohemians were engaged in an epic fight for their castle, and Cassidy and I were their foot soldiers.

At the corner, we stopped amid a crowd of tourists with cameras to watch a young black boy with bottle caps wedged into the soles his sneakers tap dance on a crate top. Mesmerized by his feet, we stood motionless for the better part of twenty minutes until, exhausted and only a few dollars richer, the boy stopped. The crowd applauded politely. However, knowing that this was probably his only routine, they avoided asking for an encore. He removed the bottle caps from the bottoms of his shoes and dropped them into his shirt pocket before gathering up the change and bills that the tourists had dropped at his feet.

When Cassidy remained behind, the young boy stared at her curiously. "What do you want?"

She shrugged. "Where did you take lessons?"

"Lessons?" He scoffed, almost as if she had asked him how to fly. "I didn't take no lessons."

"Well, how did you learn?"

"My brother taught me." He started off down the street and Cassidy ran to catch up.

"But where did he learn?"

"My daddy taught him and his daddy taught him. What, you writing a book or something?" he said.

She shook her head. "No. I'm sorry. I just. Well, thank you," she said. "Here, wait."

She reached into her pocket pulled out a wad of bills, withdrawing a five. "This is for you."

"I don't want it," he said.

"Why not?"

"Just 'cuz. Thanks though," he said. He turned the corner and disappeared into a crowd. We looked around and realized that we had walked two blocks farther than we had intended.

"Um, do you know where we are?" I said. She shook her head.

"No. I've never been off of Liberty Street. We don't get out much." She backed closer to me as the crowd increased, until she was pressed against me. I put my hands on her shoulders to steady her. An old man sitting on a bench nearby motioned us over.

"Got a dollar?" he said. I reached into my pocket, but Cassidy grabbed my wrist.

"Where are we?" she said.

"Just off Bourbon," he said. "So can I have that dollar?"

"First tell me where Marie LaVeau's is," she said.

The man closed his eyes and leaned his head back against the wall. "You lookin' at it, kid."

She released my wrist and started for the door, calling back to me over her shoulder. "Give him a dollar."

I handed him two ones and thanked him. He shook his head. "No, thank you."

I followed her through the door and closed it behind me. A string of brass bells jingled against the frame, garnering the attention of a couple of patrons and a tall woman with an orange scarf woven into her hair.

"Don't break anything," the woman said.

"We'll be careful," I said.

"Mm-hm. I wasn't talking to you. I was talking to your little girlfriend there." She pointed at Cassidy, whose backpack was trailing dangerously along a shelf of bottles. I grabbed a red vial just before it fell from the shelf and moved her pack safely from the shelf. Cassidy turned. I caught the red vial again, this time only inches from the floor.

Cassidy blushed. "Oh! Sorry."

"No problem, sweetie. Just be careful," the woman said. We made our way to the back of the store, where a candle-lit shelf hid tucked behind two shelves of books. A hand-lettered sign hanging above invited customers to light a candle, leave an offering to Madame Laveau, and say a prayer. Another sign, hung to the side of the first, warned patrons against placing a hex on others, as Madame Laveau frowned on hexes and would send them back on the perpetrator ten-fold.

Behind several rows of votive candles, between two silver candlesticks, there it was. Cassidy stared at it, reached out to touch it, but hesitated. The head was far more grotesque than it appeared in pictures. I don't really know what we were expecting to see. But there, on a wooden pedestal, was someone's head, shrunken and stitched together in pieces. The eyes were sewn shut and the little hair it had was pulled back into a tight ponytail. A wooden spike was shoved through its nose and someone had stuck a drinking straw in one of its ears.

Cassidy pressed herself against my chest again, this time allowing her hand to slip into mine. "That's it."

I shook my head. "No way. Not happening."

She rolled her eyes and glanced around for the shopkeeper. "Where did she go?"

I shrugged, suddenly cold and frightened, though unclear whether I was more frightened of the voodoo shop, the shrunken head, or my first attempt at shoplifting. "I don't know where she is."

"I'm right here," a voice said. "And that's not the one you need, girl. So don't you go think about jacking old Bob. Okay?"

"How did you–? Who told–?" Cassidy tried to say, but no words would escape past her shock. "I mean–"

"I know things, child. That's why I'm here. Come with me," the woman said. Cassidy and I started to follow, but the woman put a hand to my chest. "You wait here. Keep Bob company for me." She pulled a cord on the wall and a curtain fell between us. The shop was too dark and the smell of vanilla hung in the air around the altar. After several attempts to avoid seeing it, I looked at Old Bob. He definitely wasn't the same head from the picture in Cassidy's scrapbook. Bob was fat and smiling. The head in the ad was thinner and scowling.

Old Bob was perched on the stem of an upturned wine goblet. Scattered on the altar around him, coins representing every possible culture in the world shimmered in the candlelight. Beneath the votives, I could see bits of straw. Glancing beneath them, I cringed. Voodoo dolls. Rows of them. At first, I thought they were all the same, placed as decorations. But each face was different, each doll dressed differently. One was wearing a patch of a bandana as a shirt. Another had a turban on its head. Turning away, a doll in the far corner drew my attention. I had seen it somewhere before.

The doll was almost weightless, made out of straw like the others, but instead of having pins stuck through it at various places, its hands and feet were bound together with black string. A piece of string wrapped its head, too, a gag across where the mouth would have been. But the binding and the gag weren't what first drew my attention. It was the doll's hair. Whoever had made the doll had taken the time to weave bits of yellow yarn into its head, giving the doll a long mane of blonde hair. They had also wrapped the doll in a white sundress. I threw the doll back onto the shelf, knocking Bob over in the process.

A patron nearby glanced up from the book he was reading. "What's wrong?"

I shuddered, pointed to the doll. "It just looks like my friend."

"And it's bound," he said. "That's not good."

"Why?"

He shrugged, returned the book to its place on the shelf, and reached for the doll. "Someone took a whole lot of time with this doll."

He explained that whoever had made the doll had taken the time to make it so realistic because they wanted the voodoo to work on someone they didn't know. "You say this looks like your friend?" he said.

"Yeah. She's in there with some woman."

He eyed the curtain, chewing on his bottom lip. "Okay, listen carefully. This doll isn't what you think. It's not meant for bad. You need to take care of your friend."

"What do you mean?"

"Dolls can be bound for many reasons. The way your friend here is bound means something very particular." He flipped the doll over, examining its back, the hair, and the knots in the string. "Yeah. See?"

He pointed to a burned spot on the back of its head. "Whoever did this saw something and they made this doll so that your friend wouldn't do whatever it is she's going to do."

"How do I know what it is she's not supposed to do?"

"I haven't a clue. But I'd be very careful, if I were you." He laid the doll back in the altar. "I'd leave an offering if I were you."

As he wandered away, I fumbled through my backpack for something to leave. I withdrew a handful of change and dropped it into one of the unlit votives, not knowing whether I should say a prayer or if Marie LaVeau would just know what the offering was for. A woman with two toddlers in tow excused me out of her way, kissed a coin, and placed it beside Old Bob. "Thank you," she said, looking up at the portrait of Marie LaVeau above the altar. When she had left, I followed suit.

I stood there for what felt like hours, trying to tune out Marie LaVeau's House of Voodoo and everything that I had just learned, until Cassidy emerged from behind the curtain, smiling.

When she saw me, she threw her arms around me. "Thank you, thank you, thank you! I got it!"

"What?" I said, confused.

"She had it for me. She knew we were coming and gave it to me. We can go now," she said. She dragged me by the arm through the store and onto the sidewalk. Once outside, she dropped her backpack and opened the small box. Inside, there it was, just as it had appeared in the ad. I wanted to take the shrunken head and the diary and the poems from her, throw them all into the storm drain and drag her away from the shop. I could tell her dad about everything, and he would make sure nothing happened to her. But I couldn't. Her face was too full of joy.

"We have to get home," she said. "Like, right now."

I shrugged. "I don't know what bus to take or what."

"That's okay. I know the way home. She knew everything, Billy. Everything! Look." She opened her backpack and removed a scrap of paper. "She even gave me directions home!"

Chapter 26

Whoever had chosen the music to be played over the PA system in the waiting area of the arbiter's office had miscalculated. Rather than the quiet, soothing effect they had obviously intended, the low droning of a Bach sonata was beginning to put me to sleep and I found myself fidgeting just to stay awake.

"Sit still," Mother said. She was reading a two-year-old *Redbook* she had found on the coffee table. I sighed.

"Mom, how long are we going to have to wait?"

She shrugged. "I don't know, Billy. Buddy's not even here yet. I told you we were going to be way early."

I folded my hands atop my knees in an attempt to keep them from bouncing, trying instead to focus my nervous energy on looking around the room. There were more people floating around the lobby of the arbitration center than I had first noticed. Occasionally, someone stopped at a filing cabinet long enough to remove a folder or two before disappearing into one of the eight doors lining the room.

"So are you guys ready?" a familiar voice said. I looked up to find Buddy Quinn smiling down. "You look nice, Billy. Are you nervous?"

"A little."

"Don't be. It'll go quick," he said.

Mom's ears perked. "What? Quick?"

"These things usually are when they involve children."

She stood, stretching. "I'm just ready for it to be over."

"I'll bet. What about you, Billy?"

I shrugged. I didn't understand very much about what was happening, and was even less interested in learning. Instead of my pending deposition, my thoughts were consumed by the shrunken head and our trip into the Quarter the day before. Even after an hour's walk back to the home and through my relentless probing, I was no closer to knowing why Cassidy had wanted that head. And I understood even less why I was so preoccupied with helping her get it.

"Buddy! It's nice to see you again," said a woman across the table from us. She wore a red sweater, high-necked and too warm for New Orleans. She offered her hand and he took it, holding it politely rather than shaking it.

"And you, Karen. How are Jack and the boys?"

"Fine," she said with a smirk. "Craig's joined the track team and Bobby is captain of the football team. I hate it but of course Jack's thrilled."

"You should be proud, Karen," Buddy said. He turned to my mother. "Beverly, this is Karen Hughes. She's representing the company, but we won't hold that against her."

Mother shook her hand. "Pleased to meet you, I guess."

Karen smiled. "You too, Ms. Northrop." She turned to Buddy Quinn. "So. What will it take to make this all go away?"

He shrugged. "That's the question of the day, Karen. Beverly's all but lost her job over this. Bills are stacking up."

"Six months' salary, a transfer to another office, and a pay bump. Say 12.5 plus cost of living adjustments?" she said. I thought I heard my mother gulp. Instead, Buddy shook his head.

"No, Karen. Beverly and I have discussed it and we both think that any offer should not factor in future employment. She's had this problem once before, as you well know, and it seems to be endemic within the company," Buddy said.

I felt my mother's hand close around mine, cutting off circulation. But she said nothing, instead deferring to Buddy. Karen Hughes looked first at Buddy, then at my mother and me.

"Fine. Let's get started then," Karen said.

Stepping to the door, she motioned in three men. I recognized the first two as the men from the restaurant. The third man I didn't recognize. He took a seat at the head of the table and opened a folder.

"We're here today to discuss the matter of Beverly Northrop's sexual harassment complaint against Ken MacAdams. Let the record show that I'm Robert Carson, serving as mediator. As dictated in the arbitration and mediation agreement, Riverside Financial's counsel will begin the proceedings," the man said. He waited for Karen to nod before continuing. "I'd like to take a moment to lay down a few guidelines. While this isn't a courtroom, it is still a legally binding proceeding. Those present to give depositions in this case will be sworn in, and your testimonies will be subject to all of the same rules that govern testimonies under oath."

He glanced around the table. Everyone nodded their compliance before he continued. "Thank you. According to a complaint filed through the office of Human Resources at Riverside Financial, on or about July 12th, Beverly Northrop alleges that supervisor Ken MacAdams attempted to pressure her into accepting a second date. When she refused, Mr. MacAdams threatened to block a promotion for which Miss Northrop was eligible. Is this correct so far?" the arbiter said.

My mother started to speak, but Buddy Quinn stopped her. "That's correct."

"To continue, pursuant to company policies, Miss Northrop then reported the incident to HR Director Arthur Thompson. Shortly thereafter, Miss Northrop was placed on administrative leave, with pay, pending the outcome of her complaint. And that should bring us up to date?" the arbitrator said.

Karen Hughes stood, and her smile vanished. "We'll attempt to show, by way of her previous track record at Riverside Financial, a pattern of inappropriate conduct stretching back three years, to her time as a secretary in the Minneapolis office."

With the change of Karen Hughes' demeanor, Buddy Quinn had stiffened. When she fell silent and the arbitrator turned to him, he didn't smile. Instead, he closed his pen and laid it across his yellow legal pad. "It's really quite simple. Miss Northrop attended a social function with Mr. MacAdams. When she refused to attend another, he threatened her. Enough said."

Ken MacAdams and Mr. Thompson shuffled uncomfortably in their chairs. The arbitrator sat, patiently, awaiting Buddy Quinn's next remarks. When he realized that they were waiting for him to continue, Buddy smiled. "I'm sorry. I'm done."

Karen coughed into a cup of water. "What?"

Buddy Quinn grinned at her breech of composure. "I'm done, Karen. We can proceed."

The arbitrator glanced over the notes in a folder, turned to Karen Hughes. "Who will you be calling first?"

"Ken MacAdams."

"Mr. MacAdams," the arbitrator said. "Raise your right hand and repeat after me."

After swearing to tell the truth, MacAdams took the chair closest to the arbitrator, near a microphone. Karen Hughes stood, tugged the wrinkles from her sweater. "Mr. MacAdams, you've heard the allegations that Miss Northrop has made against you?"

"That's correct," MacAdams said.

"What happened when you first found out about the complaint?"

"Mr. Thompson came into my office and told me there was a problem. I asked him–" he began. Buddy Quinn interrupted him.

"When was that?"

He thought for a moment, and then nodded. "Sometime around June 25th."

"Thank you," Buddy said, without looking up from his notes.

"You were saying that Mr. Thompson visited you on June 25th?" Karen said.

"Yes. He informed me that there had been a complaint filed. We discussed it for several minutes. I presented my side of the facts, and he left. I figured it would end there."

"But it didn't?" Karen Hughes said.

"No. A few days later, I was surprised to learn that Beverly, Miss Northrop, had retained counsel and was suing the company," MacAdams said.

"Did anyone give you any indication why?"

He shook his head. "No."

"Thank you, Mr. MacAdams."

Buddy Quinn again closed his pen, but instead of laying it across his notebook, he tucked it into his pocket. He stood, buttoned his coat. "Mr. MacAdams, how long have you worked for Riverside Financial?"

"Twelve years."

"And in that twelve years, how many complaints such as this one have you faced?" Buddy Quinn said.

Ken MacAdams squinted at Buddy Quinn, and then glanced to Mr. Thompson, who shrugged his okay. "Four or five."

"You're management, and you've only faced four or five complaints in twelve years? That's a remarkable track record," Buddy said. He smiled the same smile from the billboards in his office.

MacAdams smiled back. "Thank you. I can only try."

Buddy glanced at his notes. "You said in a deposition that Mr. Thompson came into your office on July 10, correct?"

"Yes."

"And that you were surprised when he returned to inform you that Miss Northrop had hired a lawyer?"

Ken MacAdams leaned back in his chair. He was getting bored. "I said so in my deposition, Mr. Quinn."

"Why were you surprised?" Buddy said. "Isn't that normally what happens in these cases?"

"Yes, but Mr. Thompson had told me that it was all going to go away," he said.

Buddy Quinn made a note, and then continued. "Why did he say that?"

MacAdams shrugged. "Something about seeing Beverly in a restaurant." Out of the corner of my eye, I saw Karen Hughes freeze. Mr. Thompson shifted uncomfortably again. Buddy Quinn sat back down.

"Thank you, again, Mr. MacAdams."

The arbitrator raised his eyebrows at Karen Hughes. She turned to Mr. Thompson. He shook his head. Karen looked across the table at Buddy Quinn, then to the arbitrator. "Can you give us a minute?" she said.

The arbitrator closed his notebook and left the room. My mother leaned closer to Buddy, whispering. "What's going on?"

Buddy shook his head. "Just a minute."

Karen turned to Mr. MacAdams and smiled. "Ken, could you excuse us all for a moment please?"

"Sure," he said, obviously confused. When he had left the room, Karen kicked back in her chair, again displaying the light, almost friendly smile with which she had greeted us.

"Well, Karen?" Buddy said.

She squinted. "Two years, with benefits," she said.

"Plus attorney's fees and punitive?" Buddy said.

She shook her head. "No punitive."

"Not happening."

At Karen's offer of two years' salary, Mother's hand latched onto my wrist. My fingers were beginning to tingle. I expected her to jump up, at any second, and start screaming "Yes!" Instead, she ratcheted her hand tighter around my wrist.

Karen was busy whispering to Mr. Thompson. He would shake his head, she would counter. Each time, she became more agitated. Finally, she turned back to Buddy Quinn.

"Buddy, it's a good offer."

"No it isn't," he said. "And you know it."

He stood to leave.

"Buddy–"

"We're done, here, Karen. Thank you. Call my office with your next offer," he said. He started for the door, signaling an end to the meeting.

"Buddy?" my mother said.

He shook her off. "We're done, Beverly."

We stepped out into the waiting area, brushing past Ken MacAdams and the waiting arbitrator. We had started down the hall and were to the elevators when Karen Hughes finally caught us.

"Buddy, wait," she panted. He removed his hand from the elevator call button.

"Yes, Karen?"

"I can't make any promises. But I'll call with an offer by close of business today. Okay?" When Buddy didn't respond, she sighed, almost pleading. "Buddy, it's the best I can do."

"Today. Otherwise it's a jury and an open courtroom and– well, you get the picture, right? And I don't think Riverside Financial wants that kind of publicity, do you?"

Karen shook her head. "No. Thanks, Buddy."

"Thank you, Karen. And congratulate Jack for me on the football thing," he said. He pressed the button for the first floor. When the doors closed, Mom spun Buddy Quinn around.

"What the hell is going on Buddy?"

"Beverly, I said trust me, right?"

"Trust you? You just turned down two years' worth of pay–"

"And you'll get ten times that if we go to court." They argued for the better part of ten minutes, in the elevator, in the lobby, in the car on the way back to his office. And through it all, through everything she said about him and to him, Buddy never broke the calm coolness of his billboards ads. Pulling into the parking lot of his office, she paused for a breath.

"My turn, Bev. If you don't want to trust me, then fine. We'll part ways and that's that. No harm, no foul. But if that's what you want, all I ask is that you wait the three minutes it will take to get to the office," he said. Mom studied him for a second. I shrunk into the back seat, in anticipation of the next round of explosions. Instead, she surprised Buddy and me both.

"Why?"

"I'll make you a deal," he said. "You come up. If there's a message from Karen Hughes, you stay with me and trust me. If there's not, I'll call her and accept the two years with benefits. Deal?"

Mom sighed. "Fine."

Without another word, we boarded the elevator to the sixth floor. Standing outside the main entrance to his offices, Buddy turned to her. "Want to back out?"

She shook her head. Buddy opened the door, allowed us to enter first, and then followed. The receptionist looked up, smiled. "Welcome back, guys. How did it go?"

"Fine, I guess," Mom said. "Well, Buddy. What's next?" she said. He motioned us into his office.

She turned to thank Buddy, but the receptionist called after us. "Buddy, Karen Hughes just phoned for you and asked that you call her immediately."

He took the note the receptionist was offering to him, read it, and passed it to my mother. She read the note and then shook her head, confused. "I don't understand. What's that?"

Buddy Quinn winked. "That's just the point where we start negotiations."

Chapter 27

After we returned home from a celebration dinner with Buddy Quinn, my mother and I didn't say much. Exhausted by the excitement of the day, we had retreated into separate rooms without as much as a goodnight. I awoke before six the next morning without having bothered to set an alarm. The morning sunlight blasted through the window of my bedroom, casting its warmth across everything. No corner of the room seemed untouched by its brilliance.

Mother was still asleep, her door bolted against intrusion from the outside world. I scribbled a note on the back of an unopened Visa bill, letting her know I had left for the Home early and would not be home until late that evening. Not to worry. I'd be okay. Thus it was that I found myself walking into the Liberty Street Home almost a full hour before even Camille would arrive at seven-thirty. A woman I had never seen before looked up, dreary-eyed and bored, from behind the pages of a romance novel.

"I'm Billy," I said. She returned to her book without a word. I shrugged and started toward Hall B. Passing the door that led to Cassidy's bedroom, I considered waking her but decided instead to let her sleep. She'd be awake soon enough, and I would be able to quiz her about the shrunken head.

On Bohemian Row, I was surprised to find the table set. The faint rattle of a hot skillet drew me toward the kitchen. Alistair, with an apron fastened around his waist, was pulling a pan of fresh biscuits in his hand. He smiled from across the room.

"Now why is it that I expected to see you early today?" he said.

"I wanted to tell everyone what happened yesterday," I said. "I couldn't sleep."

He placed the pan of biscuits on the counter.

"That's the way it goes sometimes. You can help me with breakfast while you tell me about yesterday," he said. He passed a bowl of eggs across the counter, handed me a fork. "Beat the eggs, will you?"

As I stirred the eggs, I told him about Buddy Quinn and Mr. Thompson and Ken MacAdams. He would occasionally interrupt to tell me to add this spice or that season to the eggs. When I finished the story, he took the bowl. "All done," he said.

"What are you making?" I said.

"Omelets," he replied. "We decided we wanted omelets and the kitchen won't prepare them. So this, I guess, is our display of abject defiance."

I laughed. "You go."

"Excuse me?"

"It's a saying. It means you did something cool," I said. He nodded, though I wasn't sure he understood.

"Won't you get in trouble, though?"

He stopped chopping green onions long enough to consider his answer. "And what exactly do you think Mr. Downing is going to do? Throw us out?"

I peeked out down the dark hall. "So is everyone still asleep?"

"Louise and I are the only ones up," he said. "Morning people."

He peeked around the corner of the kitchen door, checking for eavesdroppers. "She has a visitor. A certain young lady found out she was a poet."

"She's here?" I said. "Right now?"

"As opposed to ten minutes ago or five minutes from now, yes. Right now."

The lights running down the halls were on a timer and had yet to kick on. My eyes gravitated to the shaft of light bisecting the hall outside Louise's open door. Alistair prodded me on the shoulder.

"Go on. You can tell them breakfast is almost ready."

Afraid that I might awaken the other residents, I tried to be as quiet as possible. When I approached Louise's door, I could hear a voice. It was Louise. "This was your mother's journal?"

"Yeah. She kept journals for her whole life. I have this one, though," Cassidy said. "I wish I had more. Maybe I could get more clues."

"Your mother was quite the poet," Louise said over the rustle of paper. "I can see why you like it so much. Read me this one."

"Read it to you?" Cassidy said.

"Yes. Poetry should be read aloud."

"Okay," Cassidy said. "But I've never done this before."

"Just read it."

I could hear Cassidy resituate herself in a chair. "Labyrinth," she began.

"Listen to happy music, says he to me.
"Let that be the knot,
tie the string to the temple column,
pull it so it's not forgotten.
Scattered bits of my mind,
dashed themes of a symphony,
still trying to sing the song,
trying to set me free."

Her voice quivered as she began the next stanza. Louise stopped her and told her to relax. She sighed.

"I'm trying.
"Dark it is, my prison,
an abyss.
Quiet trickles the water,
across my beaten legs.
Keep you here, says something,
a voice I cannot name.
It lames me, this faceless captor,
tells me I'm insane.
The prison here is my journey,
where I'm destined to reside.
Hide away joy and youth,
locked inside your heart.
Save them for your own amusement,
but never them let out.
For what pray I, I do not know.
But insanity I doubt."

She stopped again, rustled papers about.
"What's wrong?" Louise said.
"Just catching my breath," Cassidy said. "And lost my place."

"Tug the string don't pull it.
Lest the knot should come untied.
Struggle against the–struggle against the madness
fight for control of your mind.
I'm trapped inside the maze,
in dark tunnels and bare rooms.
Free me from my labyrinth,
protect me from such doom."

When the words stopped, I jumped, almost startled by the sudden intensity of silence. Louise said nothing for several seconds. "Well," she finally said. "What does that mean?"

"I have to find my mom," Cassidy said. My heart froze. "I have to help her."

The lights in the hall flickered to life, suddenly bathing me in light. I heard a chair scrape across the floor in Louise's room.

"Well, I'm sure breakfast is about ready. You're going to tell Billy?" Louise said.

"I guess."

"You should. He'll understand, more than I think you know. Go ahead and tell him now. He's in the hall," she said. She opened the door and winked at me. "Gotcha. Good morning, Billy."

Louise held the door for Cassidy. She strolled past me without word, as if she expected me to follow her. It took me a couple of steps to catch up with her.

"We need to talk," she said. "I have to tell you something about my mom, okay? But after breakfast. It's personal. And it's a secret. Only you and Louise know about it. Okay?" Cassidy said. I nodded. "Pinky promise?"

She held out her small finger, hooked and waiting for mine. I took it, and she closed the grip, shaking my entire arm with only her small finger. "Now you can't break your promise."

I had never heard of a pinkie promise, nor did I know what horrible fate for breaking such a promise might be. Somehow I knew that I didn't want to find out. Cassidy had my word and I knew this was one promise I would never break.

* * *

A morning shower fueled the afternoon's humidity, rendered the summer sun all the more unbearable. Stepping onto the patio was like stepping into an automatic dishwasher. Steam rose in small puffs from the moss-covered mortar of the pavers. Cassidy led me by the hand toward the rear of the home. I hesitated as we turned the corner but she tugged away. "Come on. Don't be scared. They're all gone," she said.

I sighed. "How did you know?"

"Camille told me about the bees when I asked why they were tearing down the shed. Don't be embarrassed."

"I was trying to help."

"I know. Come on." She waved me closer. Around the corner, where once had stood the tool shed, was now a small clearing. There was a patch of dry ground, shaded and isolated beneath a canopy of oak trees. Cassidy unfolded the quilt she had borrowed from Thaddeus, straightened a corner with her foot, and sat.

"So, are you going to tell me what this is all about?" I said. She looked away, through the trees. Sunlight in her eyes made her squint.

"I don't know how to tell you any of this, Billy. But I'll try, okay?"

"Okay," I said. I wasn't sure where she was going and wished she would get on with it.

"Don't ask questions until the end. But here it goes." She smoothed a wrinkle from the blanket, glanced around again, and then allowed her eyes to settle on me. "Eight years ago, my mother was taken hostage."

"What?" I began, but she continued.

"She was taken away by two guardians of the temple of Apollo because she had angered him. They're holding her captive and won't let her go until I've completed my quest. I have to gather to them the things that were lost over the ages. And it hasn't been easy. They only left this diary as a clue. I've had to read all of her poetry and notes and thoughts to find out what she had done to so anger the gods. And I found out. She was one of them."

I shook my head. "I don't understand."

Pulling out the weathered book I had caught her reading, she opened it to a dog-eared page. "It's all right here." She handed it to me and tapped it. "Read this."

The first half of the page she indicated was filled with incoherent jumbles of letters and

symbols. Half-written sentences disappeared behind forceful, bold scribbles. In one corner, the
unmistakable form of Snoopy the dog faded
into a seemingly endless spiral of loops. Finally,
halfway down the page, a date stood alone on
a line.

```
8-10-83
I have offended the gods.
The spark of my life has
ceased to burn. The very
essence of my happiness
has dried up, withered and
vanished at their remorseless
hands. What have I done to
anger you? Are you not still
my sisters?
```

I thumbed through the remaining pages of the
book. Each subsequent page was a study in con-
trasts. On one, there might be a poem or a couple of paragraphs. On another, a sketch of a ship
at sea, watched over by an angel. Most, though,
were filled with the same, nonsensical scratching as the one Cassidy had bid me to read. In

more than a few places, her mother's anger was made apparent by the holes ripped through in the pages by the tip of a pen. Closing the journal, I looked back at Cassidy.

"Understand now? My mother was a muse!"

I shook my head. "I don't understand. You think she was a what?"

"A muse. One of the daughters of Zeus. She was a muse. And something happened, and now they took her away," she said.

I shook my head again. "Cassidy I–"

"Just don't. Watch," she said.

For the next hour, she flipped through page after page of the journal, pointing out a drawing of a swan or a line about a prison. With each stop in the journal, I became more confused and more bewildered. Finally, I stopped her.

"What do you mean she was taken away by two angels? Taken to where?"

"When I was just a little kid, I remember the night they took her. She was upset. She and dad had been fighting about something. They were yelling at each other. I was too little to understand, but she said that he didn't get her. He didn't understand. He tried to tell her he did. But she would yell at him and he would yell at her. Finally, she started throwing things at him, and Dad locked me in my room." Just when I was beginning to understand what had happened, she stopped.

"And then what?" I said, eager to hear more.

She waved me off. "Just a second."

Excitedly jabbing at a picture in the book, she started again. "They took her. They did."

I looked at the picture. Two figures floated above the ground. Both wore matching robes that flowed behind them, almost like wings. I studied the picture for a minute and then handed the journal back to her.

"Who are they?" I said.

She sighed. "They're the guards of Apollo's temple! They took her."

"How do you know it was them?"

"Because I saw them. I snuck out of my room and down the stairs. She was still yelling at my father about how he was abandoning her. They were there, fighting her out the front door. The harder she fought, the faster they pulled her out into the light. Daddy started crying when she finally disappeared and the light faded," she said.

The tear that had been welling in the corner of Cassidy's eye finally trickled down her cheek and tumbled from her chin.

"How do you know it was them?"

"Their robes were floating behind them," she said. "And they took her back to Mount Olympus. Do you understand now?"

"I think so."

"Good. Because I know what the last thing we have to do to free her is. We need a crypt though," she said.

"A crypt? Why?"

"Because that's what we need," she said. She stood, tucked the journal back into her pocket, and pulled me to my feet. Helping her fold the blanket, I tried to slow my brain down. She smiled at me. "You understand now?"

I nodded, speechless.

"I'm glad you believe me," she said. "I knew you would understand."

She kissed my cheek and skipped away toward the patio. I hesitated in the clearing, not quite ready to follow but not wanting to let her get too far away. She stopped at the corner and bobbed her head. "Come on, Billy. We've got work to do."

Standing there, watching her step into the blazing light of a midmorning sun, I did understand. I understood so much more than I could ever share with her. And I wanted desperately to believe.

Chapter 28

The home had fallen into that relative quiet that comes sometime after lunch, when many of the residents had retired to their rooms to study their Bibles or watch talk shows. The few residents still about congregated in the social rooms around small tables, playing dominos and checkers. Making my way back to Hall B with a stack of letters and Alistair's newspaper, I tried to keep an eye out for Cassidy, who had disappeared after our morning conversation with a promise to return during the afternoon.

Eagerly awaiting word of what the next leg of our quest might bring, I had become an annoying chatterbox. Thaddeus and Anne had both breathed a sigh of relief when Alistair sent me for his paper and the mail. Turning onto Hall B, I wondered how they would receive my return and decided that I would be markedly calmer for the afternoon. With any luck, I might be able to draw Louise from hiding in her bedroom for a game of gin.

Opening the door, I heard Christopher Downing's voice echoing in the living room and stopped, not sure whether I should proceed or not. He had apparently only just arrived and was angry.

"I have graciously overlooked your defiance for the past few weeks while I alerted the kitchen staff to begin preparing meals for you. Tonight, you'll dine with the other residents. Workers will arrive tomorrow to dismantle the kitchen and begin measurements for the renovations," he said. He was holding a clipboard and flipped through the pages excitedly. Alistair, sitting in his usual spot at the table, was slightly behind him, and I had to stifle a laugh when I saw him mocking Downing.

Alistair noticed me by the door and motioned me over. "Welcome back, Billy," he said. I handed him the paper and the mail. Downing turned.

"Is there a problem?"

I shook my head. "No, sir. I was just–"

"He was delivering my mail and newspaper, Mr. Downing. I trust that that is okay with you? Or is there bureaucratic procedure forbidding mail delivery?" Alistair said.

Downing scoffed. "Mr. Lees, I would appreciate it if you would refrain from sarcasm. Considering the lengths to which I'm going to find you people adequate accommodations either here or elsewhere, you should be appreciative," Downing said, returning to his clipboard.

"You can take your lengths and shove them up your–," Anne began. Thaddeus quickly grabbed her shoulder.

"Anne, why don't you help me get our things out of the kitchen before they disappear?" he said. She scowled at Downing before following Thaddeus from the room.

"Billy, tomorrow you'll begin helping some of the orderlies elsewhere in the home," Downing said flatly. "Judge Spurgeon sent you down here to break you of the habit of vandalism, and I don't think that this is the appropriate atmosphere for–"

"I don't think that he'll be joining you, Mr. Downing," Louise said. My heart was pounding, and I was having trouble breathing. She placed her arm around my shoulder and pulled me close. "Billy works for us. And I think that you'll find just how quickly Billy's reassignment will get undone when I call my nephew and inform him that you've taken away my helper."

"Who is your nephew?" Downing said.

She smiled wryly. "Why, Judge Spurgeon, silly man. I used to drive his mother, my sister, to play bridge twice a week before she died. And I'm sure he'll think I'm a suitable role model for Billy." She patted the side of my head. "Billy's staying right here with us. And that's final."

"Mrs. Kearney, I'd like to remind you that I run things around here," he said.

She shrugged. "And I thought that we made it absolutely transparent the last time we talked, Mr. Downing. We don't give a damn. If you don't like it, I suggest you call the judge. There's a phone over there. Would you like his number?" she said. She pulled herself straight and seemed to grow a couple of inches.

Downing eyed her and then shrugged. "Dinner is served at five-thirty. If you're late, don't expect to eat."

He stormed out of the hall, the door slamming behind him. Several seconds passed until, finally, Louise sighed. "I've never in my life!"

"Nor have I, Louise," Alistair said. He was still staring after Downing.

Donald appeared from inside the kitchen, cowering around in the door. "He's gone?"

"Yes," Alistair said. "You can come out now."

"Can you believe that man?" Donald said. I thought for a moment I had heard him growl, but couldn't be sure. 'You'll come to dinner tonight at five-thirty if you want to eat,'" he said, mocking Downing's western accent. "Five-thirty my ass. I'll be there. With bells on!"

Alistair looked up from the paper he had just unfolded and raised his eyebrows. "What do you have planned, Donald?"

"You'll see," he said with a wink. "We've a dinner party at five-thirty. And guess who's coming."

* * *

Christopher Downing's visit to the Row had so taken the Bohemians by surprise that they spent the rest of the afternoon in their own rooms instead of watching soaps or working in flowerbeds. When I went to find Cassidy, Camille informed me that she had gone out with her father and wouldn't be back until closer to dinner.

Resigned to pass the afternoon alone, I returned to Hall B and settled in at the table with a pencil and my notebook. Two hours later, the sole shred of evidence of my labor was the pile of paper at my feet. I glanced over the two pages of scratched out sentences and half-written words. The diary, so fresh in my mind, made more sense than the mess filling the page before me. With a sigh, I carefully tore the pages out of the notebook and wadded them.

"What's wrong, Billy?" a voice said. Donald Lilly was standing in the hall in his bathrobe, his hair a web of curlers and oversized hairpins.

"I'm just bored and frustrated."

He chuckled. "I can understand why. Look at this place, full of decaying old people who spend too much time in bed."

"It's not that," I said. "I'm just–well I don't know."

"Where's your little girlfriend?"

"She's not my girlfriend," I said a bit too forcibly.

Donald smiled. "I understand. That's not what I meant to say."

"She's off with her dad somewhere."

"Now there's a piece of work," he said. "Her dad. We sat for a moment as the silence in the air between us grew. I drilled the tip of my pencil into the cover of the notebook, carving a perfect, tiny crater in the center of a zero in the barcode. I heard Donald's chair scrape across the floor as he stood.

"You just got here," I said.

"Yeah, but I want something to drink. You thirsty?"

I hadn't realized it until then but my mouth was parched. I followed him into the kitchen. He set two glasses on the counter and opened the small refrigerator.

"So what will it be? Iced tea? Or a root beer float?"

I smiled. "Float."

"Good call." He opened the freezer compartment and removed a pint of vanilla ice cream.

He dumped two scoops into each glass before pouring root beer over them. When it came into contact with the ice cream, the dark root beer exploded into a cream-colored froth.

"This is the best part," he said. He picked up one of the glasses and drained half of the foam off the top. "Careful, though. It'll make you burp."

Before I could respond, he belched. We both laughed. After sucking the foam from the top of my float, I burped.

"Good one," Donald replied. He poured more root beer into both glasses. This time, it remained a dark liquid, and the two scoops of ice cream bounced to the top. When I went to take another drink, the icy globs bounced against my nose.

Donald handed me a spoon. "Here, it's easier this way."

We sat at a small folding table beside the refrigerator, eating our floats in silence. Every once in a while, one of us would laugh, only to trigger another round of belching and laughing. And somewhere over root beer floats at a folding card table, we forgot about administrators and diaries and dinners. With the glasses drained and in the sink, we returned to the dining room table. Donald picked up my notebook and thumbed through the pages.

"This one isn't nearly as full as the last, Billy."

I shrugged. "I don't have anything to write about, I guess."

"Nothing to write about? What about Cassidy? Trying to save Hall B?"

I shook my head. "I've tried. Nothing comes out."

He rubbed his chin knowingly. "I know what you mean. It's called writer's block."

I looked up. "What do you mean?"

"You need inspiration. Find your muse."

He closed the notebook, glanced around the room and leaned in. "Here's a thought. Instead of writing about Cassidy or us, why not write something for Cassidy," he said.

"For Cassidy?"

"Like a story? Make something up. Just for her."

I scratched my head. "Like what?"

"You don't read in your school?"

"We read. Books like *Where the Red Fern Grows*. But I can't write a book."

"And why not?"

I didn't have an answer.

He shook his head. "And what if Kipling had decided he couldn't write a book?"

"Who?"

"No one," Donald replied. He slid the notebook and pencil across the table and started down the hall. "Write Cassidy a story about a prince or something. Girls like princes."

Before I could protest, he was down the hall and his bedroom door closed behind him. Rolling my pencil between my fingers, I sighed. What on earth could I write that would impress Cassidy? My instincts said she wouldn't like fairy tales.

Though the notebook fell open to a clean page, the swirls and scratches of aborted attempts still marred the page in the form of gouges and almost invisible lines. As the tip of my pencil traced across the grooves, gaps appeared. I became engrossed in trying to make letters and words without gaps, carefully retracing over white spaces to fill in the holes in the tail of an A or complete a circle of an O. When the phone rang almost an hour later, I had filled over two pages.

I rushed across the room, hoping to catch it before it rang again and woke the sleeping Bohemians. "Hello?"

"Billy, this is Miss Roberts. Your mother's here."

I looked at the clock. "She's over an hour early."

"So? Your mama's waiting for you. Get on up here," she said. The line went dead. Grabbing my notebook and pencil off the table, I ran from the room. I arrived at Nurse Roberts' desk, winded.

"What's up, Mom?"

"Hey. I have news," she said. She fidgeted back and forth, rocking on her heels. "Buddy called me this afternoon. It's over, Billy. It's all over."

"So you can go back to work now?" I said.

She shook her head. "No, I can't go back to work."

"I don't understand, Mom."

"I don't have to, Billy. I don't ever have to go back to work again!"

Chapter 29

Buddy Quinn had made us rich. Mom would never have to work again and we were on our way to the toy store to buy a matching pair of bicycles.

"I like red," she said. "A red one with silver trim."

"That would be nice." I still had not come to grips with everything she had just told me while standing in front of Camille Roberts' desk and then repeated in the Buick leaving the home. Though she had not told me an amount, as we pulled into the parking lot of the toy store I was beginning to understand that whatever settlement Buddy Quinn had negotiated had made us so rich that my grandfather and grandmother were coming for a visit at the end of the month in order to help my mother pack and move us back to Minneapolis before school started. They even knew of a house we could buy.

"Once we're back in Minneapolis, where do you want to go to school?" Mom said as she examined a pair of Schwinn bicycles.

"Why can't I go to my old school?" Losing my friends had been hard, and the only thing that excited me about returning to Minneapolis was the possibility of reconnecting with them.

"Billy, your old school was just a public school. I thought you'd want to go somewhere nice like–"

"If we have all of this money, why can't we stay here?"

She stopped bouncing the front tire of a mountain bike. "What? You don't want to go home?"

"This is home now. Cassidy and the Bohemians–"

"That's what this is about, isn't it? Those people?"

I shrugged. "Partly. I mean, I like them and all."

"Billy, Judge Spurgeon said you only had to stay there for the summer. I'm sure they'll be glad to be rid of you at the end of the month," she said, before returning to her examination of the mountain bike. She tested the hand brake, turned to the sales clerk who had been waiting patiently nearby. "You have one that will fit him, too?"

"Yes, ma'am. We have it in blue, red, silver."

"I like the red," she said. "Billy, do you like this one?"

I didn't answer. Instead, my thoughts were consumed with Cassidy and her mother. By the most generous of standards, my summer had been a blur. First, Zelda's stroke. Then my mother lost her job. That alone was a sufficient one-two punch to send even the most grounded adults reeling. But then Cassidy's appearance and her quest, Downing's plan to evict the Bohemians and their fight all seemed so far away from the late-May afternoon and the solarium. The entire summer was turning into an unbelievable, almost tactile blur. Perhaps Cassidy was right. Maybe her mother was being held captive by the gods. I certainly wasn't in a state of mind to dismiss the possibility.

"Billy!"

I snapped my head up from the floor. Everything was perfectly clear now, and I knew what I wanted. "I don't want to move, Mom."

"Can we talk about this later, please?" She eyed the sales clerk loitering nearby. "Is red okay?"

I turned to walk away. "I don't care."

She returned the bike to the rack and grabbed me by the shoulder. "I'm trying here. I really am. What do you want to do?"

"I want to go back."

"Then good. We'll be ready to move in–"

"No, Mom. Back to Liberty Street."

"And why?"

"Because I do. I want to be with my friends. I want to be with Cassidy," I said. Sensing her growing frustration, I considered backing off, apologizing. Instead, I stood there, my arms folded defiantly across my chest.

She stood drumming her fingers on her elbow. Several times, she opened her mouth, started to speak, but stopped short of whatever it was she wished to say. The sales clerk soon realized that we were no longer interested in the red Schwinn and had moved on to helping a woman select a skateboard for her son, but neither my mother nor I had noticed. After what seemed like a much longer time than it was, she acquiesced.

"Fine. We'll compromise. I want to celebrate. You want your friends," she said. She glanced a silver mountain bike, tucked neatly into the rows of other bicycles and shook her head. "What's her name? Cassidy?"

I nodded.

"Think she'd like to go to dinner or a movie?"

I shrugged. "I don't know. Maybe."

"Well let's find out."

* * *

Mom rapped hard a second time on the door leading to Christopher Downing's apartment. The sound of her knocks echoed up the stairs. "Maybe they aren't home," she said.

"No. They're here. It's just a really big apartment. Knock again," I said.

When she pounded on the door a third time, she winced. After several seconds, she shook her head. "They aren't home, Billy. Maybe we can–"

"They ain't here," a voice said from behind us. Camille Roberts had returned to her desk. She looked particularly more frazzled than was normal.

"I'm sorry," my mother said.

"They're out back. There is a situation," Camille said.

"A situation? Is everything okay?" Mom said.

"That depends. Go see for yourself," Camille said. She flopped down in her chair and opened a folder, apparently unconcerned about whatever situation was occurring. We started down the hall and she called after us, "Hey! Cut through the dining room. It's quicker."

We saw no one in the halls, in their rooms, or loitering around television sets. Even the orderlies were absent. We turned the corner into the dining room and into a pleasant, evening breeze blowing in through the patio doors. Several of the tables had been moved out onto the patio and were covered with dishes of food. The missing residents were crowded into the back yard of the home. Those that were able to walk had found their way, barefooted, into the grass to dance to "The Revelers." For the residents confined to wheelchairs, the orderlies stood nearby, ready to wheel them to their next conversation.

Mother and I couldn't help but smile. "What is this, Billy?"

I shook my head. "I don't know," I said, as my eyes settled on a clock. "Oh no."

"What?"

"It's six," I replied. I scanned the crowd for Alistair or Louise, found Donald in his lilac colored dress and ringlets, and grabbed my mother's hand, pulling her through the crowd.

"What is this?" I said.

Donald smiled sheepishly. "Glad you could join us, Billy. Miss Northrop, you too."

She smiled, shook his hand. "What's going on?"

"Well–" he began, but Alistair interrupted him.

"God, what a fun time. Look at Downing's face, Donald. I think we can call this a wild success," Alistair said. His cheeks were bright, a jovial smile across his face. He was drunk, and upon seeing me, he took me by the wrist. "Billy, I've been a real shit to you a few times and I'd like to make it up to you."

"It's okay, really," I said. I started to turn, but he stopped me.

"No, I want to make it up to you. I started painting a picture. You and your little girlfriend. Sound good?"

I didn't know what to say. So when my mother stepped forward to answer for me, I breathed a sigh of relief. "Oh that sounds wonderful! You can hang it in your bedroom, can't you?"

I nodded, rather stunned. Alistair had apparently not realized my mother was behind me, because he brightened even more when he saw her. "Well hello, there! Beverly, would you like a drink?"

Mom smiled at him, and the tension and anger of their previous meeting vanished. "Sure."

Alistair Lees offered his arm to my mother and led her across the patio to a makeshift bar set up on a table with cups and bottles. Two younger women I recognized as nurses stood guard over the alcohol. I turned back to Donald.

"What is all of this?"

"Well, consider it a warning shot," he said. He emptied his wineglass and started for the bar, motioning me to follow. "We decided that everyone needed to get out for a little while. If that bastard won't let us have dinner in our room because it was unfair, we decided to make it fair."

"But how? I mean, all of this?"

He chuckled. "We had help."

He nodded toward Camille Roberts, who had reappeared beside a very red Christopher Downing. They were discussing something, rather heatedly, but over the rising chords of a Buddy Holly tune and the laughter, I couldn't hear them. I looked around the patio for Cassidy, hoping she was there, but she wasn't.

Donald was still talking about how Camille had gone out of her way to help set up the barbecue. Emily and her boyfriend had gotten a few bottles of wine and other spirits, and two of the orderlies had raided their deep-freezes to provide the steaks and ribs. When he paused to say hello to one of the residents, I slipped away, back into the home. Cassidy couldn't be far away and she shouldn't miss the party.

I wasn't as familiar with this end of the Liberty Street Home, so it took me several minutes of wandering the halls to reorient myself. After arriving at two dead ends, I finally found what it was I was looking for. I slipped through the broom closet, up the hidden staircase to Cassidy's bedroom. When I got to the top of the stairs, I tapped quietly on the door. Shuffling footsteps and a slammed drawer confirmed what I had expected. Cassidy was hiding.

"Cassidy?" I called through the door.

"What do you want?" she called back.

"Can I come in?"

The door opened and she stepped out of the way, allowing me free passage into the room. The last rays of daylight cast a solitary spotlight on the alcove and her collection of treasures. The diary was there, beside the picture of her mother facing the sea. The shrunken head stood alone in the center of the second shelf of the alcove. The curtains on the window were half closed, and I could tell from the look on her face that she had been watching the party below.

"Why don't you come down to the party?" I said.

"I don't think I'm allowed. My dad would get angry."

"Why? It's just a barbecue." I took her by the hand and pulled her towards the door. "Come on. You'll have fun."

She pulled away and retreated across the room. I took her hand again and started for the door. Cassidy struggled until we reached the door. "Cassidy, I'm not taking no for an answer."

She shoved past me. "Fine. I'll go. But if I get in trouble, I'm never ever talking to you again."

When we reached the patio, my mother was in the yard, barefoot and dancing with an old man I didn't recognize. She saw me and started for me, but her partner wouldn't let her go, insisting that she stay and finish the jitterbug she had started. She threw her head back, laughing, and shrugged. With the final notes of the song, the old man twirled her and then tried to dip her, inciting yet another laugh, this one audible over the diminishing music. She thanked him for the dance, moved to pull away, but could not break free before the next song cued in the player. As they two-stepped to "Blame it on the Bossa Nova," Mom made eye contact with me and glanced at Cassidy, mouthing, "Is that her?" I nodded. She smiled approvingly, as if to say "not bad." I blushed and turned away, hoping Cassidy hadn't noticed. Luckily she had found Louise and was laughing and talking a few feet away.

Christopher Downing had taken position just inside the dining room where he could continue to peer disapprovingly at the gathering. When he saw Cassidy, his eyes narrowed. But he didn't move from his spot. Camille had joined the two nurses by the makeshift bar. She smiled when an elderly woman approached and asked for a cup of wine. "Sorry, hon. It'd upset your medication. How about a nice juice instead?" She poured the woman a cup of grape juice. Someone tapped my shoulder.

"So how's the party going now?" Donald said. But instead of looking at me, he was watching Cassidy, who was now barefoot on the grass and dancing between Thaddeus and Anne.

"Pretty good, I guess."

"You had food yet?" he said. He smiled at Leon over by the barbecue pit. "Good burgers. Even better steaks."

"Maybe in a bit," I said. I continued to follow Cassidy's dancing around the yard. First, she danced with Thaddeus and Anne, then with Alistair. For just a moment, she was near my mom and they spoke, but I couldn't hear them over the music. Then as quickly as they came together, the whirl of the dance pulled them apart.

"You should get out there and dance with her," Donald said.

"Nah. She's having a good time," I said.

I wanted to go dance with her. I wanted to feel the grass between my toes and her hands held in mine, to have her close by. But I was afraid–afraid that she might blush and run away, that I might humiliate myself or insult her. What if my mother made a big deal out of it? As much as it hurt me not to be in the yard with Cassidy, I didn't move, remaining affixed to the lounge chair, and tried to put words to what I was feeling. Why was it that I suddenly couldn't move? Couldn't breathe? Was I really that terrified of dancing or embarrassment? Donald Lilly, still seated beside me, tapped me on the shoulder. "You okay, Billy?"

"Yeah, I guess."

"What's wrong?"

"Nothing," I said. But he knew I was lying.

"Billy?"

I remained silent for several seconds, my mind still trying to put words to my emotions. Sentences wouldn't form, only random words until, finally, clarity came. I knew what it was that my mind wanted to say.

"Donald, can I ask you a question?"

"Sure. Anything."

"Okay," I said. I took a deep breath. "How do you kiss a girl?"

He almost laughed but caught himself. Instead, he kicked back in his chair, relaxed. We were just the guys now. "That's a hard one, Billy. I mean, are you talking about mechanics or what?"

I thought about it for a second. "I mean, how do you know when to kiss a girl?"

"Well, it depends on the girl, I guess. But the short answer is that you just know," he replied. He was watching Cassidy dance with another resident I didn't recognize. He nodded toward her. "With your girl, I think you'll know. But you're a long, long way from being ready for that."

"What do you mean?"

"Well, you're still young. Wait a while." He braced himself against my knee and pushed himself to his feet. He stretched his back and started for the yard. He paused to slip his feet out of the lilac pumps. "But, Billy."

"Yes?"

"First, you have to dance with her."

Chapter 30

So I danced with Cassidy.

The grass, rubbing between my toes as I took care to avoid stepping on her feet, was warm and soft, still pregnant with the expectation of late-summer rains. For hours we whirled around the lawn, beneath the embrace of the security lights. By the time the security lights automatically shut off, Downing had vanished into his apartment, and Camille had long since given up her post beside the bar. The few residents and staff that remained in the yard made little complaint as they filed back into the home. Mother's arm slipped around my waist. We paused long enough for her to polish off the last swallow of wine from her paper cup before crumpling it and dropping it into the garbage bag someone had tied to the doorknob.

"Miss Northrop," Cassidy called from behind us. We turned.

"Cass, I told you earlier you can call me Beverly," she replied. Cassidy tucked her hair behind her ear, demurred at this insistence of informality. Through her hesitation, though, my mother detected something. "Are you okay?"

"Yes, but–well." She stopped again to regain her nerve. "Could I speak with Billy for just one minute before you leave?"

"Sure, baby. Take your time," she said.

Cassidy slipped her fingers into mine and led me back into the yard. She flopped down on a lounge chair with a long sigh. We had been dancing for more than two hours, and exhaustion was weighing heavily. Even the light of a half-moon seemed too harsh to bear. She squinted against it.

"There aren't any stars here. I wish I could see stars," she said. I looked up. When my mother and I moved to New Orleans, we had come from a big city. So, the lack of stars had never struck me as particularly strange. She shook her head. "In Tacoma, there were stars."

"Is that where you're from?"

She shook her head. "We're from Texas originally. But with daddy's job, we move around."

Her gaze returned to the sky. "Do you think you can come over tomorrow?"

"I'll have to ask my mom. Why?"

"I have to go somewhere and don't want to go by myself." She didn't look at me until I asked her where. Without a word, though, her look told me.

"It's about your mom, isn't it?"

"I've just–will you come?" she said again. Through her voice and the look in her eyes, I knew that there was no way to avoid it, no way to delay her until Monday. Without protest, I promised that I would return the next morning, after church.

And so I did.

Convincing my mother to drop me off at the home on a Sunday wasn't easy. When I threatened to take the bus or walk to the home, she relented. "I just don't get it. You don't have to go every day, Billy. And not on Sundays. Why?"

The truth was that I didn't know. I had some vague notion of why Cassidy wanted me to come, needed me on a Sunday, but I couldn't tell her the truth. Instead, I said the first thing that came to mind. "Cassidy needs me to help her with her bicycle."

"Yours has a flat tire. Should we get it fixed? Maybe she wants to ride?" Mom said. When I didn't reply, she gave up. "Okay then, maybe not."

We pulled up to the home and I hopped out. She stopped me.

"Can I just call you when we're done?" I said.

"That's fine." I watched the car pull away before heading inside. Cassidy was watching for me from the waiting room. I saw her and smiled.

"Hey!"

She shot me a sideways glance. "It's about time you got here. You told me you'd be here an hour ago!"

She took me by the wrist and dragged me back outside. Half a block away, I finally managed to stop her. "Where are we going?"

"You'll see," she said. She checked for traffic before crossing the street. "Just try to keep up."

She darted across the street. When I didn't follow, she stopped in the boulevard and almost growled. "Come on!"

Thirty minutes, a bus ride and a transfer later, we were halfway down Esplanade. "It's just up the way a bit," she said. But this was the third time that our destination was just up the way a bit. Though my feet were hurting, bad walking shoes were the least of my concern. I wasn't convinced that we were in the safest of neighborhoods. "Cassidy, how much farther is it?"

"Just up the way a bit," she said.

After another hundred paces I came to the rather startling realization that Cassidy didn't have a clue where we were or where she was leading us. I stopped, resolved to go no farther until she told me what she was doing. Unfortunately, words failed me.

"Billy, keep up," she said without looking back.

I trotted a few steps to catch up. Flushed and winded, I just hoped it would end. "Cassidy, we've been walking forever!"

She ignored me. "See, I told you it was just up the way a bit."

I looked ahead to where she was pointing. A long wall flanked the right side of the road for the better part of a quarter mile. At intervals, wrought iron gates stood open. When we arrived at the first gate, we stopped. Above a gravel path leading into the cemetery, an archway hung suspended, framed by two plaques that read "Saint Louis Cemetery."

"We have to find an angel," she said.

"A what?"

"An angel. A statue of an angel."

"I'm not stealing anything from a graveyard," I said. She rolled her eyes.

"We're not stealing it, Billy." She slipped her backpack off her shoulders and dropped to her knees, digging through it for something. She withdrew a scrap of paper and handed it to me. While I read a newspaper story about vandals defacing tombs in Saint Louis Cemetery, she flipped through her mother's diary. When I finished the article, I looked up, confused.

"I don't get it."

She exchanged the news clipping for the diary. "Read here."

The passage she pointed to was a poem, illustrated in haste with a picture of an angel, falling from the sky with a broken wing. Throughout the passage, her mother had struck through lines of text. Words, unwanted or unneeded, were obscured by black globs of ink.

"You're not reading, Billy," Cassidy said. She tapped the page.

"Broken Angel?"

She snatched the book away from me. "Yes, broken angel. It's about a vision she had. And the angel got broken."

"So you want the angel?"

"No. If you'd read the poem, you'd understand. I need a picture of the angel. See?" she said. She indicated the final stanza. "We have to burn it."

I didn't pretend to understand how, but there in the final stanza was the line that sealed Cassidy's point.

"Burning images of my broken angel," I read aloud.

"See? Now let's go."

We began canvassing the cemetery, one row at a time. Tombs labeled Boudreaux and Gautreaux quickly turned into rows of tombs labeled Diaz and Sanchez. Midway through the cemetery, the names became more Anglicized. But we still had not found the broken angel from the article. Cassidy dusted off a marble bench across from a large, gothic crypt and sat. She rummaged through her backpack and removed a water bottle. After taking a sip, she offered it to me. "Thirsty?"

I shook my head, resolved to be strong and not need water. As the bottle disappeared into her backpack, I regretted not having accepted it. My throat itched and my tongue chose that moment to become dry.

Two more rows later, the relentless Louisiana humidity and summer sun had intensified so much that I thought my head might burst in the heat. The stones of distant crypts shimmered with radiated energy as if the marble and granite were an oven. We still had not found the angel, and I had quit looking down the rows, if only to avoid knowing just how many rows of tombs remained to search. Near the end of each row, a line of trees provided a touch of comfort. Neither of us admitted it, but we both knew that at the completion of each row, we turned a bit slower, lingering longer and longer in the shade.

Cassidy produced the water bottle again, this time offering it to me first. I accepted it without hesitation, handling it carefully.

"Save some for the trip home," she said when I took a large gulp.

I handed it back to her. "You had some before me, remember?"

"Yeah, but I'm a girl."

"So?"

She elbowed me playfully. We rested for another moment, leaning against the wall, out of the sun. She smiled at me, dropped the bottle back into her bag and started for another row, but she stopped to survey a nearby crypt. "How strong are you?"

"Huh?"

"Can you give me a boost up there?" she said, nodding to the top of the crypt.

"I guess. Why?"

"Help me up," she said. I cupped my hands into a step and lifted. Cassidy turned out to be much lighter than I expected, and she almost hurtled onto the roof. She landed on her feet with a snort. "That was fun. Wanna come up?"

I shook my head.

"Suit yourself." She surveyed the cemetery from atop her perch, shielding the sun from her eyes with her hand. On her second pass, she froze.

"What? Do you see it?"

She dismissed me with a wave of her hand. "I'm counting."

As Cassidy traced the number of rows with her finger, I sat, impatient and bored. Finally, she stopped. "It's four rows over, half-way down. Here. Catch me," she said.

Before I could brace for her weight, she had stepped off the roof of the crypt and was in my arms. I fell backwards and stopped, only to force her forward and into the marble. She pulled away from me with a yelp.

"Damn it!" She was clutching her elbow, in a futile attempt to stave off the flow of blood that was winding its way down her forearm. Along the marble face of the crypt, a similar red stream slowly congealed in the sun.

"I scraped it," she said, removing her hand and checking the damage. "It'll be okay. It just hurts."

Without asking, I opened her backpack and removed the bottle of water. "This may hurt," I said as I poured the water on her wound.

She winced and tipped the bottle away from her arm. "Don't use all of it."

"We'll be fine. It's not that far back to Liberty, and we can get something to drink and a band aid then."

Reluctantly, she shrugged. I emptied the remainder of the bottle on her arm. "Now. Let's go get that picture."

Two hours later, we walked through the doors of the Liberty Street Home, battleworn but victorious.

"I am so tired," I said. Cassidy didn't answer until we had reached the entrance to Hall B.

"Me too. Thirsty?" she said.

"Dying." Alistair was the only one awake, sitting at the table as always, reading a newspaper. Soon, standing at the kitchen sink in Hall B, we drained two glasses of water each, refilled, and collapsed into one another on the sofa. She rested her head, hot and heavy, on my shoulder. We quietly sipped our water until the cool, air-conditioned breeze brought respite.

Donald Lilly appeared in the hall and waved. "Hello, kids. How was the field trip?"

Cassidy smiled. "Great. We got it."

"Good for you," he said. "Got what?"

"What we went for," I said. I didn't know how much Donald knew or cared to know. Cassidy apparently had no objection, as she quickly changed the subject.

"Last night was so much fun! When can we do it again?"

He shrugged. "I don't know. Probably not any time soon. Your dad wasn't too happy about it."

In all of the excitement of the party, of Cassidy's quest for her mother, of the lawsuit, and suddenly, of moving back to Minneapolis, I had forgotten about Downing's plans, and now it all came rushing back over me in a flood of anger and resentment.

"I think he's stupid," I said.

Cassidy lifted her head from my shoulder. "What?"

"Making everyone move. Why is he making them move?"

She shrugged off my anger. "I don't know. Maybe he thinks it's best?"

Alistair closed the newspaper and folded it back into a neat bundle. He stood, stretching. "Did you get your picture?" he said.

"Yes, sir," she replied. She showed him the Polaroid of the angel with the broken wing.

He squinted at it through his bifocals and nodded. "Well, there it is indeed! Look here, Donald. Just like she said it would be."

Donald Lilly examined the photograph. "Very good, kids. Well, we'd best be getting ready for dinner. It'll be here any minute."

"Here?" Cassidy and I said in unison.

"Yes," Alistair replied. "Mr. Downing has agreed to let us take our meals here until we move. We can't cook them ourselves, but he will have them delivered. A compromise."

Donald nudged me and winked. "But we're not moving, are we?"

Cassidy smiled. "Not if we can help it."

Chapter 31

Come on, Billy. It's Monday, sweetheart," Mom said. She shook my shoulder again. "Wake up, or you'll be late again."

I rolled over. "What time is it?"

"Almost seven-thirty. Get dressed." She closed the door behind her. I sat on the edge of the bed for a minute, affording my eyes time to adjust to the morning glare. I could hear her muffled voice from the kitchen. She was talking on the phone.

After brushing my teeth, she was still on the phone, waving her hands as she wandered from the refrigerator to the pantry and back to the refrigerator.

"I'd want to see it before we bought it, Mom," she said. She mouthed an apology to me about being on the phone. "Mom. No, don't. I–yes, I'm sure it is a really great deal. I've just–Mom, you don't have to–yes. Okay. Love you too."

She sighed. "Mom wants us to buy a house we've never seen. She says it's a really good deal and close to all of the good schools."

Houses in Minneapolis were houses in Minneapolis and, as such, sparked no excitement or curiosity in me. Such houses were too far removed from my memories. I had exiled the familiar friends and places of home to some detached part of my mind until they were little more than a vague awareness of a place somewhere up north. They were streets and faces that I no longer considered home. Mother continued to talk about the houses my grandparents had found. One had a pool, she said, while another came with its own barn. All of the houses she mentioned were larger than two people needed with things that neither of us could reasonably expect to use. When she dropped me off at the home almost an hour later, she stuck her head out the window. "Are you excited?"

"About what?" I said.

"This is your last week, silly," she said. Myrtle squealed away, bathing me in a cloud of dust and confusion. How had I forgotten that this would be my last week at the home? Maybe she was wrong. This couldn't be my last week here. The afternoon behind David Hebert's mansion wasn't that long ago. But standing in front of the doors of the Liberty Street Home, I tried to remember what the shattering glass sounded like, how Camille Roberts first grunted and sighed at me. Closing my hand around the knob, I tried to come to terms with everything that had happened over the course of my summer.

I found Camille at her desk, just as she had been sitting that first Monday almost three months before. She looked up from the ubiquitous stack of folders and smiled. "Good morning, Billy."

"Morning."

"What's wrong?" she said.

"Mom just reminded me this is my last week."

"So it is. You must be very excited?"

I shrugged. I imagined that any other twelve year old would have been more excited at the prospect of returning to freedom. And freedom is what I would have for two weeks at least. Schools in Louisiana started much earlier than schools in Minnesota, so I would have a small vacation after we moved.

I arrived to find the doors to Hall B propped open. Inside, Christopher Downing stood with two men studying the construction plans spread before them on the dining table. Downing stopped mid-sentence when he saw me. He pointed to the kitchen, where the Bohemians had gathered to watch. "Wait with them."

We stood silently as he finished discussing the lighting scheme. "And the fluorescents. They'll be sufficient to light the space?"

"Yes," one of the men said. "Without walls to obscure the light, you can cut electrical consumption by sixty percent."

"Sixty percent? Well, thank you, gentlemen. You can see yourselves out?" He shook their hands. They disappeared around the corner, and he turned.

"I don't know how to say this to you, so I'll just say it," he began. "The renovation plans have been approved, and we plan on starting immediately."

"What is immediately, Mr. Downing?" Alistair said.

"Monday."

The Bohemians shuffled uncomfortably and mumbled to one another. Alistair waved them down. "Mr. Downing, what will become of us?"

Christopher Downing reclined against the table. "Well, that's the good news. We've found homes for all of you."

"Together?" Anne said.

He shook his head. "Unfortunately, no. The other government-assisted homes in the city are operating near capacity. I understand your desire to remain together, but it just isn't feasible at this time."

"Need," Louise said. "Need, Mr. Downing."

"Excuse me?"

"Our need to stay together," she said. "We are a family."

Anne began to cry, excused herself to the kitchen. Thaddeus stepped forward. "Mr. Downing, we've been together, some of us, for twenty years. I don't know what will become of us if you break us apart."

"You'll be adequately cared for at one of the other homes in the city," Downing said. "There is really nothing you or I or anyone can do about it."

"You could let us stay here," Donald said.

"No, I couldn't." He flipped a page on his clipboard and began quoting figures about food consumption, about electricity costs, about the amount of space only people occupied. The cleaning costs alone, he insisted, could save the Liberty Street Home.

He tossed the clipboard onto the table. "It's like this, guys. The Liberty Street Home is bankrupt. We can't afford the luxury anymore. This renovation is necessary. Otherwise, we won't be able to care for the other hundred and thirty-seven residents who depend on us."

Camille Roberts arrived, carrying a stack of envelopes. She handed each of the Bohemians an envelope with their name typed on the front of it. As she faced Alistair, I saw the tears in her eyes. "I did my best, old man."

"I know," he replied, fighting back a tear of his own. He rested his hand on her shoulder, repeating, "I know."

"Your new homes are in the envelopes," Downing said. "We'll of course assist you in moving in any way you need."

"We won't be needing your help," Anne said. She opened her envelope, read the paper, and then exchanged assignments with Louise. They both sighed with relief.

"At least we'll still be together," Louise whispered. Anne didn't reply. Instead, she retreated into the kitchen.

Downing started for the door, but Alistair called after him. "Mr. Downing, what would happen if we refused to leave?"

He stopped. "Excuse me?"

"We aren't going," Alistair said. "We have decided not to leave."

Downing bristled. "Mr. Lees, I assure you, you will leave. Now, please make this as pleasant as possible."

"Guys," Nurse Roberts said, stepping between them. She placed a hand against Alistair's and Downing's chests. "You, go to your office. And you, go to your room."

Downing stood motionless for a moment, then smirked. "Whatever. Pack, Alistair."

He stopped at the door, turned back to Nurse Roberts. "Your people really know how to stick together don't they?"

"Excuse me?" Alistair said.

Downing shook his head, muttered something that I didn't think I had correctly heard, and disappeared down the hall.

Alistair made to follow him, but Camille stopped him. "Just let it go."

"But you heard what he called us! Eighty years I've fought that–" he began, but stopped. After several seconds, he walked past us and closed himself inside his bedroom.

* * *

"Cassidy?" I whispered through the crack in the door. I had been standing at the top of the staircase for several minutes, waiting on her to return. "Cass?"

The door opened and she motioned me in. "Shh. Dad's in the other room. What happened back there?"

I told her about the envelopes and the confrontation between her father and Alistair, about

Camille stepping between them. She sat silently for several seconds after I finished.

"I'm…He's just doing his job, Billy. He's under a lot of stress," she said.

"He called Alistair and Camille niggers, Cassidy. Why?"

She shook her head, suddenly distant and detached. "I don't know. I don't. He's never talked like that before."

"Well, he's an idiot."

"Hey! He's my dad," she snapped. She had stood, abruptly, and in the process knocked over the shrunken head and a glass of water. "Look what you made me do! Now I have to start over."

I bent to help her clean up the water, but she shoved me away. "I don't need your help."

"Cassidy, I–"

"Just leave!" she shouted.

A chair scraped across the floor in a distant room. Cassidy's eyes darted to the door leading into her closet. Within seconds, her father burst through the door. His eyes darted around the room from the alcove to the window, and finally to the bed in the corner.

"What's going on here?" he said. Cassidy stepped forward.

"Nothing, Daddy. We're just–"

"What are you doing here?" he said to me.

"He's just here, Daddy. He's just–"

"Shut up," he said. She shrank back into the corner, hiding her face. Christopher Downing closed the distance between us in two steps and took me by the shirt collar. "What are you doing with my daughter?"

"Mr. Downing, I'm not doing anything. I was just helping."

"I wasn't born yesterday, boy. Why are you in my daughter's bedroom?"

"Daddy, let him go!" Cassidy shouted. Downing released my collar, and I stumbled backwards.

"Cassidy, this is none of your concern. Whatever this boy was doing–"

"He wasn't doing anything, daddy. He was trying to help me get to Mom!"

Downing's shoulders fell. He glanced at the floor, stooping to pick up the shrunken head and her mother's diary. He flipped through the pages. "Cassidy, what is all of this stuff?"

"It's Mom's. I can get her back," she said. She opened the diary and showed him the same poem she had shown me in the clearing. Her voice rose excitedly when she told him about seeing the shrunken head on their first day in New Orleans. Everything had fallen into place after that. And now they had the last piece. Her mother would be home that night.

Her father sat on the edge of the bed, still clutching the shrunken head and the diary. "Cassidy, I don't know what to say. I mean–what made you think you could get your mom back with all of this stuff?"

"She knew what was coming, Daddy. Don't you see?"

He shook his head. "Baby, your mother's dead."

"No she's not." He tried to pull is daughter to him, but she fought free. "Don't say that! She's not dead!"

"Cassidy, baby. She was sick. She wouldn't get better. We put her in the hospital, but she didn't get well," he said. He opened the diary again, this time reading the poems to Cassidy.

He told her about her mother's condition, tried to explain depression, but Cassidy wouldn't listen. Instead, she shook her head harder and harder until, at last, her face flushed with anger, she stormed across the room and slapped her father's chest.

"She's not dead! She's not dead! She's a prisoner. It's right here!" Cassidy shouted. Her father grabbed her hands and tried again to pull her to him. He succeeded in pinning her arms at her sides, trying to soothe her, but she just kept screaming at him to let her go. Suddenly, her father shouted in pain, released her.

"Damn it, Cassidy." He clutched his hand. A trickle of blood ran down his wrist, disappearing into his sleeve.

"Leave me alone! You're not my dad," she shouted. He stood there silently, in the center of the room, watching Cassidy sob in the corner. She was rocking back and forth, her knees drawn up to her chest. It took me a minute to make out what she was chanting. "She's not dead. She's not dead. She's not dead."

Her father knelt beside her, slid his arm around her shoulders. "Baby, your mom committed suicide when you were four."

Cassidy stopped rocking. "What?"

"She was sick, baby. When she went into the hospital, I sent you to Grandma's for the summer. She killed herself before you got home," he said. She returned to rocking in the corner, but this time she didn't chant.

Downing straightened his pants as he stood. He looked at the bite marks in his hand, blotting the blood away with his handkerchief. When he saw me standing in the corner, he looked surprised.

"Billy, I'm sorry. I didn't realize you were still here," he said. He tried to smile but failed. "Look. Maybe you should head back to Hall B. Come back later, okay?" he said. I nodded and fled. I stopped at the bottom of the stairs in the janitor's closet and threw up into a garbage can.

Chapter 32

The next two hours on the Row passed with excruciating slowness. Thaddeus's soap opera provided very little relief from the image of Cassidy cowering in the corner of the sleeping porch. Even when Alistair offered to let me watch him paint, I declined, instead preferring to sit on the sofa and search for an explanation for Cassidy's dismissal. But no matter how deeply I searched, I found no answer. I don't know how long I had been on the sofa when the door opened and Christopher Downing walked in.

"Billy, would you join me in the dining room for a minute?" he asked. I agreed and we made our way across the patio to the dining room. Downing held the door open for me. "Have you talked to Cassidy?"

I shook my head. "Not since this morning."

"She won't talk to me. The last time I checked on her, she was still in the corner." He sunk into a chair, burying his face into his hands. "I just don't know what to do, Billy. I mean–I really didn't know."

I didn't know what to say or do. I straddled the chair across from him, my head resting on the back. He talked for almost thirty minutes about his wife, about how they had met and how he had been so enthralled with her and her artistic temperament. By the time their first anniversary rolled around, though, he knew that they were in trouble. So much had her hatred for him grown that she would shy away whenever he moved to touch her. So it was no small miracle that, in their third year of marriage, she became pregnant. A baby, he had thought, would pull her out of her depression and maybe draw her out. But it didn't work.

"Post-partum depression," he said. It wasn't clear now if he was speaking to me or to himself. "The doctors said that she would pull out of it within a few months. I kept waiting."

She hadn't pulled out of it, he said. When they finally had her committed, Downing was so consumed with trying to save his wife that he had to send Cassidy to his mother's in Seattle.

"And that's when it happened. I came into the bathroom one night and found her." He looked up, his cheeks wet and glistening. "She had crawled into the bath tub and slit her wrists. I just always assumed that Cassidy knew."

"Well, she didn't," I said.

He shrugged, as if to knock the weight of the story he had just shared off his shoulders. "She won't talk to me, won't even acknowledge I'm there. Billy, could you maybe to talk to her?"

"Why me?"

He heaved a sigh. "Because she chose you."

Standing in front of Christopher Downing, I tried to process everything that had happened. This was not the same man who only an hour before had burst into the sleeping porch and found me with his daughter. This version of Christopher Downing was too soft, almost vulnerable. Something in his request wasn't right, but my mind wouldn't settle on it. As I mounted the stairs through the janitor's closet, I still had not figured out why I was worried to go up those stairs, as if at the top of the dark staircase Cassidy would be waiting with a shotgun.

"Cassidy?" I called. There was no answer. I pushed the door open. The room was empty, just as I remembered it, except the alcove beside the door was empty. The linen drape was crumpled on the floor beneath it, and Cassidy's artifacts were gone.

The door leading through her closet was open, and through it, I could see motion in her bedroom. "Cassidy?" I called again.

She stopped in the middle of her bedroom but didn't turn. "Go away, Billy."

"I just wanted to see if you were–"

"I said go away."

I stepped through the closet and into her bedroom. The piles of dirty laundry were gone. The books were all upright, filling just two shelves of the bookcase. The only signs of disorder in the room were a pile of laundry on her bed and shredded scraps of paper on the vanity. She had reduced the photos of a happy childhood that had adorned the mirror into a pile of shredded scraps. I ran my fingers through the bits of faces and vacations and shuddered. "What's going on, Cass?"

She hadn't moved since I had entered the room. There was no emotion, no feeling, and her eyes were dead.

I reached out to wipe a strand of hair from her face, but she knocked my hand away. "Leave me alone."

I moved the strand of hair and tucked it back behind her ear. "Are you going to be okay?"

She returned to stuffing the pile of dirty clothes into a laundry bag. "I'm a big girl. I can handle anything."

"Do you want to talk about it?"

"No, I don't. I don't ever want to talk about her again. Ever. She doesn't exist." She shoved another wad of laundry into the already full bag and winced. "Damn it!"

She withdrew her hand, clasping her wrist.

"What happened?"

"I jammed my wrist. What do you think?"

I tried to pry her hand away, but she shoved me off again. "Billy, I'm fine. I'm fine. My mom's dead and I'm fine."

She flopped back onto her bed with a sigh. "Why didn't you say anything to me?"

I looked up. "Huh?"

"You knew, didn't you?"

I shrugged. "I dunno. Maybe. But that's not important."

"Not important? You should have said something. Then things would have been different."

I flopped down beside her, careful not to pull her hair. "I'm not sure how."

She rolled over, rested her head against my chest. "Because then I wouldn't have to hate you too."

"Cass, I–" I said.

She interrupted me with a kiss on the cheek. "It's okay, though. I understand. This is the way things have to be."

She stood, extended a stiff, cold hand. "Goodbye, Billy Bradshaw."

"What?"

"I said good bye."

I stood, speechless and confused. I tried to speak, but there were no words to describe the swell of pain and fear welling up from the pit of my stomach. "Cassidy, I'm not sure what's going on."

"Leave. I'm through with you."

"But you're my best friend."

She withdrew her hand. "And you were mine, and now I'm through with you. So leave."

Standing in the middle of her bedroom, I saw the memories of a summer speeding away and didn't know how to stop them. The girl standing before me wasn't the girl with the apple or the girl from the cemetery. I could not see this version of Cassidy poring over diaries and mythology books, excitedly trying to explain the history of the muses. Instead, that image was replaced by the steely face of a girl who had just stomped in my chest. Fighting back tears, I started for the door.

"I don't want to lose you," I said.

"You should have thought about that before." She closed the door between us, and I heard the lock click.

Twice again that afternoon I returned to Cassidy's room. Both times, the door was locked, and she didn't answer when I knocked. On my third trip up the stairs, I found the door open.

Her alcove was emptied of her mother's artifacts. The diary, the shrunken head, the photographs were all gone. On my final trip, shortly before five o'clock, I resolved to step through her closet to see if she was in her bedroom. When I tried the knob, though, it was locked from the other side.

Camille found me in the hallway a few minutes later and informed me that my mother was here. She stopped me at her desk. "What the hell happened earlier, Billy?"

I told her about how Downing had discovered the hidden room and his wife's things, how he got angry, how he told Cassidy about her mother's suicide. Camille shook her head. "That explains the box of stuff he took to the dumpster."

"He what?" I said.

"He and Cass took a box of stuff to the dumpster and then left. Haven't seen them since."

"Where?"

"I don't know. He said they'd be back later," she said. "You be safe, now, Billy. Okay?"

On the drive home, Mom jabbered incessantly about houses and vacations and the things we would buy when the money came. She wanted a new kitchen, she said, complete with a restaurant-styled gas stove, ignoring my point that she didn't enjoy cooking. Turning onto our street, she shrieked.

"Oh! I forgot to tell you. Your grandparents are coming down next week to help us move."

"Cool," I said. But she knew by my tone that I lacked enthusiasm. Once inside our apartment, she cornered me.

"Sit down," she said. She sat down beside me on the sofa. "Sweetheart, why can't you get excited about this?"

"I don't know, Mom. I just–I like it here."

"You liked it in Minneapolis didn't you?"

"I guess."

"Well, there. You'll probably like it again."

I didn't reply.

She stood with a sigh. "I just don't know, Billy. I don't know what to say or do to make you happy."

That night, while lying in bed waiting for sleep to come, I thought about happiness. I had been happy in Minneapolis. We lived in a neighborhood there with other families and a park nearby. Twins games and trips to the movies were regular occurrences. If Mom had a date, I got to spend time with my grandparents. But we moved away from all of that. At first, I had been excited about the move. Eventually, that excitement was replaced by the realization of everything I had been forced to leave behind. Now that I had those things again, I wasn't anxious to leave. I tried to make lists of the reasons we shouldn't leave, but exhaustion had already begun to overtake consciousness, and the lists quickly became nothing more than a string of unrelated words.

A car horn in the parking lot woke me an hour later. I sat up with a gasp. But I couldn't get back to sleep. Instead, my mind was consumed with a singular image: the diary, in the box, at the bottom of the dumpster. I resolved that I would retrieve it for her the next morning. Then she could complete whatever journey it was she was on. Or at least get to try. Tuesday, I would return with her quest complete.

I had almost dozed off when I awoke again. What would I do if the garbage were emptied in the morning before I got there? Without hesitation, I flew from my bed, dressed, and silently slipped out into the hot, dank New Orleans night. By the time I got to the street corner, I had worked out the fastest way to walk to the Liberty Street Home. My backpack, emptied and slung over my shoulder as an afterthought, knocked hollowly against the small of my back with each step. A few blocks from my apartment, I began to think about the shadows, the creeping crawlers that might lurk there, waiting for a boy making his way through the night. I began to consider the purpose of all the things Cassidy had amassed. Flying in the face of gods couldn't be a good idea. What might those gods do to a young boy wandering through the darkness if they found out? And the voodoo of Cassidy's doll didn't bode well. I quickened my pace.

The city looked different by the light of night. There was little traffic, and what little there was consisted mostly of cabs and delivery trucks. Normally full of pedestrians, the city looked lifeless. The only indication that it was populated at all was the piles of garbage bags, placed with little care by the street to await eventual collection.

"Hey kid," a scratching voice called out. I didn't stop. Instead, the footsteps behind me sped up. "Hey kid. Where ya going?"

"Nowhere," I said.

"Don't be scared. You got a buck?" the man said. I shook my head. "K. Just asking. Thanks."

I sped up. His pace matched mine. "You want company?" I shook my head, but he didn't pay attention. He reached out and tried to grab my backpack. "Whatcha got in there?"

"Nothing," I said. I turned abruptly and tried to disappear into the shadows. By the time I turned onto Liberty Street almost two hours later, I was nearly running. I stopped in the driveway, panting. Halfway there, I thought, as I started to the dumpster.

It was filled to overflowing with garbage. The kitchen had been the last to empty. Half-eaten sandwiches and noodles oozed across red bags labeled biohazard. I took a deep breath, reached in, carefully searching for a hard corner in the pile. My fingers closed around the edge of a box and I tugged. Two bags of newspapers toppled down noisily as I pulled the box out of the dumpster. The diary and pictures were the most important artifacts. They went in first. When my backpack was as full as I could get it, I zipped it shut. Only the shrunken head and a few jars of dirt remained. They would have to wait until the morning. After hiding them beneath a bush in the flowerbed and returning the newspapers to the dumpster, I started the journey home, confident in my safety. I had conquered the dumpster. I could conquer anything.

* * *

Mother shook her head. "No, Billy. Not today."

"I'll take the bus," I said.

"Why do you want to go back there again today? Haven't you had enough of it?" She tossed another egg into the skillet and stirred it with the whisk. "Toast or bagel?"

"Toast," I said. I eyed my backpack in the corner. Mom still hadn't found out that I had left the night before. I wasn't about to tell her. "Please?"

"No, Billy."

"It'll make me happy."

She slammed the skillet down. "Damn it, Billy. Don't start that."

"Well, you asked me yesterday," I said. She stared at me down the tip of her nose. I wasn't backing off. "So?"

"Fine. Whatever."

I rushed for the door, grabbing my backpack. She called after me. "What about breakfast?"

"I'll eat there!" I shouted as the door closed behind me. On the bus, I noticed several people that I had seen on my first bus trip to Liberty. They had gone out of their way to get to know me over the course of the summer. The woman across from me had twins my age and made her living by cleaning apartments across town. She smiled at me as I took my seat.

"Well g'morning, Billy. You look kind of tired."

"Yes, ma'am. Long night."

She returned to reading her book. I considered telling her that we were moving and she wouldn't be seeing me anymore. But I had learned over the past months that people on buses come and go, and you just don't ask questions about it.

The bus arrived at Liberty Street, and I hopped off. In front of the home, an ambulance and two police cars blocked the driveway, their lights still flashing. I shook my head, wondering which of the residents had died. There was a police officer standing outside the front door. My heartbeat quickened as I approached. He stopped me as I mounted the stairs.

"There's nothing to see here," he said.

"I work here, sort of."

He turned over his shoulder. "Ma'am, he says he works here?"

Camille Roberts appeared. Her eyes were puffy and red. She had obviously been crying. "Billy! What are you doing here, son?"

"I came to see Cassidy," I said. She started crying again and turned away. I stepped past the officer and tapped her on the shoulder.

"What's going on, Miss Roberts?"

She pushed me down the hall, past her desk. "Go wait in the back. Okay?"

I didn't want to go without knowing what was happening, but I didn't dare resist either. Instead, I made my way back to Hall B. The Bohemians were gathered around the table. The radio was silent, the television off, and Alistair's paper was lying unread on the desk beside the phone.

When they heard the door close, they all looked up.

Alistair stood. "Billy. Son what are you doing here?"

"I came to see Cassidy, but Camille sent me back here," I said. Alistair's cheeks were flushed and damp. He'd been crying as well. "Alistair, what's going on?"

Thaddeus pulled the chair next to him out. "Have a seat."

I shook my head. "No. What's going on?"

"Billy," Anne said. "We have to tell you something."

Louise walked over, slid her arm around my waist. She led me to the sofa. The others followed. Alistair was the only one who didn't sit.

"Billy, Cassidy–I don't know how to say this." He took a deep breath, held it for a moment. "Cassidy died last night."

"What?" I said, thinking I hadn't understood.

"She died, Billy," Louise said. Anne rushed away down the hall. Louise flinched when we heard the door slam. She looked up at Alistair. They were crying again.

"Someone tell me what happened. Now," I said. When no one volunteered to answer, I stood up. "Someone tell me what happened, please."

"She uh–" Thaddeus began. Alistair sat on the edge of the coffee table across from me.

"She killed herself last night, Billy," Alistair said flatly.

My chest seized. I shook my head, tried to breathe, but could not force air into my lungs. I tried to scream, but nothing came out. The room began to spin and my vision grew blurry. The last thing I remember was Louise's hands on my cheeks trying to calm me and Donald Lilly standing over her shoulder. "He's hyperventilating," Donald said, just as I blacked out.

Chapter 33

I spent my adolescence searching for a meaning in the tragedy. It wasn't until almost ten years later that I grasped the key, a key that had been there since the beginning. Through the week of endless interviews with police officers, a trauma specialist, and more than a few psychologists, through endless questions about her quest, the religion she had constructed on her mother's mystery, inquiries about her relationship with her father, the one question they never asked was the one I couldn't answer. They knew then what I know now, that there can be no answer to the question "Why?" But tell that to a twelve-year-old boy, lying on a bed after passing out from shock, and you'll learn futility at its truest.

When I came to, I at first thought it had all been a nightmare. But as my eyes focused, I saw that I was in Zelda's room. Outside the door were voices, muffled and hushed. One of them I recognized as my mother's. She was quizzing Alistair. He told her everything he knew, about the quest, about the fight with Downing. That explained my mood the previous night, she said. He told her how Christopher Downing had found Cassidy in a bathtub, already dead, how she had slit her wrists with a pair of scissors, just as her mother had done eight years before. I thought I could hear my mother crying. Finally, she knocked on the door.

"Billy, hon?" she said. I didn't look at her. "Billy, it's Mama."

She knelt beside me, stroking my hair. "Baby, talk to me."

I rolled over to face the wall.

"Billy, what can we do?" Alistair said.

"I just want to be alone for a little while," I replied.

"I don't think that that's such a good–" she began. Alistair cleared his throat. I heard her stand. "Well, I'll be right outside the door, okay?"

I lay in bed, thinking about my backpack. Bulging with books and papers and photographs, the memories of Cassidy's Mother. When I had first seen the diary, even that morning when I had slipped away from my apartment, I hadn't understood how important it was to her. Now, lying in a bed that wasn't mine, I understood that my backpack contained Cassidy's life, her entire world.

Opening the door, I found my mother standing in the hall, still talking to Alistair. She ran her fingers through my hair. "You okay, Billy?"

I brushed her hand away. "I think so."

Alistair forced a smile. "We'll get through this, son. I promise."

Mother led me to the table. Louise appeared with a glass of orange juice and a cold biscuit.

"Eat this," Louise said. "It'll make you feel better."

I took the biscuit, but didn't eat it. Instead, it lay untouched on the table before me. I sipped the orange juice, still numb. When I had emptied the glass, I set it back on the table.

"How long was I out?"

"About thirty minutes," Anne said. "You hyperventilated."

"It happens," Thaddeus said. He had taken the seat across from me and was pretending to read the front page of Alistair's newspaper.

I stared down at the table. Nothing made sense. Over the years I've read about studies of how children react when first exposed to death. I've always viewed such studies with skepticism. No researcher ever asked me. Sitting there at that table, I knew that my life would never be the same.

I looked up from the table. "I want to go home."

"Okay. I'll get your things," Mom said.

"No, I will," I said, perhaps too quickly. But she didn't notice. I found my backpack on the floor behind Emily's desk and slipped both arms through the straps. When my mother noticed me standing by the door, waiting, she apologized and said goodbye to the Bohemians.

We met Camille Roberts, coming towards us in the hall. Her eyes were still red, but she had reapplied her blush in an effort to hide that she had been crying. She stopped my mother. "I'm glad I caught you."

"We were just heading home," Mom replied. "It's been a rough day."

"Well, I think it may get a bit rougher, baby," Camille said. "Billy, would you give us a minute?"

She pulled my mother into an empty room off the hall, out of earshot. I stared at the floor, waiting. When they returned, my mother looked at me and sighed. "Billy, baby, the police would like to speak to you before we leave. Are you up to it?"

I probably wasn't up to it, but the way Camille asked left me with the impression that we didn't have a choice. I turned to my mother. "Will you be there?"

"Yes, of course."

Camille led us into Christopher Downing's office and told us to wait there. She excused herself to the hall and picked up the phone, informing whoever answered that we were waiting. Within moments, a male and female police officer joined us. The woman sat down beside me. She smiled at me, but I could tell that her smile, like Alistair's, was forced.

Behind her, in the hallway, I noticed the paramedics wheeling a stretcher out the front door. Camille stepped in between me and the stretcher and closed the door, but not before I saw the white sheet, tucked neatly around a lifeless form that was so unnaturally small it looked foreign.

The female officer placed her hands on my knees. "Billy, my name is Officer Holland. But you can call me Allison," she said. "I'd like to ask you a few questions. Would that be okay?"

* * *

We arrived at Cassidy's funeral with the Bohemians in a borrowed minivan. They had insisted that they come with us, and I think my mother felt touched that they wanted to be there for me. Only Alistair had shown any reluctance to attend. Accepting Cassidy and me had not been an easy task for him, and her death had been a wound to his very soul. In the days leading up to her funeral, he had appeared broken. His towering physique had become stooped, and his eyes were perpetually hazed over with tears.

For two days, Alistair adamantly refused to consider attending her funeral and rarely ventured from his room. At first, everyone assumed that he was simply venting his sorrow into his paintings. But Anne sensed it was more than that. When I found him sitting in his room staring at the half-formed painting of Cassidy and me, I almost ventured into his room. The fear of what outbursts might occur because of such an intrusion stilled my desire to talk to him, and I remained in the hall instead. But I knew what was behind those eyes. For reasons of his own, Alistair had found promise and hope in Cassidy and me. With her gone, that hope vanished. Only after Anne cornered him after lunch a day later did he agree to attend her funeral.

Cassidy's father had chosen to hold only graveside services for his daughter. Beneath the unrelenting sun, the seven of us stood across from Downing and Cassidy's grandparents. The minister spoke of the fragility of life, that delicate balance with which God entrusts us. Cassidy was taken too young, he said. We should all learn from her the value of each day of our lives. Each time he said her name, I found myself unable to avoid looking at Christopher Downing. I had not seen him since Monday evening. He wasn't crying now, as the minister blessed the small coffin. But somehow I knew that it wasn't because he didn't feel. I wasn't crying either, for the same reason. We both had run out of tears.

After the last prayer, we formed a line and one by one filed past Cassidy's coffin. My mother was ahead of me, and she paused, said a brief prayer, and then moved on. It was my turn. I tried to step forward, but couldn't. Donald's hand, reassuring on my shoulder, pressed me forward. "Take your time, son," he said. "She'd want that."

I took a deep breath, stepped up. My foot kicked a clod of dirt down into the open grave, and then I looked back at Alistair. His grief-stricken face had frozen into something resembling anger.

I hastily fished in the pocket of my trousers for a moment before I found the chain. The locket couldn't be far. I let it slip from my hand and into the grave. Though I had not wanted to part with it, I knew that Cassidy needed it with her. I hadn't told anyone other than Donald that I had her mother's diary, the necklace, and the photographs. He agreed that there was no reason for anyone to know. The answers didn't lie in a pile of sentimentality.

I kicked another a bit of dirt into the grave to conceal the necklace as best as I could before walking away. Following my mother, I shook hands with Cassidy's grandparents. When it came my turn to face Christopher Downing, my blood ran cold. I looked at him, wanting to blame him for her actions, but I couldn't. If anything, Downing and I were co-conspirators in her death, both equally to blame for the bad choices of a disillusioned girl.

We arrived back at the Liberty Street Home almost an hour later. My mother and Camille helped the Bohemians out of the van and up the steps. As we stepped inside, it occurred to me that this was the first time they had left Bohemian Row since I had known them and quite possibly for many years.

Alistair had bolted from the passenger seat and into Liberty Street almost before the van had come to a stop. He bounded up the steps to the front door two at a time with surprising agility. Donald was the last out of the van and the last inside. Instead of heading down the hall, he stopped in front of Camille's desk.

"Beverly, may I have a moment?" he said.

"Of course," Mom said.

"We know this isn't the best time, but there isn't a better time. This has been a tough week for Billy, a tough week for all of us, I guess," he said. He stared down at his feet for a moment. "We know that Billy missed his birthday on Thursday, but we had already gotten him a present. And I was hoping that—well, maybe this isn't the most appropriate time, but we are leaving tomorrow."

"Of course," Mom said. "I'll just wait here."

We arrived at Hall B, greeted by the crash of furniture and a torrent of obscenities. No one said anything or thought to point out the obvious. We simply entered, accepting of the fact that Alistair was venting his anger—finally, thankfully—though we were fearful that he might get hurt. Donald made me sit at the head of the table. While the other Bohemians retrieved my birthday gifts, he ventured into Alistair's room, and the tantrum ceased. When the

Bohemians returned, they were carrying a stack of packages, each wrapped with care in a page of the *Times-Picayune*.

"My touch," Thaddeus said when I noticed the wrapping paper. He slid the largest of the three packages to me first. "Open this one first, or else the others won't make any sense."

The package was heavy and solid. I carefully untied the string holding the paper in place, unfolded a corner of the paper, then undid the other. The last fold revealed a new journal, leather-bound like Zelda's. "All writers should have one," Louise said.

I opened the cover and tried to smile. On the first page, each of the Bohemians had written a short note and signed it.

Alistair slid the second package to me. "Open this one next."

The second package contained a carved wooden box. Inside, I found a fountain pen. I immediately recognized it as the same pen Zelda had used in her own journal.

"She'd want you to have it," Donald said. I felt the weight of the pen and the grip, where it had been worn smooth by years of steady use.

The third package was a box of ink cartridges. "To get you started," Donald said.

In the car on the way home, Mom patted my leg. "I was really proud of you today, Billy. You were so brave."

I didn't know what she meant. "Brave?"

"You've been through a lot, kiddo." She drummed her fingers on the steering wheel, keeping time to whatever song was playing on the radio. After several minutes of silence, she sighed. "One hell of a summer, eh?"

I shrugged. "I guess."

"Well, it's almost over. Grandpa and Grandma get here on Tuesday. Are you excited to see them?"

In all honesty, I hadn't thought about it since Monday. Everything else had faded in the aftermath of Cassidy's suicide. I forgot that this chapter of my life would end that night when the clock struck midnight. At midnight, the summer was over. The Bohemians would have a new home and we'd be moving back to Minneapolis with my grandparents. I scooted over in the seat, slipping my hand in my mother's.

"Yeah. I'm excited to see them."

The phone rang the next morning at five o'clock. Through the paper-thin walls, I heard my mother answer it. "Hello? What is it?" she said. "Oh no, what happened? What? Last night? I mean, we just. God, Camille. This is too much. Yes, yes of course I'll tell him. Thank you for calling. Goodbye."

I heard the phone rattle back into the cradle, followed by the click of her door opening. When she opened my door, she found me sitting on the foot of my bed. She sat down next to me. "That was Camille Roberts, Billy. I've got some bad news."

"What happened?"

She sat there for a moment, trying to find the words. "Donald Lilly died last night, sweetheart. He had a heart attack and passed away quietly in his sleep."

Chapter 34

My mother refused to allow me to attend Donald Lilly's funeral two days later. Cassidy's funeral had been enough, she insisted, adding that she didn't think I could handle any more exposure to death. Instead, she suggested that I write a letter to his family, sending it care of the residents of Bohemian Row.

"They'll know the right people to give it to, sweetheart," she said. But I understood a fundamental truth that had always escaped her: the Bohemians were the right people. So I wrote the letter, placed it in an envelope, and addressed it to Alistair Lees at his new address. Downstairs at the mailbox, I discovered that the postman had already run. Inside our box was a letter with "Mister William Northrop Bradshaw" scribbled across the front. Whoever had addressed the envelope had failed to write a return address. So my only clue was the postmark: New Orleans, four days earlier. I turned the envelope over several times, examining the weight and texture of the paper. I'd received mail many times before, usually a Christmas or birthday card from relatives. But this was something wholly different. Someone had written me a letter.

Careful not to rip the single page inside, I tore the envelope open. My eyes immediately fell to the bottom of the page, where the signature made me think I had seen a ghost–or was at least was hearing the voice of one. For across the width of the page, in a looping signature, was the name "Donald Lilly."

Dear Billy,
I would imagine that this little note comes as a shock to you, and wish I could see how your face looks right now. But I can't. So I wanted to explain a few things that I've not had the time to say.

Having you around these past months has again opened my eyes to the wonders of life. There is so much more that you will experience as you grow, and I'm thankful that I again got to experience part of it all with you.

I don't much expect that you understand the choice I made now, but you will. I spent my entire life looking for a place where I would be comfortable, maybe not accepted, but tolerated. I do not wish to search again, and having seen what life can be, I don't wish to go back to where I was before.

I know I don't have to say anything about who to tell about this letter and when. You'll figure that out.

```
Your friend always,
    Donald Lilly
```

I very gently folded the letter, returned it to the envelope, and tried to ignore how hard it had become to breathe. Through my own paralysis, the world around me continued to move. A delivery truck passed by, its brakes screeching to a halt somewhere up the block. Just across from our building, two women gossiped on a porch, occasionally erupting into laughter. Sitting there, Donald's envelope in clutched in my hands, I wondered if those two women realized just how pointless life could suddenly become. I stood, dusted my pants, and climbed the stairs, wanting nothing more than to sleep.

* * *

Sitting up, I blinked twice to wet my eyes, which had stubbornly decided they did not wish to focus on anything beyond the edge of the sofa. The phone chirped again. I stumbled into the kitchen and reached for the receiver as it rang a fourth time.

"Hello?"

"Billy, this is Emily, from Liberty Street?" a girl's voice said. It took me a moment to couple a face with the voice.

"Oh. Yeah, hey."

"Miss Roberts wanted me to call and tell you she has some things for you," she said.

"What things?"

"She didn't say. She just wanted me to call you and ask you if you maybe could come by tomorrow and pick them up."

Running through a mental inventory of everything I might have left behind, nothing stood out. Maybe Camille knew about Donald Lilly, or at least had suspicions, and wanted to quiz me about it. Someone had known about the letter. They had tipped her off. The last thing I wanted was another week of interviews at the hands of the police.

"Billy?" Emily said.

"Sorry. Yeah. Tell her I'll come by in the–" I paused, looked at the clock on the stove. I had enough time to catch the afternoon bus to Liberty Street and still make it home before Mom's return. "Tell her I'll be there shortly."

Donald's letter was lying on the coffee table. I shoved it into my pocket before breaking into a run for the bus stop. On the bus, I thought about the letter and all the questions it raised. Why had he written me instead of Alistair or Thaddeus? Wouldn't Anne Moore have been a better choice? After all, they had been his friends longer than I. Why me?

"Don't bother asking," said a woman's voice from across the aisle. I looked up and recognized the orange scarf. The woman from the voodoo shop.

"Excuse me?" I said.

"That question you were just asking yourself. Don't bother. Because you'll never really know the answer." She winked.

"I don't know what you're talking about."

She smiled again. "Sure you do. You were wondering why."

The apparent shock across my face must have given away my surprise because she laughed. "Oh honey, it doesn't take a genius to figure it out. You have the look."

"What look?"

"That 'why me' look. You know," she said.

I saw little point in trying to figure out what she saw and how she had known or why she was on the bus. Instead, now I wanted to know what she meant.

"Why isn't there an answer?"

"That's life, hon. Things just happen and we don't know why. Sometimes it's good, sometimes it's bad. But," she said as she grasped a handrail and pulled herself to her feet. "Things always work out in the end. Hang in there, kid."

And with that, she stepped off the bus. I turned in my seat to wave, but she was gone, almost as if she had vanished or was never there. In New Orleans for over a year now, I had grown accustomed to the ghosts that haunted her streets.

The bus struck a pothole and, with a hard bounce, turned down Liberty Street toward the home one last time. Outside, a trail of dust flowed down the steps to a pile of construction debris beneath the portico. Stepping around the pile, I noticed a chunk of drywall atop the pile with a swatch of flower-print wallpaper still attached, flapping in the late August wind. I immediately recognized it as the wallpaper from the kitchen of Bohemian Row.

Inside, Camille Roberts' desk was empty, as was the desk behind the window where only three months earlier Ellie had leaned over to see me. I considered momentarily that Ellie was but one of the many question marks hanging over the summer. Like so many others, Ellie had simply vanished. The door leading to Cassidy's apartment was closed. I looked down the hall, hoping to catch a glimpse of Camille or an orderly, but only an old man confined to a wheelchair was there, padding his way along the corridor.

"Well, you weren't kidding when you said a few minutes, were you?" Emily said.

I looked around. Camille wasn't with her. "Where's Nurse Roberts?"

Emily pointed down the hall. "Back on the Row—I mean Hall B," she said. She shook her head. "It doesn't seem right to call it—"

"I know," I said, interrupting her. "Thanks, Emily."

When I arrived at the back of the home, I almost thought I had come to the wrong place. The small hallway that connected the old house to the Hall B expansion was gone, replaced instead by a gleaming tile corridor lined on one side with a nurse's desk and on the other with a low vinyl couch. Where the doors had once stood, the tile changed from the standard white to a grey tile, speckled to look like granite.

Beyond the corridor, where Bohemian Row had flowed from room to room, partitions divided the vast space into small cubicles, miniature spaces designed to afford a modicum of privacy to those who no longer required it. At the entrance to each cubicle were empty brass slots awaiting nameplates for each of the future residents.

Camille Roberts appeared at the entrance to one of the spaces, made a couple of notes in the patient's chart, and started toward me. She stopped at the vacant nurse's station and opened another chart.

"Glad you came, Billy," she said without looking up. "Give me just a second, will you?"

I took a seat on the sofa. The upholstery crackled as I sat, reminding me once again of the newness of everything. I missed the sounds of jazz blaring from the radio and the rustle of Alistair's newspaper. Where the smell of bacon and biscuits had greeted me just two weeks before, there was now the stench of floor wax and fresh paint. I even missed the old, thread-worn couch on which we had spent so many afternoons watching soaps.

Nurse Roberts closed the chart and sighed, rubbing her hands across the small of her back. "I swear this place is going to be the death of me," she said. She glanced at me in that way she had of looking as if she were at once curious and bored. "Come on, Billy. I have something for you.

I followed in silence back to her desk and waited patiently as she gave a stack of folders to an orderly I didn't recognize.

"Take these back to the nurse's station on B and file them, please," she said.

Camille smoothed her hair back, sat down, and rested both hands on top of her desk. "Now. Where did I put it?"

"Put what?" I said.

"Just something I ran across during the cleanup. I think Anne Moore left it for you," she said. She lifted several folders, knocked a couple on to the floor and then exclaimed, "There!"

She reached down onto the floor behind her desk. When her hand returned, it contained a photograph. Scrutinizing it, she shrugged. "I wasn't sure I was going to give it to you. But, I think you deserve it. Here. This is yours," she said as she extended the photo across her desk. It took a moment to recognize my own face pressed against Cassidy's.

At first, I thought I might start crying again, but instead I found myself unable to stop smiling. The picture, snapped during the barbecue, managed to catch us dancing. Around us, the lights, the grass, the trees, everything blurred together. But there, in the center and perfectly focused, were our faces. Cassidy's face, red and flushed with laughter, was more alive in that picture than I remembered it ever being.

"Billy," Camille said.

I looked up. "Ma'am?"

"You gonna be all right?"

I smiled. "Yes, ma'am. I'll be fine."

She patted my head and walked from the room chuckling. She paused at the corner. "See you around, Billy."

I turned back to the picture. "Yeah. See you around."

I placed the picture inside my notebook, slipped it back into my backpack and started for the door. But as I turned, my backpack caught a stack of folders sitting on the desk, sending a cascade of loose paper to the floor.

I bent down and began sorting things back into order until I came to a black nameplate. I traced my finger through each of the letters, confused and bewildered. Zelda Groves. It had fallen from one of the folders. Unable to resist, I found Zel's folder and read the single document stapled inside. It was a letter from Christopher Downing to Zel's niece about the "many benefits of Liberty Street's new long-term specialized care facility."

I closed the folder, returned it to the stack on Camille's desk, and smiled. After everything he had tried, everything that he had done, Downing had still failed to clear the Bohemians out of Hall

B. Zelda Groves would be the first resident in the newly-renovated wing.

I opened the heavy door and stepped out into the sunlight. My eyes adjusted just in time to see the green stripes of my bus sputter by. I shrugged and started off down the street, wondering how long the walk back to our apartment might take.

* * *

Many nights in the years that followed, I often considered what became of my friends, the Bohemians, after they left Liberty Street. While I lingered in that space just between consciousness and dreams, I would picture them. They have all found a place together and are still gathered around the dining room table, as they were the first time I met them. Anne and Louise sit almost imperceptibly closer to each another than to the others. They share a sideways glance as Thaddeus and Zelda tie into yet another argument. At the head of the table, Alistair quietly pretends to ignore them in favor of his morning paper. They all smile when Donald appears, dressed in his best linen dress and ready for a day outside.

But I'm not so foolish as to think that such a happy ending is possible for my friends. After they left Liberty Street and I returned to Minneapolis, I wrote them each, regularly, and they replied. But the pattern was always the same. A letter would go unanswered. A second letter to one of them would arrive back in my mailbox marked "Sender not at this address." True to form, Alistair outlived them all and wrote every month until the very last. At first, our letters were short, very succinct, and devoid of any mention of everything that had happened. But slowly, over the years, our tension thawed. He apologized for not completing the painting he had promised. After Cassidy's death, though, he never picked up a brush again. One name that we never mentioned was Christopher Downing.

It may sound strange, but as hard as I've tried, I cannot blame Downing for anything that happened. He was but one of many catalysts in a causal line that began with a World Series game behind a condemned mansion and ended with two deaths. We weren't to blame. We were just factors, links in the chain. Some might ask, if given a stick, a rock, and twenty or so feet of empty grass between a wall and me, would I swing again?

Absolutely.

The End

Dear reader,

We hope you enjoyed reading *Anything But Ordinary*. Please take a moment to leave a review, even if it's a short one. Your opinion is important to us.

Discover more books by Michael DeVault at https://www.nextchapter.pub/authors/michael-devault

Want to know when one of our books is free or discounted? Join the newsletter at http://eepurl.com/bqqB3H

Best regards,
Michael DeVault and the Next Chapter Team

You might also like:

Dasvidaniya by W.L. Liberman

To read first chapter for free, please head to:
https://www.nextchapter.pub/books/
dasvidaniya-literary-fiction

About the Author

Michael DeVault lives and writes in the quite southern town of Monroe, Louisiana. His previous novels include Partiot Joe Morten, and A Glimpse of Tuscany (SaucyVox, 2002). Michael is also a journalist whose non-fiction has appeared in local and national print and Web publications. The Patriot Joe Morton is Michael's fourth novel. You can visit him online at: www.michaeldevault.com